Weeping may endure for a night,
but joy cometh in the morning.
                              —*Psalms* 30:5b

MARILYNN GRIFFITH

Happily Even After

Steeple
Hill
Café

Published by Steeple Hill Books™

STEEPLE HILL BOOKS

ISBN-13: 978-0-373-78598-8
ISBN-10:   0-373-78598-4

HAPPILY EVEN AFTER

www.SteepleHill.com

Printed in U.S.A.

ACKNOWLEDGMENTS

Every book I write seems to require more and more help. I'm thankful to have a great family, good friends and a great publishing team to help me out.

Fill, Ashlie, Michelle, Fill Jr, Ben, James, John and Isaiah:

Thank you for putting up with me while this book came together. I hope that all the harried hugs and microwave dinners leave you no worse for the wear. Each of you is an amazing story that I'm blessed to be able to read every day. Without you, none of this could happen.

Calvary Chapel Tallahassee and all the amazing moms I've met over the years in the nursing mothers' room:

Thanks for your support and your friendship. You're the best.

Jessica Alvarez, Diane Dietz, Joan Marlow Golan, Megan Lorius and all the Steeple Hill Books staff who worked on this book:

Thanks again for believing in me and allowing me to tell another story with you. I appreciate it.

Mom, Maurice, Shay, Mya and Maxwell:

Thanks for giving me plenty to laugh about while writing this book. You all are incredibly talented and giving. I miss you much.

Claudia, my wonderful mother-in-law, and Grafton, my father-in-law who treats me like a daughter:

Thank you so much for your love and support. (And for giving me your son. He's a keeper!)

Mrs. A. Smith, Mrs. Dupont, Mrs. Sperling, Mrs. Shaner, Miss Dot, Miss Sonia, Mr. Gillmore, Mr. Hankerson, Principal Gayle, Miss Wimberley and all the other teachers and staff who have cared for my children this year:

Thank you. Your hard work has been a blessing to me and my family. Sorry I haven't always been around. This is some of what I was doing.

Dave Talbot, Rachel Williams, Dick Foth, Sharon Hinck, Susie Aughtmon, Wendy Lawton, Cyndy Salzmann, Janet Eckles, Marci, Vicki Tiede and everyone from the Mount Hermon shuttle van:

Thanks for the great time at Mount Hermon 2007. It helped me a lot with this novel.

Mair, Barbara Joe, Jen, Staci, Amy, Angie, Jess, Heather, Gail and all my other writer friends:

Thanks for putting up with me when I disappear. I believe in you.

For all the readers who continue to support my work and my family by buying my books and telling others about them:

Thank you. You make it all worth it.

Jesus, who picks me up when I fall:

You did it again.

Chapter One

All hail the Queen!

My gold dress drapes the floor as I approach, taking my seat beside the King of all creation. He's called me forward, invited me into His throne room. I'm blessed and embarrassed. I haven't seen Him all week. With only a slight tiara adjustment, I stand before the King and step onto a tiny, tiny scale....

"Tracey! Don't you hear this baby crying out here? You've been in that bathroom for, like, an hour! And now you're in there screaming? What's that about?"

The heavenly throne room faded. My velvet gown became a pink terry-cloth bathrobe. The toilet in my secret bathroom, the only one of the six lavatories in my home far enough away from my bedroom for me to feel safe enough to step on a scale, was no longer my throne. The overhead fan, which usually drowned out my screams when I stepped on the scale, must have finally failed. It was my favorite and most dreaded day of the week.

Sunday.

Church with my mother-in-law and weigh-in day wrapped into one morning. And after months of escape in my purple bathroom, my husband had found me out. Was nothing sacred?

"Coming!" I grabbed my throat, realizing that I was still speaking in my regal tone. I paused in front of the mirror and removed the plastic crown my friends gave me for my last birthday. No time to remove the face paint or the body glitter, though. Oh well. After almost two years of marriage, Ryan should know that I'm a little crazy by now, shouldn't he?

Armed with a wet washrag, I scurried out of my secret room, scrubbing my face like a dingy wall as I went. By the time I reached my bedroom on the other side of the house, my husband was snoring, with Lily, my baby daughter, resting on his chest. I sighed with satisfaction at the sight of them. As I tiptoed back to my retreat, though, I groaned at the sight of myself in the hall mirror. Despite my spa treatments, not much had changed.

I'm no queen. I'm not even a princess. I'm just Tracey Blackman, a fat girl from Illinois.

Stop it. You are not fat anymore.

Okay, well, I used to be a fat girl. Sometimes I feel like I still am, like I'm one Oreo away from inflating into a balloon and floating out my window.

I wondered if my husband would notice.

Probably not.

My baby girl would notice, though, since I'd be taking her favorite sources of sustenance, also known as "the girls," which were currently overflowing my nursing bra, with me. (I like that word, *sustenance*. It's so…purposeful. Don't you think?) Since I've got the booby juice and because I know that Ryan really loves me, I'll forgo the Oreo and settle for my life as a slightly lumpy postpartum person. I read that in a parenting magazine over the weekend, that men can get postpartum depression too, so the term should apply to "postpartum people." I canceled my subscription after that, though the laughing fit did keep me from finishing a pint of ice cream that I hadn't realized I was even eating.

That's how I became a fat girl, silently polishing off the ends of cartons and bottoms of boxes like an efficient little machine. My grandmother taught me not to waste anything. Perhaps I internalized that message a little too deeply. I wish she'd lived long enough to see me at this size, let alone the size-six wedding dress packed up in the attic.

I felt like a fake that day in that itty-bitty dress. I still feel like that sometimes, though a lot less often since my dress size has doubled to a twelve. I walk around thinking that any minute somebody is going to find me out and scream, "fat girl undercover!" Once I was on the elevator and a big girl got off and a lady started joking to me about how overweight the woman was. I felt like some kind of spy from the fat side. After several attempts to say something nice without becoming physically violent, I explained that I thought the girl was beautiful. That was one quiet elevator ride. About as quiet as it is in my bathroom now.

After the weigh-in trauma, I was usually in here getting my praise on with Donnie McClurkin or Fred Hammond, but this morning it was just me, God and my scale. And one of us was saying the wrong thing.

Maybe I wasn't standing up straight. Right. That was it. I looked around my royal bathroom for a good laugh, taking in the purple-and-gold decor and crown furnishings. I keep it locked all week and far as I knew, my husband didn't come in here. I sure hoped not. This place was for praying, pampering and fighting the digital dragon also known as my scale.

The whole thing started with collecting princess decor for my daughter's future bedroom. Every little girl wanted to be a princess, right? Then one day I found myself crying after a tongue-lashing from my mother-in-law, Queen Elizabeth (yes, that's really her name). I decided to claim a throne of my own. Sure it's a gold-plated toilet seat from eBay (it had never been opened, don't worry) but I'm so glad I did it.

Not wanting to take the chance of Ryan waking up again, I locked the door and took a deep breath before climbing on the scale one more time. I leaned forward, looking past the belly my La Leche League leader promised would be gone by now ("Nursing really burns those calories, you'll see!"), so that I could see the numbers, numbers that I never thought I'd see again.

161.

There it was in bright red numbers, making a fool of me. Before I got skinny and got married I would have celebrated a scale that showed me those numbers (it'd probably have a bathroom to itself) even though it would have been defective. But now, a hundred pounds and four karats later, those LCD digits scare me silly, especially with today being Sunday. Though this scale is accurate to the pound Queen Elizabeth (I call her Liz to annoy her) can size me up to the ounce.

"You're almost one-sixty, you know. About a quarter pound from it. You'd better push back from the table, baby. You can't blow up like you did before. You have a family now," she said to me last Sunday on her way to the sanctified section at the front of the church. I'm surprised nobody heard the air hissing out of me, she deflated me so fast.

All that air must have followed me home from church last week and puffed me back up, because despite little sleep, little food and more exercise than I've done in I don't know how long, I gained weight. Again. And what scared me most was that I was starting not to care. When that happens, watch out, because Queen Liz hadn't seen anything yet. I can blow up faster than an air bed when I put my mouth and my mind to it.

I paused for a moment and closed my eyes, picturing myself exploding out of the tiny skirts my mother-in-law keeps buying me and splattering a crowd of people. I guess it's like being an alcoholic or something except I'm faced with the reality of my food addiction at least three times a day.

Though my husband thinks I'm kidding, I've told him more than once about the binge that could be around the corner. It could happen at any moment if I'm not careful. And I'm not usually; careful, that is. Counting things—calories, points, carbs, pick your poison—makes me nervous after a few months. I just have to believe that my thinking has changed at this point, even if I am little jumpy most of the time.

I was a much calmer person when I was fat, even if a cardiac event was imminent. Though the pictures of me back then are pretty shocking, I never really felt as fat then as I do now. Looking down at the numbers on the scale, I feel something that I'm not familiar with—desperation.

Last week, I overheard a woman in the grocery store blaming her belly on her son. He was the twenty-year-old pushing the cart! My daughter is six months old and I'm running out of excuses. After hearing that lady, I vowed to lose at least a pound. Instead, I gained two.

Figures.

Before Queen Liz shrunk me down (or blew me up) to size, I'd actually thought I was looking cute last Sunday at church. This week, I look a hot mess…and I know it. Seven nights of a colicky baby crying paired with two server crashes for my Web design clients leave a sistah looking a little tired. Not that Queen Liz will accept that as an excuse. To hear her tell it, all I need is a good hair relaxer, better use of my college degree and of course, one good round of Jenny Craig.

"We don't have to mention it to Ryan or anything. It'd be just between us girls. You can rip off the labels on the meals and tell him that they're TV dinners. By the time he figures it out, you'll be too cute for him to care!" my loving mother-in-law typed above the forwarded e-mail with the latest Jenny Craig special. She'd tucked a Weight Watchers gift certificate in the diaper bag she bought me months before.

Since I never mentioned the gift certificate and obviously didn't use it, the Queen moved on to Jenny Craig, citing a friend's success with the program. "That girl was big as a house before."

Wow, Mom. That makes me feel good, I remember thinking. Yeah, Mom. As evil as she can be, that's what the Queen wants me to call her. The sad thing? I want to call her that. Getting a wonderful husband would have been enough, but getting a mother seemed too good to be true....

It was.

This probably would be easier if I had more memories of my mother or if my grandmother was still alive, but I don't and she isn't. I thought I'd worked through all my "Are you my mommy?" issues until I got married and had my own baby girl, my sweet Lily. She looks a lot like my mother, same cinnamon skin and upturned nose. Nobody else recognizes it though since my mother isn't around. What people do notice about Lily is Ryan's eyes and laughing mouth, everything from him, nothing from me. Sometimes my husband works so much that the most I see of him is in Lily's eyes. Except for Sundays.

Sundays are the days when my husband turns off his phone for a few hours and leans into me, whispering funny things in my ear. Sundays are the days when we sit in the pew knee-to-knee, arm-to-arm. Together. A family. So, fat or not, I've got to get moving. Jesus is waiting by my prayer stool, calling me to put on my battle gear, to settle my soul—

"Tracey! What are you doing in there? Didn't you hear me before? Lily's hungry. She doesn't want me."

Oh well, so much for soul settling. Duty calls.

Ryan had stayed up too late working. I could hear it in his voice.

Lord, don't let it be one of those Sundays.

"Sorry, honey. Here I come." One kick sent the scale back under the sink (which felt good even if it hurt my toe). When I stepped into the hall, they were both there, my husband and my baby. They both looked happy to see me.

Ryan held a finger to his lips and shook his head when I reached for Lily. "You know what? She's okay. Sorry for yelling. I had a long night. Do you forgive me?"

I nodded and caught my breath, surprised as I often am by how good he looks, even in the morning. He is what my friend Dana calls "carelessly handsome," so good-looking that he doesn't even seem to be aware of it. Every woman in the church is aware of it, though, especially me.

He kissed Lily's forehead before kissing me lightly on the mouth and looking me up and down, pausing at all the parts I was trying so hard to hide. "You look so pretty this morning that it doesn't make sense. I'm supposed to be thinking about God, you know. It's the Lord's day. You do know that you're beautiful, don't you?" He took my hand and led me—us—to the baby's room where he put her in her crib.

Words didn't seem adequate for the moment, so I ran a hand up my husband's arm instead, thinking of how good he was to me, even before I lost the weight. His mother would have flipped if she'd seen me then. Ryan saw me, though, all of me. And he looked at me then just like he was looking at me now. Words came to me in a rush as we headed back to our room. "You look good this morning, too. Maybe we should take a few minutes to thank the Lord for what He's made."

Ryan opened the door to our room and pulled me inside. "I think that's a wonderful idea."

"Babe, can you do something with Lily? I can't drive with her screaming like that. Seriously." Ryan switched lanes and took a back street before stealing another glance at his watch. Late is not in my husband's vocabulary. Unfortunately, when you look up that word in the dictionary, you'll find my face beneath it. Though abstract concepts come easily to me, I'm often easily

confused by the basics, like the location of the only skirt
I can currently fit into. It's a cute skirt, thank goodness,
but since we lingered too long over our thanksgiving for
one another this morning, Ryan's probably done with
me for a while. At present, he's a man with one mission—getting to church before his mother.

He didn't have to worry about me fighting him on
this one. For once, I had his back. I prayed like crazy
on the passenger's side, all the while reaching back to
comfort Lily in her car seat. Things seemed much easier
when she was tiny and still facing the back. I guess
there's a limit to how much black leather a kid can look
at, because she always fell asleep in spite of herself.
Now, with a whole blaring world in front of her, there
was a lot to be fussy about.

Her daddy seemed to think so, too. "Oh, come on.
Get out of the way. That's not even a parking space.
What in the world is wrong with this guy? Can't he see
that I'm trying to get around?" Ryan honked the horn
and hung his head in disgust.

I did the same, minus the honking. When Ryan's like
this, there's no room to give, not a second to spare. If
he could, my husband would leave the car right here and
sprint to the sanctuary just to keep from being a few
minutes late for service. Knowing how painful this is for
him and that's it's pretty much my fault, I touched his
elbow, made him an offer. "Sweetheart, I'll park and
bring the baby in. You go on ahead."

His head snapped up. "You sure?"

See? I know him so well…in some ways. "Absolutely," I said, though I didn't sound totally convincing, even to myself.

Ryan picked up on it, too. He sighed. "Thanks, but no. You're just trying to help and I appreciate it. We're a family. We should go in together, late or not." His jaw set into a tight line.

I got out of the car, still stuck behind the line of traffic in front of us, and walked around to the driver's-side door. I opened it and tugged at Ryan's arm, gave him a kiss on the cheek. He didn't respond in kind. It's okay. I know he was just worried about the time. In my head, I was thinking of Adrian, Dana's husband. He's a model guy, the kind of man women want their daughters to marry, but he can't stand being late, either. He'll leave Dana at home on a Sunday morning in a minute. Ryan could have easily done the same. "Go on in, honey. I've got the car."

He looked relieved as he got out, but then the cars moved and he saw it. We both did. A salmon-colored Lexus parked in the pastor's space.

Queen Liz had struck again.

My first Sunday at my husband's church, I'd been amazed at the procession of ladies. It was amazing to watch, no matter how many times I saw the women file into Promised Land Worship Center. The first row curved in sharply, much shorter than the others. Those seats were reserved for Pastor Dre and First Lady

Hyacynth, along with the other ministers, full-time staff people and their families. The first lady's friends, the special ladies of the First Ladies and Friends Society, sat there also, usually in matching hats. On occasion, my stomach lurched at the sight of them.

My mother-in-law, on the other hand, looked as though her mouth watered when she saw those women. Ryan had told me before he married me that his father had served as an interim pastor of this church for a few years, but that another man had been sent to take his place. The son of that man served as pastor now and Queen Liz didn't seem too happy about it. Once one had a taste of the first row, evidently, it was hard to take being moved back. And moved back she was.

Row number two was what I like to call the Mama and 'nem section, reserved for all the cousins, aunties, parents and assorted other relatives of the pastor and first lady. The only person I could point out on that row was Pastor Dre's mother, who despite her advanced age would sport a pair of stilettos and a fierce suit in a minute and walk better than me while doing so. I need to get to know her better....

The third row, Auxiliary Alley, I call it, is for the older women of the church who did most of the work: the Altar Club, Missionary Circle and Women's Auxiliary all sat there, though none of us had any idea what most of them did. Queen Liz sat prominently on that row, even though no one, including her pewmates, was sure which ministry she belonged to. Personally, I thought she belonged to the I-ain't-sitting-back-no-farther-than-this club, of which she was both founder and president.

All the other ministries, groups and programs filled in the remaining seven rows that comprised the top ten. To try to pose your way into one of those rows was to invite scorn that could last a lifetime. I'd tried to shake hands with a woman at the restaurant we went to after church and Liz had almost karate chopped my wrist. "She's that woman who lied about being in the choir. Don't fool with her."

It turned out that the incident in question had occurred when she was in the fifth grade. Church drama dies hard. So does the ill will my mother-in-law sends my way every Sunday when I take my seat with Ryan in the back near the door. It's as far as I can get from the Queen and still be in the sanctuary while also offering the option of quick exit. Best seat in the house. Although there is a place in the balcony that would be just perfect….

Ryan won't hear of it, though. He tries to act like he's so different from his mother, but he has a thing about the balcony. "That's for latecomers, sleepers, visitors and other nonessential folk," he'd told me in the only imitation I'd ever heard him do of his father. The message hit home. I was all of the above except maybe a sleeper. Pastor Dre wasn't boring, that much was for sure. If his preaching didn't keep you up, the reflection of the lights off his cuff links, watch, bracelet and other assorted bling could definitely do the job.

And Hyacynth? Well, let's just say that though all

that stuff in my bathroom was a joke to me, the first lady probably had the real thing in her house. Howard undergrad, Harvard graduate school, Miss Black America two times over. Yeah. That's what I was dealing with. The few times I'd talked to her she seemed pretty down to earth, though. For a beauty queen, anyway.

There I was, being ugly again and in the house of God at that. My real problem wasn't with any of these people, but with my scale and my mother-in-law.

Your real problem is with God, I dared to think for just a second. That would have to keep for later, especially with my husband next to me about to break into a sweat.

"Why did Mama have to park in Dre's space? Can you tell me that? Sometimes I think she just wants some attention."

You think?

For my husband to be such a computer genius and great businessman, he could be a little dense when it came to his mother. Okay, a lot dense.

I settled myself down into the movie-theater-type chair, wondering for a moment if I'd have been able to fit in it a couple years back. Probably not. Black folks need pews. Room for your butt, your purse, your program and of course, a few inches to swing your mortuary fan if it came down to it. We had fans here. I'd seen them, but I'd never seen anybody use one. It was all about climate control these days.

The service started and no one noticed as I sprang the trapdoor on my nursing blouse. Lily gulped once or twice, but the music was too loud for anyone to hear. Everything seemed to lift off me as the choir sang, that is until the songs ended and they got to the announcements.

Ryan shifted in his chair as the first message blinked across the screen in all caps.

PLEASE DO NOT PARK IN THE PASTOR'S SPACE. IT IS PERMANENTLY RESERVED AT ALL TIMES.

It was all I could do not to laugh and not because it was funny, but because I was terrified. Queen Liz could get a little crazy sometimes and Ryan didn't do well with public displays of madness. He liked to keep his crazy at home.

As she did in my nightmares, Ryan's mother stood in the third row, talking to the church secretary as if there weren't fifteen hundred other people in the room.

It was hard to hear her, but I'd been cut by the Queen's sharp whispers enough times to make it out.

"I don't even appreciate that, Pastor. Who gave you that space, anyway? I've been parking there for thirty years."

I looked over to see what Ryan had to say, but it was too late. The brothah had used my exit.

My husband was gone.

Chapter Two

"Sometimes I think you make this stuff up," Dana said on the phone the next morning as we ran through the updates for her bath-and-body Web site. She had a new product line for babies, called Water Lily. It was based on the products she helped me make for my daughter's sensitive skin.

Lily hasn't had one rash since I started using the products and all the moms at church ask me what I did for her. I felt good about that until I realized it meant my baby must have looked bad enough for everyone to have noticed. I told them about Dana's shop, Made of Honor, and most of them knew about it already since they're franchised all over Illinois, but she hadn't made the baby stuff available in her stores yet. Some drove a few hours to Leverhill, unable to wait. Thanks to my daily needling, she'd finally agreed to at least put it on the Web.

The keys clicked under my fingers as I typed the

changes she'd given me. "I wish I did make this stuff up, Dane. It'd be a lot funnier to watch on TV or something. But you know what they say, truth is stranger than fiction. It happened just like I told you."

God must have been with me to let me get some love in before service, because after his mother's announcement about how that parking space had been hers for thirty years and she didn't notice the five-inch-tall neon letters saying Reserved for Pastor, I hadn't gotten so much as a kiss out of Ryan. He'd dived back into work a day early and he'd dived deep.

I've only seen the back of him, wandering down the hall, his voice shouting into the phone, since. I must say, though, it wasn't a bad angle. I could have done without the screaming, though. He needed a management-style makeover. And he needed it, like, yesterday.

Just then, an e-mail from Dana popped into my box with attached photos and descriptions of the new products. I'd twirled the phone cord around my elbow, about to explode with glee. Nothing like a click-chat, where we talk and e-mail back and forth. It drives Ryan crazy, but a man who e-mails people in the same house with him has no room to talk. None. Besides, everybody can't go blind and break their thumbs on a PDA like him. The prescription on my glasses is strong enough as is without trying to read some tiny screen.

I opened the files and smiled with satisfaction at the product photos. "I really like how these came out. I don't know why you seem so reluctant about the baby line. It's some of your best stuff yet."

I could almost see Dana shrugging two hours away. "I don't know," she said. "I guess it's the baby thing. I don't feel qualified. The wedding stuff I can do in my sleep, though sometimes it's a nightmare. I'll have to tell you about our latest bride when we have more time. Remind me. Anyway, I almost feel like this is your line, Tracey. I made suggestions, but you researched everything, tested everything…"

Wow. Dana sounding insecure? Too weird. Too much like we were discussing infertility treatments. "Wait? Are you guys trying to get pregnant or something? Is that it?"

A pause on the line. A long breath. "Yes, we're trying. Sorry I didn't tell you. I guess I thought we'd be pregnant the first month and all I'd have to announce was a baby on the way. It's turning out to be harder than we thought. God knows, though. I guess I shouldn't have been so concerned when you got pregnant so fast with Lily. You were the lucky one."

Sometimes I wonder. "Don't sound like that, okay? Now that I know you guys are trying, I'll be praying and available for random Googling on any topic you need. You know I'm good for that."

"Yeah."

The gaping silence, a rarity between us, widened until we both fell in. Refusing to accept it, I climbed out first. "Okay, I'd love to sit here and quietly contemplate this with you, but the boob buzzer is going to go off any minute now, so if you want to talk about it—"

"I don't."

Right. No more than I wanted to talk about the comment Queen Liz gave me after church on Sunday.

"Oh come on, Tracey, what size is that skirt, a fourteen? You're better than this. I know your mother died, but she must have taught you something." She'd said this easily, my mother-in-law, like a knife slicing through butter.

I refrained from telling Liz that despite our short time together, my mother did teach me something that seemed to have been left out of her own home training: *If you don't have anything nice to say, don't say anything at all.*

As the alarm next to my breast pump rang in the bedroom, I hung up with Dana and scrambled down the hall, stopping to smile at myself in the mirror on the wall. If there's one thing that thirty years as a fat girl had taught me, it was that I had a pretty face.

Such a pretty face.

Ryan was the first guy I dated who didn't say that. He was more fascinated that my laptop had a Linux partition. Go figure. Now it seemed I was doomed to just a pretty face again. Only, this time, it didn't look quite so pretty.

Please join the Queen for a breakfast of scones and tea on the veranda....

I wake up then, just as I'm about to drown in my bowl

of Raisin Bran. Not a very royal way to die. I sit up in the tub and push the bath tray forward so that I can stand up. Dana always thought it was weird that I could eat breakfast in the tub. What she doesn't realize is that I could live in there (at least for a weekend). A good stock of food, a stack of books and basket of Dana's products and Princess Tracey would be good to go.

Today, though, I've just got to go. I pushed my reign back a day this week, so as not to encounter the natives. Lily was sleeping on the floor in her carrier. It was her first time in the royal restroom, but I thought she could be trusted.

I got out of the tub, toweled off with my secret thousand-thread-count towel and applied Smooth, my favorite product in my friend's new product line for mothers. This week's scent was Mango Mama and I was feeling it from head to toe.

"This number does not define you. God does," I whispered to myself as I stepped onto the scale, adorned only with my crown and a hopeful smile. My belly looked smaller in the mirror at least. I got up the courage to look down, again having to strain a bit to see over my stomach. Mirrors were deceiving. The numbers, happy ones, blinked back up at me.

159.

Maybe my scale worked after all. I certainly hoped so. Funny how the numbers on this thing appeared so rosy and cheerful all of a sudden. Last Sunday, they looked like something out of a horror movie. I glanced into the steamed-over mirror, and traced the circles under my eyes with the tip of my finger. I should have added a facial, as well. No time now. Despite the good news about my bubble butt and its imminent demise, my face looked like I'd been kicked around the farm a few times.

Then Lily started screaming, like she'd been doing for the past five days. Straight. One more reason that I was just now getting to wear my crown. I didn't think I'd make it this week at all. We were going to the doctor today to see what was wrong. Of course, that meant another day's work pushed back. Another all-nighter. I patted my cheek.

A queen has to do what a queen has to do.

Today was supposed to be Ryan's day to watch the baby so that I could catch up on my site maintenance and start working on the new logo for the church, but with the way Ryan's been acting lately, I didn't bother to remind him.

A call to our family physician got us an appointment that I hope will answer some questions. Both Lily and I are going crazy. It would have been nice to have Ryan tag along, but again, I'm not going to bring it up.

One feeding, a diaper explosion and two outfits later, we were on the road, heading to the doctor. Ryan remembered that it was his day to watch Lily, called to apologize and said he'd meet us there.

More than an hour after his call, I tried to stay away from a bunch of sick children in the waiting room. I wasn't holding my breath waiting for the doctor or Ryan to appear. Ever the optimist, I gave my dear husband a call. "Hey, you anywhere near?" I asked in my neutral, just-checking-in voice.

He answered back with the force of a megaton blast. "No, I'm not anywhere near! I'm working, okay? I would think that you could handle taking the baby to the doctor alone. I wanted to make it, but there's some stuff going on."

I'll say. Our little nuclear family has had another explosion. Man down! Man down!

"No problem," I said, although there was definitely a problem. My man was losing his mind. Ryan's business had always been pretty much his life, but now I was worried that it would be the death of him, too.

Something would have to give, but right now I was more concerned with getting Lily well so that she and I could get some sleep. She had to be as tired as I was. Or at least as tired as I knew I was going to be when I looked up and saw my mother-in-law coming into the doctor's waiting room. And she was smiling.

Oh, Ryan. Why?

For a moment, a millisecond perhaps, the Queen seemed normal and I wondered, not for the first time, if I'd just pegged her wrong. She was wearing her sugar-cookie lip gloss and wheat-colored linen suit. Her open-toed Coach slides matched her bag. She was one hip grandma, to be sure. As I softened toward her, her words rained down on me from where she was standing above us, like a bucket of hail.

"Well, look at you! You've lost what, two, three

pounds? I can see it in your face. Definitely in the one-fifties again. Good girl." She patted me like a stable horse before plucking the baby from my arms. A woman chuckled behind us while flipping through a six-year-old issue of *Sports Illustrated.* Her husband, a little plump himself, looked on in horror while trying and failing to hold in his own stomach. I felt his pain. And mine, too.

"Hello, Liz. You needn't have come, though I do appreciate it." Did I appreciate it? Yes, I did. I think. I didn't like it, necessarily, but I did appreciate it. She was my family. "I know you're not much for doctors. You don't have to stay. We can meet for lunch later if you'd like."

She glared at me at the mention of lunch. "No, thanks, dear. I'm not hungry. I usually fast lunch from the approach of spring through the end of summer. Then I have a big salad for dinner. You should try it. Even when I miss my walks, it keeps the numbers down. Besides, this is what grandmothers are for. I wouldn't think of leaving."

I didn't have to ask which numbers she was referring to. The same digits that had made my morning, of course. Liz would have needed a sedative, though, if she'd seen the numbers that I'd rejoiced at today. Her scale has never gone that high. Ever. Not even when she was pregnant with Ryan. "Doctors didn't just let you eat for two in my day," she'd said when I explained that my doctor recommended that I gain at least twenty-five pounds with Lily since I'd been underweight by their chart when I conceived. Now that I'd added another fifteen pounds to that, Liz and Dr. Thomson were last on my list of people to see.

The nurse called us back just the same. "Lily Blackman?"

I tried to take the baby from my mother-in-law, but she was already up and sashaying down the hall with my daughter. She moved like only a former model can. Liz looked very comfortable chatting with the nurse, who was about her same size. Lily was weighed and had her temperature taken and we were led to an examination room. Once inside, Liz whispered to me that the nurse had four children and that perhaps I should talk to her to get some tips.

My throat tightened as I remembered the tips that my friends had tried to give me when Ryan and I had first started dating. "This thing with his mother, how he always talks about her, always calls her on the phone? Don't you think that's weird?"

In too deep and stupid enough to think such things endearing, I didn't think it was weird. Now? We'd left weird a year ago. We were firmly residing in the desert of madness and I needed a drink of water.

Living water.

Lord, please don't let me act a fool with Liz today. I know that she means well. Show me how to love her.

There wasn't long to contemplate that thought. Dr. Thomson entered the room with a big grin. His booming voice filled the room with Caribbean notes that reminded me of the preacher who'd presided over Dana's island wedding. The good doctor shook the Queen's hand. "Morning, Grandma. Nice to meet you."

Queen Liz didn't look very happy to have been so easily identified as a grandmother. Most people took her to be my aunt or friend. Though she was obviously disturbed by his greeting, Liz gave him her best smile just as well. "Hello, Doctor."

Before I could explain about Lily's problem (and my problem, all fifteen, no forty, pounds of it), the doctor picked up my daughter and cradled her as though she were his own grandchild. "Fussing, are we? No sleep for your mother? That means less milk for you, young lady, which is no good. No good a'tal."

Lily promptly smiled and fell asleep as she always did with our doctor, who'd raised nine children of his own. Sometimes I wanted to ask him how much he charged for house calls. At least maybe I could take a nap. At present, my spare thirty-minute block of the day was spent doing workout DVDs. It had worked this week though, so I couldn't complain.

"Coughing?"

"No."

"Just crying then?"

I nodded. "Yes."

"Before feeding or after?" Lily whined once. He bounced her one good time and she went quiet again. Amazing. He should bottle that for Ryan.

"After."

Dr. Thomson nodded, then looked over his glasses at me. "Have you lost weight?"

My mother-in-law beamed. "Doesn't she look good?" She gave me an affirming look.

The doctor gave a disapproving one. "Tracey, now is not the time for dieting. I told you that. Trust me, the weight will stabilize after the first year of nursing. Right now, though, you are building your daughter's brain. Your body is holding on to fat reserves so that it can make milk. Your daughter doesn't have colic, honey. She just doesn't like the skim version of her food."

Words escaped me. I just sat there, blinking. Could this be true? Had my dieting turned Lily's stomach? Sure, I tried to avoid nursing her after I worked out because some of the books said it soured the milk, but surely I wasn't starving the kid. I mean, look at me!

My mother-in-law recovered much faster than I. "So what you're saying is that perhaps it's time to switch to formula so that both mother and baby can get what they need? It's the only sensible solution based on what you've just said."

Dr. Thomson peered over his glasses. "It is not the only sensible solution, Grandma. It's not even a solution that I want to consider at this point. I realize that in our generation, breast-feeding was frowned upon, but my goal for all the mothers in this practice is to breast-feed as long as possible. For a year, at least."

Liz looked faint. "A year? Why, that's downright… strange. The baby will be walking by then. Talking, practically. It's gone on too long as it is. And the way it makes Tracey eat, Lily's brain will be too big for her head with all that fat milk. It may even make her fat, too—"

"I'm going to have to ask you to leave now." The doctor turned sleeping Lily away, as if hearing such things would crush her psyche. "Words are medicine, too, and I'm afraid you've come equipped with poison today. Your daughter-in-law is courageous and smart. She and her husband asked me to support them in the decision to breast-feed. I can't do that with you here confusing things. And for the record, Tracey is not big. You're just very…petite." The look on his face said the rest—that Queen Liz could stand to gain a few pounds and a better attitude.

It would have been easy to gloat as my mother-in-law huffed toward the door, but I didn't. I couldn't. She was Ryan's mother, even if I never would be able to accept her as mine. She gave birth to my husband. That meant something. It had to. "Please stay, Queen," I said, before I realized it. My friend Rochelle would have been proud of me. Dana would have thought me gone soft. Maybe so. It'd be fitting. The rest of me had congealed into a Jell-O sculpture, so why not my heart, too? Wasn't that what God wanted of me, anyway?

My mother-in-law wiped the corner of her eye and sat down.

I bit my lip. Usually there's no stopping the Queen's dramatic exits. My husband came by that honestly. "Thank you for your support, Doctor. And don't worry about protecting me." I took Liz's hand. "You know how mothers and daughters are. She just wants what's best for me. Ryan and I are determined to continue nursing through this first year. Don't worry."

My doctor bowed low toward the Queen before giving Lily back to me. "It's not Ryan that I'm worried about, Tracey. It's you. So many strong women come through this practice changed by motherhood into insecure little girls. I never thought that you'd be one of them. Your mother-in-law may be a queen, but so are you. You've just got to learn how to rule your own roost." With those wise words, a big hug and a menu plan for nursing mothers, Dr. Thomson left Queen Liz, Lily and I alone in the room.

As we left, I realized that my mother-in-law was still holding my hand. Tight.

I closed my eyes for a quick prayer. We weren't alone at all.

Chapter Three

We had a fight in the car on the way over. A pretty bad one. Almost as bad as the blowup with Ryan's software business earlier in the week. He assured me that everything was okay, while he tried to retrieve files one of his key employees had deleted. He whispered words like "solvent" and "litigation" when he thought I wasn't listening.

"Look, we're here now, okay? Let's just try and get through this. Dre wants me to step up and do some things in the church, but it seems like the harder I try to serve God, the more whack things get. I don't even know what we're fighting about."

I blinked back tears. "Me either. Not really. I think we're both just tired. All this stuff with your business has had you on edge. Some lawyer keeps leaving messages, by the way. Something about the articles of incorporation."

Ryan gripped both sides of his head as if trying to hold it on his neck. "Yeah, whatever. Look, I don't want to think about any of that right now, much less talk about it. Let's just go in here and see what the Lord has to say to us."

Sounded like a plan to me.

For once, Ryan didn't pop up out of the car and move inside the church at lightning speed. Whatever was going on with him, helping the pastor seemed to have him dreading going inside as much as I usually did. Today, though, I was trying to get a move on. A few minutes more and someone might take my back-corner seat. And that would be totally unacceptable.

I gave Ryan a little nudge as I grabbed the last of Lily's things. "Come on or somebody might get our seats. And you know I won't know how to function then. You might look up and see me in the balcony."

Ryan laughed, but I wasn't kidding. It just might come to that.

"We can't sit in the back today, Tracey. I forgot to tell you. We need to sit in the front, at least until after the announcements."

A rapid succession of blinks from me followed this insane information. "When you say front, just exactly how far front do you mean? Ninth row? Eighth?" All of a sudden I wished I had a paper bag in my purse. This was enough to make me hyperventilate.

"Third row, babe. With Mom and the other ladies. Don't look at me like that. It's one Sunday, okay? I know that my mother gives you fits, but she's my mother. Help me out. Just for today."

Famous last words. I knew better than to believe them. For one thing, whatever this front-row business was about, it wasn't just for today. Ryan dealt with things on a need-to-know basis, especially when it came to the Queen and I. I had a feeling that I'd be needing to know this same information next week as well. Still, she was his mother and he was my husband. "Okay. Just promise me that you won't let her clown on me in front of all those people. You know I hate that."

He kissed my hand and took a bow. "No problem, Your Majesty. Your wish is my command," he said as we passed one of the older deacons, who readjusted his glasses after we went by.

So, he'd been in my bathroom after all. He was so dead when we got home. For now, though, it was time to face the Queen. Wearing a prepregnancy skirt for the first time since the baby, I was feeling pretty good, too. It had elastic in the waist, but the Queen wouldn't be able to tell that. Okay, so she would, but I didn't care.

Ten minutes later, we were on the third row and far enough from Liz to keep things civil without having a fight.

Or so I thought.

Even with a hat more than a foot in diameter, three-inch heels and two-inch nails, Queen Liz managed to squeeze through twenty people to get to us before I could escape. And she had the nerve to drag a friend along for the ride.

I waved goodbye to the confused people who'd just

been reassigned farther down the row without their permission. If only I could get off as easily.

"That skirt is cute, but frumpy. Did you get my e-mail?" She lowered her voice to a whisper. "You know. Jenny Craig. No one has to know. I promise."

My eyes could have worn a hole in Ryan's shirt from the way I stared at him, but he was so caught up in his own distress (over what, I wasn't sure) that he left me defenseless. "Hey, Mom. You look good this morning. Nice shoes."

Obligatory or not, that was more than any compliment I'd been given in a long time. I took a deep breath, reminding myself not to be jealous. That was just what she wanted, to set us against each other.

"Thanks, son. You look good, too." She paused. "So does my sweet little grandbaby." She moved in for the baby kidnapping, always her ultimate goal. "Here, I'll take her."

My mother-in-law's hands came toward me in a flash of pink and green. My eyes focused on the pearl insets on the designs on her nails. She was in rare form today.

Instead of clutching Lily to my chest as I usually would have and trying to explain that in a few minutes she'd need to eat and I didn't want to disturb the service with Lily's crying, I let go. I let God. If the baby cried, she cried. Nobody would die. For whatever reason, Liz needed to make her friends think that she had me under control. (I knew enough from the dynamics between my friends and me to know when a woman, even an older woman, is showing off for her girls.)

My husband looked relieved. It had been a long week for him at work and at home. Though this seemed more serious than any problems Ryan had dealt with before, I still wanted to help. The difference now was that he didn't confide in me or ask my counsel the way he did when we were dating and first married. It was as if he thought I'd break since I'd had Lily, like he had to protect me from everything.

That, and the orchid climbing out of the lady's hat two rows in front of me was really starting to get on my nerves. Okay, so I had a baby. Women have been doing it since time began. I admit that it's more challenging than I thought it would be. Okay, a *lot* more challenging than I thought it would be, but God is helping me do it. Sure, there are days when I'm so tired that I fall asleep while I'm typing, wakened only by the blare of my nursing alarm, but hey, life goes on. I appreciated the way people looked out for me when I was pregnant, now I'm wondering if I'll ever be Tracey again. Not that I don't like the sound of Lily's mom....

I was doing it again, letting my mind wander in church of all places. Ryan took my hand and gave me a smile. Very nice. Now if I could just concentrate and stop making menus and to-do lists in the margin of my bulletin, I'd be making progress. I didn't know why, but ever since I'd had Lily, some of my most creative moments had happened in church. Usually, though, I was holding Lily, so I didn't get to write any of it down until I got home. Right there, as the choir was finishing, I thought of a concept for the logo for CurlyDivas.com, a site for black women with natural hair. I was enjoying that project a lot, even picking up a few tips for my own tresses.

Today I was wearing my half-ro in twists, set off by a middle part and sporting the copper highlights that my former hairdresser was kind enough to come to my home and put in. I'd tried to make appointments with her several times, but something always came up with the baby. And as much as Queen Liz wanted everyone to think that she was the perfect grandmother, outside of church and other public events, she didn't want to fool with Lily at all. When I asked her to babysit so that I could get my hair done, she suggested I call a friend or switch Lily to formula so that she could be sure that she'd sleep most of the time.

I got that my choice—our choice—to breast-feed made things a little unconventional for everyone. That was why I pumped my milk, too, so that the Queen didn't have to worry. It didn't matter, though. If I could just make it through the first year, things would get better. They had to. The good thing was, I was never, never doing this again. Ryan would have to play catch with someone else's son, because another baby in this body just wasn't happening. As soon as I was fertile again, I was going to—

"Here." Lily dangled from my mother-in-law's arms like a little golden dishrag. Her face was red from crying. Was I so into my thoughts that I hadn't heard my own child? The music was loud, but still….

She felt warm against me, pushing her face into my shirt. For all the hard times, there were good ones, too. I loved my baby in a way I hadn't known it was possible to love anyone. Tapping my foot to the music, I cradled Lily in the crook of my arm and pulled a blanket up over her. My nursing shirt was like some sort of James Bond contraption and with one flip of a button, all the goodies were flowing and totally out of view.

"'Lizbeth? Is that child pulling out her breast-asssissss? Lord have mercy. I do believe that I have seen it all." One of my mother-in-law's friends, Miss Bea, looked as though she was about to faint. She grabbed a mortuary fan from the back of the pew in front of her and started fanning so hard that I had to close my right eye.

I should have closed the left one, too.

Maybe then I wouldn't have seen the Queen's face coming at me like some sort of eighties 3–D movie. She wasn't smiling. She didn't even scream, which was what I expected from the look of her. What she did do was something new, something inexplicably terrifying.

She whispered.

And not to me.

"Son, get your wife up from here and take her to the nursing room. Now."

Ryan, who'd obviously been doing some daydreaming of his own, looked confused for a moment himself. "What, Mom? Tracey nurses Lily in here every Sunday. What's the big deal?"

Miss Bea started to wail. The organ faltered and

someone missed the entrance to the chorus of the song. The Queen took the fan and tried to comfort her friend, still speaking with the vicious whisper that made me want to look behind me to see if there was a sniper in the church balcony, waiting to take me out at any moment.

There wasn't. I peeked.

"Now, Bea, calm down. I told you. The girl has no mother, no home training. Don't you get yourself all upset now. I'm going to take care of this, if I have to drag her out of here myself." She turned and stared at me with the coldest look I'd ever gotten from her (and that's quite a collection).

Lily burped while her grandmother pushed up the sleeves on her mint-green suit. She meant that thing, as Dana would say. She was going to try to drag me out of here. I had to pray then, because the first thing that came to my mind in that moment was the almost forty pounds separating myself and the good Queen. Every ounce would come in handy if she tried to put her hands on me. Every ounce.

You are in church. That is your mother-in-law. Get up and go—

I was thinking it. I was praying it. But I guess I took too long about it, because the next thing I knew, Lily and I were up on our feet and a diaper bag was shoved onto my shoulder. My husband took my hand and led me out of the pew, providing a clenched smile to the two hundred or so people in our vicinity. This was past embarrassing, it was humiliating. Despite my resolve, a tear tickled my nostril as I stepped onto the carpet covering the aisle.

Ryan walked close behind me as though he had a gun to my back. I thought to myself that it seemed as though his mother had a gun to his. A loud sniff escaped when the pastor's wife waved and I tried to smile. Ryan's phone vibrated in his pocket, but he didn't stop for that, either. He pushed me along with purpose, even when I paused and tried to turn to him and speak, to say that this was insane and that we should just sit in the back of the church together and try to talk some sense into his mother later, there came a gentle pressure of his arm across my shoulders.

His words, hot on my neck, let me know that sitting in the back wasn't going to happen. "Keep moving, Tracey. For goodness' sake, just keep moving."

For goodness' sake, Ryan? Or for your sake?

Either way, I kept going. Smiling and crying like some sort of Miss Mom USA without her Prozac, I stumbled out of the only place I felt God in my life anymore and into the cold empty hall. Once the doors closed behind us, I turned to my husband and gave him a look worthy of the Queen herself.

"Don't look at me like that," Ryan said in a voice too loud for a church hallway but much quieter than his usual tone in such situations. He pointed down the hall at the door I'd passed so many times, but never gone inside. "Come on. You're going to have to go in there."

More tugging and pushing. Him trying to take the

baby, me taking her back. Him trying to take the diaper bag, me taking it back. Him throwing his head back as if he wanted to scream, me doing the same. Like a bad zit on prom night, things were coming to a head and this wasn't the place for the mess.

Though we'd both dug in our heels, mine were a little too cute to endure for the long haul. Just as my wedges started to wobble, Ryan took my hand and kissed it before steadying me. "Baby, please. Can you just come on? I need to get back in the service. Pastor asked me to do something special today and I'm going to miss it. I know Mom is out of line. I do. It's just not the time to deal with it." He led me down the hall, toward the door I didn't want to enter.

I followed, thankful that in the midst of the whole mess, Lily had somehow managed to fall asleep. Must be nice. "You always say that, Ryan. 'I know Mom shouldn't have said that. I know that hurt you. I'll talk to her. It's just not the right time.' You know what I'm starting to think? It'll never be the right time. I think you know that your mother will never accept me and you don't really care. Well, I do—"

"Get over it." Ryan folded his arms, rolled his eyes and pointed to the door. "You've got to go in there, so just do it and be done with it."

I looked deeply into my husband's eyes, wondering if he really saw me standing here, if he heard me breathing. It was me, wasn't it? Tracey Blackman, business owner, graphic designer, new mother, his wife? I'd never had to wonder who I was before, but since marrying him, bearing his child, I found myself searching for identity more than ever. And my husband had just told me to get over it.

Mother Redding, the wife of the former pastor, who also happened to be the mother of the current one, stopped to smile at me on her way into the sanctuary. Liz (the only person people seemed to call Mrs. Blackman these days) said the former first lady was mean, but she'd never been anything but nice to me. I looked for her every week just to see what she was wearing. This morning she wore a bright orange suit with flames going down the back of her skirt. Fire climbed her shoes, too. As she reached the door, she gave me a wink, then straightened her shoulders and went inside the sanctuary. Her son's booming voice burst through the door as she opened it.

My eyes looked back and forth from the door I'd come out of to the door it seemed I had no choice but to go into. Now I was going somewhere else, somewhere new, and I wasn't sure how I felt about it. I stared at the mahogany door once more and took a deep breath while reading the words engraved on the brass plate.

The Cry Room.

I remembered again why I'd never wanted to go inside previously. Who would want to spend a church service in a place with that name? Though I'd never been inside, I'd deduced that this was a place for mothers to take their crying babies. Did I mention that

Lily wasn't crying? I was the one about to burst into tears. At the beginning of my pregnancy, I'd enjoyed the way people had offered me a seat or given me special privileges, but even that had gotten old. Being escorted out of church and into a special room by my husband and mother-in-law was just too much.

This wasn't the first time I'd gotten this kind of reaction to feeding my hungry baby, of course. I'd nursed Lily in hot cars, bathroom stalls and guest bedrooms. Church had been the only place in my life where all of the pieces of me—Christian, wife and mother—could exist at once. And now, even at church there was a special place for me to go, away from my husband, who seemed to be slipping from me by the second, from the pleading look in his tired eyes.

Maybe this wasn't such a bad thing, this forbidding door in front of me. Maybe it was time for me to find my own place, both in our marriage and in our church. I attempted to square my shoulders like that flaming-hot church mother had done, but I was too weighed down by the diaper bag on my shoulder and the baby in my arms. Instead of standing straight, I almost fell over. Again.

My husband sighed, but reached out to support me again. "What are you doing, Tracey? You're going to drop the baby on the floor. Look, I've got to get back in there before Mom comes back out here and makes a scene, okay? It's not a big deal to go in the Cry Room. Almost every church in Illinois has one of these now. There's a window in there where you can see everything. And who knows, maybe you'll make some friends here. It might be good for you."

I took a deep breath. "Maybe I should just take Lily to the nursery and stay in the service with you. Maybe *she'll* make some friends in there."

Ryan lifted an eyebrow. "Don't try to be funny, okay? You know Lily hates it in there. After the diaper rash and the screaming last time, we agreed that she'd stay with you. Since Mom is acting so crazy about you feeding her in the church, I guess that means we'll be apart until you stop nursing, but don't turn this into a big fight. Not now."

Until I stop nursing? What was that supposed to mean?

He pulled back from me as if he'd touched something not so nice and straightened his tie, a silk one Rochelle had hand-painted and sent as a gift for his birthday. Right now, I wanted to wring Ryan's neck with it and get in my car and drive the two hours back home to Leverhill, where Rochelle, Dana and my other friends from the Sassy Sistahood e-mail group still lived. My heart went back there for me, back to my old church where they let mothers feed their babies under a blanket and people knew how to say hello. Where—

"Tracey!"

As my husband raised his voice to the tone he used with his insubordinate employees, a baby on the other side of the door let out a piercing scream. My husband folded his arms and made an I-told-you-so face.

"See? There's a reason for this. If that child was in the service, no one could hear and then the mother would have to get up and try to get out from between all those people—"

The door to the Cry Room jerked open and a woman I'd seen many times before stormed out with her crying child. Tears were streaming down her face, too. "Excuse me," she said as she pushed past us.

I watched in amazement, first at the dark room revealed when she opened the door, and second at her exit from the one place that was supposed to be for crying. She wobbled on her high heels across the foyer to the nursery. I gasped in disbelief.

The door opened again and a smiling face appeared, a deacon's wife whose name I couldn't remember. Sister Hawkins, maybe? That sounded right. She ran the Mother-to-Mother ministry and had very definite ideas about what being a mother meant. Running my graphic-design firm, In His Image, from home and putting Lily in part-time day care did not fit with her concept of mother-hood. Probably the only reason Mrs. Hawkins (that was her name!) still spoke to me was because I nursed Lily instead of giving her formula. She'd never say that, but it was the only thing she'd discussed in our brief conversations.

Ryan formed a tight smile as the woman stepped forward with one hand behind her to buffer the sound as the door closed. He narrowed his eyes at me a little, just enough that only I would notice. "Sorry about the noise. It's our first time. It's a little bit of an adjustment."

Sister Hawkins leaned forward, speaking only to

my husband and barely above a whisper. "We really like to keep it quiet here so that everyone can hear and the other babies stay peaceful. That baby—" she pointed down the hall toward the path that the mother who'd left had taken "—he wouldn't take his bottle. Not much we could do to help with that…." She paused to quiver at the idea.

"Anyway, Brother Ryan, your wife and daughter are more than welcome to join us. We've been wondering why she hasn't come in before now. I know that I sent her an invitation." She smiled wide, revealing the gold front tooth that had surprised me the first time I saw it. Now it just made me want to giggle. There were a lot of things we could do to hide our pasts, but some things just told the tale for us. The light hit the gold tooth from all angles. My husband blinked as if someone had just taken his picture. I was too mad to laugh.

I forced my mouth shut when Ryan squeezed my hand. I hadn't realized it'd been hanging open. I don't know which thing stunned me more: Sister Hawkins's gold tooth or the fact that babies couldn't cry in the cry room. What was the point of the place then? I decided to ask. "So it's not really a cry room, is it? It's a place for moms to nurse their babies?"

The woman turned to me. "Yes, that's it exactly. They're called Nursing Mothers' Rooms at some churches, but the Cry Room was what the building committee chose. I know it seems different at first, but it's church policy. With Brother Ryan advancing in favor with the pastor and the other men, you don't want to be disobedient and hold him back, right?" She patted my arm, then held it tight.

Feeling like a homesick kid on the first day of school, I gently pulled away. "I do want to follow the policy, but the church I grew up in doesn't make the mothers leave the sanctuary to feed their babies. Our pastor wanted all the families to stay together—"

Ryan frowned. "He's not your pastor anymore. And that's not your church. This is. Now go on in, hon. I've got to get back." He brought down his tone for Sister Hawkins's sake and gave her a polite nod as well, but not before whispering, "I'm sorry," out of the corner of his mouth.

I dropped my head. I was sorry, too. Once again, I was proving his mother right. That look on my husband's face had said it all. Though he loved me, his mother seemed convinced that I would never be quite right for the job of being his wife or running his house. I'd heard her whisper it to him more times than either he or I would admit. Queen's doubts had always made me feel bad, but this morning I wondered if she wasn't right. I couldn't help thinking too that Dana had told me not to marry Ryan. At the time, I'd thought she was jealous, since they'd gone out a few times. But now…

The woman's hand gripped my arm again, and before I knew it, the dim room enveloped me and the door shut behind me. Lily wiggled awake in my arms. I could imagine her blinking to adjust to the darkness the way she did in her crib at home. She knew she was somewhere different, somewhere that seemed far away. I smiled down at her, hoping that she could see me.

That's right, honey. They've put us out of the church of all things.

Chapter Four

"The changing table is over there. There's a rocking chair and baby swing in the corner. There are footstools under most of the chairs to use when you're nursing. There are some nursing pillows over there," the deacon's wife said, pointing to a stack of pillows and blankets in the corner. "If the baby falls asleep, you can walk her down to the nursery and put her in one of the cribs. They'll call you if she wakes up and starts to cry. The number will flash right out there."

Sister Hawkins pointed toward the panel of glass running across the front of the room. Beyond it was my new church family, milling about and shaking hands. High above their heads was a black square with blinking red numbers, each one assigned to a different child when they signed in to their classes. I saw a woman duck through the crowd and rush out the side door.

I pushed Lily upright and over my shoulder to keep

from showing my disappointment. The woman who'd run out had a three- or four-year-old, so this separation thing wasn't as temporary as Sister Hawkins made it seem. What if Lily felt the same way about the toddlers' class as she did the nursery? Would I be stuck in here for the next five years? Maybe I had it all wrong. I hoped so. "It's very nice. All of it. I was just wondering, though… How long do I have to stay in here?"

Sister Hawkins gave me her signature look of disapproval. Her children probably knew it well. "It's not a prison sentence, dear. It's an honor. Being a mother is a beautiful thing. It's a pity more young women don't realize that. Again, we ask that you use the Cry Room as long as you're breast-feeding your baby or whenever your child is crying during the service and not in the nursery. You'll like it so much, though, you won't want to leave. I've been in here seven years myself, ever since they built the new church."

"Yeah, this is her own personal pulpit," someone whispered, followed by a few giggles.

"Hush," the woman said in the sharpest, sweetest tone I'd ever heard. "Here, honey, sit down." She offered me a seat between her and another woman, who was the head of the Planning to Homeschool group or the Mothers of Many ministry, one of those women that I found both amazing and intimidating. I considered taking the seat she suggested to try to get to know that woman better. Rainy Styles was her name. I was sure about that. Ryan and I had been reading up on homeschooling and all other aspects of child rearing and I had a ton of questions to ask.

Still, I wasn't ready to spend my first Sunday that close to Sister Hawkins's scrutiny. Instead, I smiled at both of them and took a seat on the end of the back row in case Lily started crying and I needed to make a quick exit like that other woman had done. "Thanks, but I'll sit here for now."

·The deacon's wife looked a little insulted before fixing her smile, so much like my husband's a few minutes earlier, firmly in place. The church mask, my old roommate used to call it as we set out on Sunday mornings. She'd tug at her cheeks and forehead, determined to leave all fakeness behind. I had no name for the false Sunday smiles, but I hated them. Church for me was a place to be vulnerable, not a place to cover up and be perfect. There was the rest of the week for that.

Attending the church that Ryan had grown up in, the church where his mother still attended, gave me plenty of opportunities to need Jesus. My old friends had wondered how things would go with me coming to a church where Ryan had a past and I didn't, but Rochelle had said it best: "Go where your husband goes. God will go with you."

I had amened the sentiment then, but sometimes now I wondered if God had gotten lost in the move. My mother-in-law didn't just attend this church. From the way she'd had me kicked out of the sanctuary this morning with my husband's approval, it seemed as if

Liz just about ran the place. Now she'd have a whole team of women trying to whip me into a suitable wife.

Sister Hawkins attempted to whisper to someone about me. She didn't do very well with it. She needed to take hissing lessons the Queen. "They're talking about making her husband a minister, but I don't see how it's going to work with her acting a fool like that. Talking about her old pastor and such. Doesn't she know how things work around here?"

Evidently I didn't know much of anything at all.

The only light in the room came through the glass in front of us, so it was hard to make out who she'd been speaking to, but I knew that the speaker was the woman who'd escorted me in. My jailer. The pastor wanted to make my husband a minister? Surely this lady was confused, or at least I thought so at first, but after re-counting Ryan's nervousness this morning, I quickly realized she might be right. Gossips like that might get the details confused, but they generally got the big things right. Ryan was being considered for something. Why hadn't Ryan told me anything? Maybe he had….

I've got to get back inside….

Hmm…

Dana's husband, Adrian, was a minister now, though at the Messianic fellowship they attended, it wasn't nec-essarily called that. Rochelle's husband, Shan, was a deacon at his church, too. Still, my friends were real. Honest. Did I have to become some kind of Christian robot in order for my husband to become a leader?

I hugged my baby closer and shut my eyes before they stung with tears. Maybe Sister Hawkins was right. Though I felt I had a point, the sanctuary wasn't the place to prove it. I should have just come into the Cry Room like I'd been asked and talked to Ryan about it at home. The thing was, we didn't talk at home. Ryan barely talked to me at all, and when he did, that stupid cell phone seemed attached to the side of his head, or his BlackBerry, laptop or some other piece of equipment was in front of his face.

Lily pushed forward with her feet, digging her heels and toes into the cup of pudding that had once been my abdominals. I'd almost laughed when the woman mentioned nursing pillows. I didn't need any—I was one. Though I'd stood up at my wedding almost two years ago with a stomach flat enough to cook on, giving birth to a ten-pound baby had stretched me into some kind of rag doll. Body parts had left their original positions and shifted to new locations. Where my six-pack had once lived, there was now an empty Hefty bag, hanging over with just a little bit of trash in it. Or at least that's the way my husband described it right after the birth. I laughed with him then, but it wasn't funny anymore. Nothing was, especially not this room.

Lord, I love being a mother, but does this mean I have to stop being a woman? A person?

A pregnant woman on the other side of the glass paused in front of us, checking her hair. She smiled at herself in what she must have thought, as I once did, was a mirror. I bit my lip remembering how my own face had stared back at me from that glass when I was pregnant. I'd finger-combed my little Afro and kissed my lips together thinking how cute I was, just like this woman was doing now. I wondered if she knew what awaited her on the other side of the glass, a life of watching other people worship through a window, of running out of God's presence when your number blinked red. I wondered if she had any idea what this new motherhood was all about. I certainly didn't.

"She's missing the corners," the woman next to me whispered. "I love when they use it for a mirror, but I always want to turn up the lights real quick and wave so that she can see there's, like, thirty women in here watching her check her lipstick. We used to have fun in here, but that was before…"

I choked back my brewing tears and smiled, squinting a little to see the woman beside me more clearly. From her voice and sense of humor, I knew she was the one who'd made the crack before about this room being the other woman's own personal pulpit. I wasn't quite sure what she'd meant by that, either, but if I got to know this lady better, I'd be sure to ask. With her blond curls clearly in view, I realized with a shock, this must be the model-thin mother all the men spoke about, the one who always wore her old jeans back to church after each baby. The one husbands compared their wives to. Perhaps I should have taken the seat next to the other woman after all.

A friend must show herself friendly.

I sighed. Over and over, I'd prayed for friends at the church and every time, this scripture came to my mind. Today, I needed to suck it up and obey. I'd made enough messes for one morning. "You used to do stuff like that before? Before what? It sounds like this used to be a fun place."

The woman moved closer, extending both hands. Her baby must have been the little boy in the swing. "It was a fun place. But like I said, that was before…all the cliques, all the rules."

"Shh! Please be quiet back there. The Word of God is about to go forth. Have some respect," the deacon's wife said in a much less friendly tone than she'd started with in the hall.

The woman next to me laughed quietly. "That *means* her service is about to begin. Listen up, you'll get an earful. I have a feeling you're going to be our object lesson for the morning. Don't let it get you down, though. And don't let this room get you down, either. It used to be called the Breathing Room. It's only the Cry Room if you let it be."

"Quiet, puleeeeeze!"

Lily started crying at the sound of Sister Hawkins's loud voice, the same way she did at home lately when Ryan screamed into the phone while talking to his business partners. I tried to hush her quickly so I wouldn't be sent out of yet another room. I'd thought myself so blessed when I got married. Ryan had what every good girl dreamed of, especially one who'd been fat all her life and never had a date.

He was a Christian, a genius and fine, to boot. No other guy loved computers the way I did, and talking with him about open-source software and graphics programs had taken many of our dates long into the night. What had never come up was his workaholic tendencies. Oh, and his freaky relationship with his mother. That one was most definitely left out of the equation.

As Dana pointed out, though, I should have had a clue when his mother took over all the wedding planning and ordered those ugly pink bridesmaids' dresses. Straight out of *Gone with the Wind* those things were. I think back now and know how good my friends were to even wear them. I wasn't thinking about my friends at the time, though; I had only one thing on my mind, becoming Ryan's wife.

Lily tugged at my shirt and I gladly obliged her hunger. At least I could meet someone's expectations today. Slightly louder than the music had been, the pastor's voice filled the room. The baby grabbed my finger at the sound of the man's rich timbre, one she'd heard often when I replayed sermons in the house.

If I was honest, Pastor Dre, the younger son of the Reverend Redding, the man who'd pastored during Ryan's youth, was a much better orator than my pastor back in Leverhill. This young pastor's sermons were lively and contemporary and he had a great sense of humor, but like many other up-and-coming pastors I'd met, he didn't seem to know how to connect with people. Sometimes he seemed so focused on his programs that I wasn't sure he even liked the members, let alone loved them.

The people seemed to regard him more as a prince than a servant, and the gold lacquer thrones that he and his wife sat on behind the pulpit had almost sent me running out of the sanctuary my first Sunday here. Still, this was my husband's church, and somehow, I had to make it mine, too. Even if it meant losing me in the process.

"We see through a glass darkly," the preacher said. "We look in the mirror and think we see who we are, but we're not looking in God's mirror, we're seeing the reflections of other people and who they want us to be. You need to take a look in the mirror of God's Word and see what things are really looking like. That nice suit might be looking good in the natural, but in the spiritual, well, you could be wearing rags. You might look in the mirror and see a mother with dark circles under her eyes, but when reflected in God's Word, you are a beautiful woman, wise and valued far above rubies."

The tears I'd been holding back broke free and streamed down my face. I'd been looking at myself, at this church, at my husband through the mirrors of everyone but God. Sure, Ryan was different from my friends' husbands, but I was different from them, too. So breast-feeding had made me gain weight instead of lose it as everyone said it would. I was doing something good for my baby. Maybe this room, this place I'd fought tooth and nail to stay out of, would be a blessing, too.

My neighbor's fingers reached out for mine. She held my hand tightly for a few seconds and then let it go. She didn't turn to look at me or even say a word, but it meant so much just to have someone touch me, to have someone care.

The room blurred as I held my baby closer and let the pain of the morning run out of me with hot, wet tears. Unfortunately, Lily was used to my silent crying and she finished her feeding quietly. The morning had started off with me on the pew next to Ryan, praying he'd notice my new perfume and the prepregnancy skirt I'd worked out every day the week before to squeeze into. (Again, there was elastic in the waist, but still…it counted for something.)

I tried to remind myself that Ryan had fallen in love with me while I was heavier than this and he loved me now that my pregnancy pounds seemed stuck to my frame.

But today, he didn't notice my skirt. He didn't notice me at all. He'd spent most of the time before service explaining to his mother why I didn't usually pass Lily down the row to her and the other older women.

"Lily will start to spend more time with you as she gets older. For now, though, Tracey's trying to be a good mom and I think she's doing a great job." He'd actually sounded proud of me in that moment and I remember smiling and feeling beautiful. Feeling strong.

Those feelings were short-lived.

Ryan was the king of church etiquette now that we'd moved back to his home church, though he'd been a free spirit when we were both in the singles' group back at Broken Bread Fellowship in Leverhill. No matter how much you think you know a person, you never really know every part of them. You're lucky if you really get to know yourself. Dana tried to tell me that, too. Oh well.

Although the embarrassment of being ushered out of the sanctuary by my own husband weighed heavy on my mind, it was his words that pressed the hardest against my heart, not his actions.

Get over it.

It was the same thing he told the managers of his company all the time. Still, he'd never said it to me.

Until now.

"Church family, please welcome the newest member of the ministerial team here at Promised Land Worship Center, Ryan Blackman! Many of you will remember his father, Robert, who served here for many years. Ryan is an accomplished businessman, as well. Some of you are running his software on your computers at home. His wife is back there with the baby, but you can shake both their hands on the way out today. Ryan will be heading up the youth division of Christian Education. Give him a hand!"

My tears stopped and the Cry Room came into view again, this time allowing me to see my husband approach the pulpit. Say what? The minister of whom? My heart seemed to stop as Ryan took a seat behind the pulpit, next to the pastor. I could hear Sister Hawkins groaning from where I sat. My heart seemed to stop, but I knew it couldn't have, because I was still breathing. (I was, wasn't I?)

"All these years that my Reginald has been a deacon here and then Pastor goes and puts another young guy on the ministerial staff. Well, that's how it goes, I guess." Sister Hawkins looked over at me, no longer beating around the bush. "You'd better get your act together though if you're going to deal with those ministers' wives…they'll eat you alive, honey."

"Like she would know," my new friend the next seat over whispered, barely moving her lips.

I could only watch in shock as my husband was congratulated. Youth? Was this some kind of joke? Ryan barely had time for his own daughter. How could this be happening?

The woman next to me extended her hand again. (Why couldn't I remember her name? Probably because I'd been calling her Skinny Woman in my mind since coming here.) Brenna Ross. I'd seen her name and face on the screen as one of the ministers' wives. Her husband was the minister of music, a dark-haired hunk who all the visiting college girls went crazy for. At least I didn't have that to deal with. She pulled me toward her and hugged me.

"I hope you were listening to the sermon," Brenna whispered. "Get the tape and hear it again. See yourself as God sees you. You don't have to look good in anyone else's mirror. Keep your eyes on Christ. He's got his eyes on you. Call me. I'm in the directory."

I nodded and swallowed hard as she let me go, thankful for what seemed to be my first real friend since coming here. Thankful too that the glass separating me from my husband, the glass that I'd once thought was a mirror, seemed to have a different purpose after all—to make me see a new me, a woman made into Christ's image instead of her own.

Chapter Five

Though I'd relished the closeness of Sunday service, I could really do without the posturing of the lunch that followed. I understood that people were happy for my husband, but I wasn't prepared for the onslaught of huggers who approached us at every turn. It seemed a little silly to me actually. He was a youth leader, not a rock star.

My smile stuck fast until the hand-shaking and hugging was over. If that wasn't bad enough, Queen Liz had joined us in the line, shaking each person's hand before they got to me.

The woman was out of control.

I was out of control, too, even pausing to break my texting-is-for-idiots rule to send out an SOS call to my friends. After the way the morning had gone, I prayed that Ryan would tell his mother that we needed to go home and that we'd catch up to her another time. I should have known better than to think he'd do that, though. It was too much like common sense.

"Sit up straight, baby." My mother-in-law said the words without moving her lips better than most ventriloquists. "Don't make Queen Elizabeth have to pinch you now." She demonstrated the correct posture by holding her head high, drawing acknowledgment from other high-ranking church ladies across the restaurant.

I'd wanted to go home and be alone with Ryan, to get a clear answer on how he'd been made a minister without me knowing anything about it. Mother-in-law wasn't having it, though. Now that Ryan had sat in one of those gold pulpit chairs, she insisted that we go to the restaurant frequented by all her friends. I had a feeling that she knew more about Ryan sitting up there than he probably did.

Queen Elizabeth smiled at me, but I didn't smile back. All my fakeness had been used up this morning. Hearing her refer to herself in the third person had even wiped out the little home training she thought I had.

Though I'd celebrated my first wedding anniversary, the mention of my mother-in-law's name, Queen Elizabeth, still made me want to laugh sometimes. I'd thought Ryan was kidding the first time he told me his mother's full name. During her years as an educator, people had called her Liz, but at church and anywhere I happened to be, she was definitely the Queen. Today, though, her name didn't make me want to laugh. Today, it just made me mad.

"Forgive me if I'm not sitting erect, Mother, but my back hurts from carrying Lily and that diaper bag all day." I didn't add that the hours I huddled over my laptop typing furiously while Ryan and Lily slept probably didn't help, either.

"Just call me Mom, honey. Didn't we go through this already? And if you would just give that baby some formula, you could be sitting here like a princess. People, namely myself, would carry that baby everywhere you have to go. Since you insist on playing nursemaid, you must understand how it's going to leave you—" she sat up straight and patted her chest "—hunched and hanging. And make no mistake, no man likes that."

In my mind, I compiled several retorts, but I was too tired to do battle with Queen Liz today. What bothered me more than anything she said was the way my husband sat there silent, never interjecting a word in my defense. Or his own.

I turned away from Queen Liz to check on Lily, sleeping in her carrier at my feet. She looked so peaceful that I envied her a little, before thanking God that she was a baby and far from a woman. I leaned in to Ryan, circling his elbow with my arm, I pulled him toward me. "You looked handsome in the pulpit, baby. You should have told me and I would have brought a camera. Do I need to get ready to hear your trial sermon now or what?" I couldn't do ventriloquism quite like my mother-in-law, but I gave it my best try, hoping that being turned away from her and talking low would somehow keep her from hearing.

Fat chance of that. "Oh yes, honey, you're going to have to get ready for a lot of things. Ryan's father preached in that church many a time. He was interim pastor and would have taken over, but the denomination sent Pastor Redding, and the rest is history. We're about to make some new history, though, ain't we, baby? Pastor Blackman, now, I like the sound of that."

So much for my voice-throwing skills. And my life.

Queen Liz didn't know me as well as she thought she did, though. I knew how to play her games. Being a fat girl on the sidelines for most of your life gives a person time to watch close and learn everybody's tricks. "Head pastor, honey? Really?" I threw my arms around his neck. "This is so exciting. I knew you loved the Lord, but to give up your business and go into the ministry full-time? Where do you think we might get our first church? I heard there's some open churches in Wisconsin. Racine, I think. Wouldn't that be something?"

Confusion furrowed Ryan's brow. "Hold up! Slow down. Take a time-out. Both of you. I'm not giving up my business for anybody and I'm not going to be a preacher full-time. Look, Mom, I appreciate that becoming pastor of the Promised Land Worship Center was your and Daddy's dream, but it isn't necessarily mine. Now, Tracey and I have had a rough morning and the baby is tired, so if you don't mind, we're going to eat and get on home."

Now I felt like smiling, but my mother-in-law definitely didn't look like she'd appreciate it. She stared at both of us in total shock.

"Ryan? Baby, have you lost your mind? Are you talking to your mother this way in front of your wife and child? Now I know better than that, sunshine. I know that you wouldn't disrespect your mother, would you?" she asked in a voice so sinister it even scared me.

Ryan lowered his head. "No, Mom. I'm sorry. I'm just tired."

"That's my sunshine," his mother said, reaching across me to pinch his cheek.

Did she just elbow me or was that my imagination?

Either way, this whole scene was totally unacceptable and although I'd tried to be the quiet, nice person everyone needed me to be, this was too much. Way too much. My hunched back suddenly straightened. "Liz, don't worry. You're right. Ryan would never disrespect you. He reserves all that for me."

"Lower your voice." It was both of them together, mother and son, screeching their words between clenched teeth like a bad orchestra.

"I will not." That was me, opening my mouth wide for the first time in what seemed like forever. I was tired of swallowing my pain, chewing my problems like a piece of hard candy. Whatever had been holding me back had snapped and as my friend Rochelle would say, only Jesus could help us now.

I wrapped up two chicken legs in a napkin and

shoved them in my purse. That, and the look on my mother-in-law's face when I did it, made me crack up laughing. Totally a Dana move there. I used to hate to go to a buffet with that girl. I was about as hungry as I was mad, though, and didn't care who knew it. I stood up, dusted my skirt for crumbs and started gathering Lily's things.

"Tracey, I'm going to need you to sit down, babe. Everyone is looking." Ryan wasn't wearing his church face, but his real expression, the face I'd fallen in love with. The one I waited days on end to see, but rarely saw. It was a shame I had to loud-talk him in a restaurant to produce it. Still, it was too little and too late.

Lord, I've tried to be good, to do right, but I need somebody to do right by me. I'm sick of this.

"Ryan, I'm going to need you to give me a call when you decide who you want to be married to—me or your mother. I love you and I pray that we can work this out, but I know who I am and what I can bring to a man, to a marriage. And this just isn't it."

He reached for the baby carrier, but I already had it in hand.

Queen Elizabeth shook her head. "Let her go, sunshine, but don't let her take my grandbaby. That's your child. Put your foot down and—"

"Mom, will you be quiet? I want both of them. Tracey is my wife and you need to accept that."

That stopped me cold. How I'd longed to hear those words. I reached for his hand and started to say something, but Queen Liz beat me to it. Her hand knocked mine away as she laced her fingers with Ryan's.

"I told you she wasn't what you thought. She can't even take care of the baby. And look at her. She'll be big as a house again before you know it. Mark my words."

I closed my eyes and swallowed hard, waiting for Ryan's defense.

He didn't say a word.

Neither did I. The only sound was the squeak of my wedges against the linoleum.

Without looking at his face, I stepped toward the door, still not knowing what I was doing or where I was going, but a plan was forming in my mind. It was Sunday and in a few hours, Dana's daddy would be frying fish or cutting a ham and all my friends would be sitting around that long table, laughing and talking. Loving. Healing. Hoping. As I walked to the door, I decided that I'd be there with them, too.

Ryan ran behind me now, but a busload of church folk from across town entering from the side door cut him off before he could get to me. I jogged a little, with Lily's carrier banging against my knee and tears blinding my eyes. Why did it always have to be like this with Ryan and me? With him only expressing concern for me when I was running away? Mother Holloway from my old church said that some men just couldn't take good treatment, that you had to treat them bad to get some attention because that's all they'd ever known. She said some women were like that, too.

I didn't want to be one of them.

As I pushed through the first door to the outside, the outer door opened. A tall, handsome man with a goatee and designer sunglasses stepped inside, holding the door open for his wife, just as tall and twice as beautiful. Pastor Dre and his wife, Hyacynth, also known as Miss Black America in my head. I made a mental note to stop giving people these names, especially since Brenna seemed so nice. I wished she were here now instead of Sister Hawkins, who I'd passed a few booths back.

The pastor's eyes narrowed at me as he took me in and looked behind me at what was no doubt Ryan chasing me from behind. "'Morning, Sister Tracey. Wasn't that wonderful this morning? We're so glad to have Ryan on our team. We'd love to work more with you, as well. Will you be at service this afternoon? I loved those logos you sent over. I want to talk to you about taking over the entire Web site."

"Ryan and his mother are back there. You can leave me a message with them." I squeezed past them and through the door, still held open by Pastor Dre. I turned and ran for the car, wincing each time the baby seat banged into me. It would probably leave a bruise, but right now I just had to go, to get out of here. I needed to be with people who loved me, who wanted me around. Playing church wasn't my cup of tea.

I stopped at the car and keyed in, leaning inside to click the baby seat into its base. A million thoughts blasted through my mind. Had I really done what I thought I did just now? Had I run out on my husband in front of the whole church? Had I loud-talked his mother and snatched the baby and ran past the pastor?

Lord, what am I doing?

"Nice skirt."

My head hit the overhead light in the car as I jerked around, thinking it was my husband. He'd come to save me from myself, save us from falling apart. I eased out of the car and pivoted quickly, ready to collapse into his arms.

I caught myself just in time.

Almost.

It wasn't him.

I'd never live it down.

Running out on my husband at the local buffet had been bad enough, but being seen in the parking lot falling all over another man definitely wouldn't help things. True enough, the man, Mark Johnson, had been my personal trainer back in Leverhill and still made my stomach flutter to look at him, but that was beside the point. That his cologne made my toes curl was even more irrelevant. I was having a marital crisis, one that I'd created all on my own. Poor Mark had nothing to do with it.

That I'd had a crush on the guy the whole time he was training me (before I realized that he was nice to all the sweet, fat people at the gym paying him fifty dollars an hour) had absolutely nothing to do with anything. But what was he doing here? Now?

"Tracey? Is that you? You look…amazing." Mark's breath caught in his throat in a way that let me know he really meant it.

Was I blushing? I hoped not. "Well, I've picked up about thirty pounds or so. I just had a baby. She's in the car. See?" I pointed into the back seat and scanned the parking lot quickly. Though I was totally freaking out over the present situation, I had to wonder what had happened to Ryan, the husband I thought was chasing me. I did see a woman approaching, though, a tall girl with blond dreadlocks and a tailored dress that fit in all the right places. She walked up behind Mark and snaked an arm around his waist, despite his being bent over to look at the baby.

"Hi, I'm Willow, like the tree," she said, extending her other hand.

It sounded like a stage name, but it was definitely fitting. "I'm Tracey. Mark used to train me a few years ago."

Mark nodded and pulled Willow to the window to look at sleeping Lily. How she'd endured the knee-knocking run to the car without waking, I'd never know.

"Look, Will. This is her baby. Isn't she cute?"

Miss Tree recoiled as if he'd been showing her a snake. "Um-hum. Real cute." She looked me up and down again. "So you trained her in Leverhill at that little gym you told me about?"

Little gym? Temple Maintenance Fitness was one of the biggest gyms I'd ever worked out in, and my business took me all over the country. Or at least it used to. I hadn't been on the road much since Lily was born except for weekend trips back to Leverhill. I got the feeling Willow had never been there, but assumed that anything outside Chicago was nothing. I wanted to remind her that we were in Naperville, a suburb of Chicago and not the city itself, but I had a feeling I'd be met with the same reaction that Mark was.

Whatever.

I had to get going anyway. That little town she described had a lot of people who loved me in it and right now, I needed them more than ever.

Mark laughed a little. "It's a huge gym, Willow. Better than the one we train at here, in fact. Tracey and her friend, um, Diane was it?"

"Dana."

"Right. Tracey and Dana were two of my first clients there. They took a chance on me and signed right up. Tracey lost a good bit of weight with me, like what, fifty-two pounds?"

I smiled. He had a great memory. "Fifty-three."

"Right. But it looks like you've lost, what, another fifty? Sixty, maybe? I know I said it already, but you look amazing." Without warning, Mark pulled away from his girlfriend and gathered me up in a hug, lifting me off the ground. "I am just so proud of you, girl! You did it up big. Well, small. Anyway, it's nice to see you and congrats on your baby."

I tried to find my voice. There it was. "Thanks. Nice seeing you again. And nice meeting you, Willow."

As I turned, I gave the parking lot one last sweep for Ryan and a quick glance at the restaurant. In the window booth where we'd been sitting, I saw my husband, wearing a new face, a sad one I'd never seen before. Beside him was my mother-in-law, talking animatedly and waving her hands and pointing toward the door, no doubt recounting my little scene.

I squinted to see who she was talking to, then sighed when the other occupants of the booth came into view. Pastor Dre and his wife. I jumped into the car and slammed the door, wishing all I had to do to fix this was run into some room behind a piece of glass. I'd come to the restaurant worried about Ryan becoming a minister. I pulled away from the parking lot wondering if I'd have a marriage to come home to.

I also wondered something else, something that scared me. I wondered if Mark Johnson and Willow were married.

Chapter Six

I didn't have to say a word.

My friends knew what had happened without me even speaking. I guess Ryan and I had become pretty predictable. I'd secretly hoped that the problems we'd had at the beginning of our marriage stemmed from me getting pregnant on our honeymoon and us moving away from the church we'd met and married in. I'd prayed that having a baby would bring us together, and would make things better or at least give us something to talk about again. Instead, it'd driven us apart.

Today, it'd driven me away from my home and husband in Naperville, Illinois, and over the Ronald Reagan Memorial Parkway, back to what still seemed like home. For me anyway. Lily hadn't stopped crying since we hit the interstate. How she could sleep through anything at home and scream on a peaceful ride that would have put most babies to sleep, I never would understand.

I saw Adrian Norrell, Dana's husband, first. He was taking out the trash, which meant they'd probably barbecued ribs. They were good, but messy, especially with all the kids running around. I'd downed those two chicken legs fifty miles ago and knew that in my present state of mind, me and a plateful of barbecue were going to be a dangerous combination. There'd be something healthy, though, since Dana had had a stroke the first year Ryan and I were married. (I sometimes think my marriage contributed to it, but there was a lot going on that year.) Since then, there was usually something healthy at the Sunday dinners.

You have bigger things to worry about.

I cut my engine and parked, realizing that though I'd texted Dana, she always turned her phone off on Sundays. Too bad my husband didn't try that, too. I squeezed the steering wheel. I'd dreamed all my life of getting married. I'd served with Dana as a bridesmaid in nine weddings, with me usually looking like a giant piece of fruit. I thought once you got the guy, the happily-ever-after was automatic. Now I was just praying for a happily-*even*-after. Even after he hurt me. Even after I ran out on him at a restaurant....

Adrian dropped the trash can. "Tracey? Is that you? Are you okay?"

Before I could answer, Adrian had the car door open and was hoisting me up over his head like when we were kids. I'd been chubby even back then, but Adrian had somehow always managed to pick me up. "Okay, you're not bleeding. Girl, you scared me! Is the baby okay?"

"She's fine. It's just…" Adrian's concern made me start crying all over again. Though Dana had married him, Adrian had been my best friend, too. Many of my expectations of a husband had come from growing up with Adrian opening doors for me and treating me with respect. Dana didn't know how good she had it. Well, I guess she'd figured it out. She married the guy.

"Lily's in the back seat. She just went back to sleep. She's been wailing like a wounded animal the whole ride."

Adrian didn't answer, he was already in the car, unlocking the car seat from the base and grabbing the diaper bag. He reached back for my keys and slid them into a pocket on the bag.

I swallowed hard. He'd done more for me in that moment than my own husband had cared to do all day. It wasn't that Ryan was insensitive, his mind was just overloaded. As the CEO of a company that had grossed over eight million dollars in the past two years, the last thing on his mind was my diaper bag.

Before his mother had chimed in with her opinion, Ryan and I had agreed to hire a nanny to fill in while we alternated days with the baby. His mother quickly changed his mind on that one. "You don't need to do a thing for that baby. That's what your wife is for," she'd said. Ryan disagreed with her in private but his actions since said that he believed her words much more than he let on. As my old pastor loved to say, "When you believe a thing, you behave like it." Good or bad, that was true.

Adrian took my hand and helped me over the sidewalk. He blinked furiously at me, which meant he knew how bad things were. Adrian didn't always talk a lot, but if you watched all his blinking and head rubbing and carrying on, you could pretty much figure out what he was thinking. Today was no exception.

He stopped and took a long sniff, which meant he was looking for a new candle scent and something had caught his nose. A year or two from now, when the new scent came out, I'd figure out what it was he'd smelled. I hoped it was something wonderful. I couldn't wait to go to the store he owned with Dana and fill my trunk with candles and soaps. After the scolding I was likely to get from Rochelle, the resident mama of our little crew, for how I'd acted today, I was going to need some serious pampering. Why hadn't that thought occurred to me until now? Suddenly I wasn't in such a rush to get upstairs.

Adrian paused on the bottom step to their second-floor apartment, which Dana had shared with me for three years before I married Ryan and moved out. He ran a hand across his bald head. "Now listen, T-Bone, I don't want to pry or anything—"

I punched his arm. "What did I tell you about calling me that? Don't make me have to get your wife on you." The first time Adrian saw me after I'd lost my weight, he'd christened me T-Bone to the delight of everyone. I'd banned him from using the title, though, and until now he'd honored that. I wasn't mad, though; it was an unspoken rule between us that when the situation demands it you can break the spoken rules. If it wasn't okay to do that sometimes, he and Dana might not be married now. I had to do an awful lot of negotiating to get Adrian to my wedding with Dana's no-Adrian-anywhere-that-I-am rule. So I could let this T-Bone crack slip.

Adrian and I took the next set of steps in silence, but he paused on the landing. "Okay, now you know they're going to pounce, right? Especially Rochelle. You want to work your story out on me or are you going to plead the Fifth? I can back you up on that if you want me to."

I started crying again.

What a sap I am today.

"What's wrong? Did I upset you?" He wiped my face. "Do you want me to go and get Dane? I just didn't want them to jump on you without knowing how to back you up. You know how family is." He smiled, showing that place where Dana had chipped his tooth in second grade. I'd been there watching, on the sidelines, the place I knew best. Now I didn't know where I was. Who I was.

That's not what you told your husband today.

My little I-know-what-I-can-bring speech came back to my mind and stung me like a recoiled rubber band. I shook my head at Adrian. "You didn't upset me. It's just so overwhelming for someone to have my back, to consider how to defend me, how to support me. I miss that so much. I need it now more than ever."

I paused to take a breath and got a mouthful of tears. "I walked out on him, Adrian. In a restaurant full of people he grew up with, people we go to church with. His mother, well, she's just become impossible and I don't know what happened. Something in me just snapped."

Adrian looked down at Lily, probably to be sure that she was sleeping, and set her carrier down on the steps in front of us. He took a seat, too, and patted the space beside him. It was all so seventh grade. He rubbed his temples now. Confusion.

Why don't I know Ryan this well? Why did I marry him without knowing him like this? What was I thinking?

"Tracey, of all of us in the group, you and I don't snap. We mess up, we freak out, but we don't really get angry very often. This lets me know the same stuff from before is probably still going on."

I gripped the edge of the stair. "That and a lot more. I know you and Ryan are friends, too, so I don't want to get into it. If he wants to tell you, he can, but I doubt he would even think there's anything to discuss. He's a very different person in Chicago, that's all I can say."

"We all are." Adrian put his palms together. "That's one of the reasons I came back here. I had to get real, you know? The city is alive and I love it. Dane and I are even talking about moving over there maybe half the year. We can handle it now, but not two years ago. Not even last year."

I wiped my eyes and nodded agreement. Time. It had passed so slowly when I was single, but now I grabbed for it and it slipped through my fingers. Something new was always being added when I never felt as if we ever resolved any of the old things, like how we got together in the first place. I'd admitted to my friends about having sex with Ryan before we were married because I was afraid of losing him, but my husband and I had never really got before the Lord or each other and hashed it out. We'd both apologized to each other and asked God for forgiveness and maybe that was enough, at least for Ryan. Maybe it was me who needed to work things through, like why I'd done so many things that went against who I was since getting with him.

I sighed. One of the Sassy Sistahood rules was to avoid self-analysis. It was a task best left to friends. I smiled and stood up. "There's no point putting it off; let's go on up and let them put me on the hot seat."

Adrian's phone rang at his waist. He reached down and clicked it off without missing a beat. I bit my lip to keep from crying about that, too. Once inside the apartment, Dana ran for me first. Everyone else went for the baby. Rochelle kissed my cheek and offered me a ride home.

"Thanks, Chelle, but I've got enough folks telling me what to do at home. Stay here with your family. I got myself here. I can get myself home," I answered firmly.

Dana leaned back a little and looked me up and down. "Okay, where is my Tracey? I don't think I've ever heard such words come out of your mouth since you got up the nerve to ignore me and marry Ryan." She smiled. "Which was a very wise choice, by the way. I didn't know that then and I'm sorry I tried to come between the two of you."

You were wiser than you know, girl.

I shrugged. "It's okay. You had some good reasons for being concerned. Reasons that I need to learn to live with now. Not that I'm perfect, either. I acted really crazy today. It was like I had been wound up so tight so many times that there was just nowhere to put it. I tried to do what I always do and just lay it down, but there was no more room to put anything else. I had to get up and get out of there."

Rochelle nodded. "Girl, you know what I say, when it gets like that…"

"Only Jesus can help you!" They all said it together, even Shan, Rochelle's new husband. I hadn't had a chance to get to know him very well yet, but he and Ryan had become fast friends. I felt bad airing all my mess in front of him. Oh well, being around our crew, I knew he already had his share of secrets and stories, too. It was the nature of things.

I tugged at Dana's shirt. "Guess who I saw today? And in the parking lot when I'd just walked out on Ryan no less?"

Dana twisted her mouth. "I have no clue. Who?"

I hesitated, wishing I'd waited until the husbands were in another room to tell her, so I could give her the full scoop. Later for that. "Mark Johnson! Our old personal trainer? I don't know if you remember him since you quit after the first couple sessions, but—"

Adrian snorted. "Oh, she remembers him all right. Mark, the *fiiiiiiiine* personal trainer. I remember everything y'all say."

Dana cracked up laughing. "That isn't fair. We were just friends then, you and I, Mr. Husband. You can't hold stuff that I said against me. And besides, baby. I love you, you know I do, but as you tell me about Halle Berry, fine is fine."

Rochelle gasped. "Adrian, did you say that? To your wife? Now, I know better than that." She wagged her finger at him in a mock scolding. "Anyway, Halle ain't all that. Now Denzel on the other hand…"

Everyone laughed, including Shan.

Adrian scooted over near Shan. "Now, see, this man here has the good sense to be quiet, but he won't even cut in to save a brother."

Dana pinched her husband. "Now we're even." She turned back to me. "I can't believe you saw Mark. I saw him a few times after I left the gym, right after I quit going. I was trying to hide from him then since I was slipping on the program, but it was unnecessary. He walked right past me. After all this time and as different as you look, did he remember you?"

Oh yeah.

"Yep. Not at first. He was just walking by and said 'nice skirt' and then realized who I was."

Adrian nodded. "That is a nice skirt, by the way. I

forgot to say that on the way up. Good color on you, too."

Everyone stared at Adrian. It was moments like this when his growing up being friends with a pack of girls really showed.

Adrian shrugged his shoulders. "What?"

Shan shook his head. "You guys never cease to amaze me. I love it. I wish I'd known y'all back in the day."

Tracey couldn't resist saying what they were all thinking. "Shan, you were in junior high when we were coming up."

He laughed first, letting everyone know it was okay to follow suit, although Rochelle was still a little sensitive to comments about their difference in age. They were a perfect fit though, anybody could see that, especially all of us. We were glad to have her back to her old churchy self again. For a minute there, she was getting laid back like Dana and I and that would have totally thrown off the balance of the group.

Ever the thinker, Adrian cut through our laughter. "Shan, you're stuck with us for the rest of your life, man. Believe me, that's long enough."

He turned back to me. "Well, I can understand Tracey not wanting to be escorted home like a child, and it's getting late for the baby to be on the road again. What about me going to pick up Ryan and both of you staying over?"

I choked on my watermelon. "I don't think—"

"Yes. That's the perfect solution." It was Dana's father.

How long had he been standing in the corner behind us? "In fact, I called Ryan when Tracey arrived and invited him to come and stay the night. He's already on his way."

I sighed, trying not to be mad. Dana's dad was the closest thing to a father I had, but sometimes he pushed too far.

Shan, who was famous for the homemade barbecue sauce, brewed for weeks at a time, licked some of his legendary sauce from one of his fingers and took a deep breath. "One good thing about hanging out with folks who love the Lord, they'll feed you, listen to you and help you out, but in the end, you're right back where you started—at the feet of Jesus."

I pressed my lips together and thanked God for adding Shan to our little group. He definitely fit in.

Ryan came.

And he left his phone at home…on purpose.

I'm not sure if Dana's father threatened him or what. I really didn't care. What mattered to me was that Ryan cared enough to make the effort to drive here and to leave his work at home.

"Thank you for leaving your phone," I said as the room cleared and the lights dimmed. Though there'd been bustle and noise a few minutes before, upon Ryan's arrival, my friends had whisked sleeping Lily away and escorted us to the guest bedroom. Adrian used it to test new candle scents. Tonight it smelled like cherries and cream.

Ryan took my hand. He pressed my fingers to his

lips. I took his other hand and wrapped it around mine. "I'm sor—"

"No, I am." He pulled me to his chest and held me tighter than I think he ever had.

I closed my eyes, taking it in. This was real. This was what I needed to remember. "I said it first. And it's true. I really am sorry. I don't know what's wrong with me. First this morning, then the restaurant. I just made a big deal out of everything. Like you say, I just need to get over it."

He kissed my neck. "No, I need to get over it, babe. I need to get over myself. I need to get over my mother, my business. I know it's messed up, believe me, I do. I just don't know how to change it. My mother needs me. My business needs me. But—"

"We need you, Ryan. Lily and I. Do you know why I didn't want to go in the Cry Room today? It's because that's the only time in the week when you're not working, when you'll talk to me without a phone to your face. The only time when you touch me. Do you know that I need you to just touch me? Not only when we're in bed, but all the time."

Ryan pinched his eyes shut, then opened them again. "I guess I don't feel like you need me, Tracey. I watched you for years in the singles' group before we ever got together. You're smart, friendly. You know everything about, well…everything. I guess I never really feel like you need me."

He looked toward the door. "And when we lived here, well, you had your friends. Believe it or not, I often felt about them like you feel about my mom. I didn't have time to hang out with you guys, so I just never really fit in. I was always the bad guy." He ran his hands through my hair. It felt so good that I sighed louder than I meant to.

Ryan laughed. "You like that, huh?"

I pressed myself against his chest. "I do. You don't do it anymore. You don't do any of the things that make me feel like you love me. That scares me."

He turned off the light and pushed me toward the bed. "You don't do any of the things anymore that show me that you need me, and that scares me," he said, sliding off his shoes before pulling back the covers. "I know that you're out of my league. I've always known it—"

"What?" I was glad the lights were out so that he didn't have to see what had to be my bewildered expression. "Are you kidding me? Honey, you're a genius, you're rich and you're handsome…. I'm just regular. Normal. A fat girl who got fine." I reached down and covered my belly. "For a minute anyway."

Ryan didn't laugh like I wanted him to. For a long time, he didn't say anything. With every second that ticked away, I grew more confused. How could we both have things so wrong?

He pulled my hand away and said fiercely, "You are a beautiful woman, Tracey. My mother was out of line today. I thought you were beautiful before you lost the weight, while you were losing it, and now that you've had Lily, well, you're even more beautiful. Please know that."

It was my turn to go silent then. I just didn't know what to say. Not to mention that I was trying to memorize those words for all the times I'd questioned Ryan's love or my own beauty.

Finally, Ryan rolled onto one elbow and stared down at me for a few seconds before kissing me. It was the kind of kiss we'd shared when we were dating. That kind that made a woman feel wanted. Loved.

He took my face in his hands. He looked serious, like he looked when studying a spreadsheet or a sales projection. "You told me at the restaurant today that you know what you bring. Who you are. You don't. I can only hope you don't figure it out before I get myself together."

I didn't know what to say to that and he didn't give me a chance to respond, the kisses came like rain, fast and furious and then quiet and steady. I took them in, trying to take each one as though it were the first, as if this were the beginning. In many ways it was. It would have to be.

I fell out of bed.

"Babe? Are you okay?" Ryan sounded stricken at first, but once he knew I was okay, he started laughing. "That king-size bed has you spoiled, see? You woke up on a full and flipped onto the floor."

Still not quite awake despite the impact of my fall, I took a deep breath and tried to gather my wits. Cherries and cream. Candle-wax burns on the carpet. I was at Dana's. In the guest room.

With my husband.

That part made me smile. For a few seconds anyway. Then I started to lose it. "What time is it? I'm sorry. You didn't have your phone to wake you up. Do you need to call Sam? Which office are you at today? Should you be out of town? I'll get the baby…." I stood up so fast that I felt dizzy, but I'd be fine once we got on the road.

"Get back in the bed, Tracey."

He didn't have to tell me twice. I dived in. "Yes?"

"I took care of all that before I came. I'm off today, that's why I left the phone. There's really nothing that Sam can't handle and if there is, then God will take care of it. I worked through our whole honeymoon for goodness' sake."

"You made it up to me." As much as such a thing could be made up to a woman.

"We both know it can't be made up for. Even the wedding. I was running all over with my cousins and not with you. I can be a moron sometimes. I know it. My mother's a little crazy, but I know what to do to make her happy. You? You're so much harder. You don't just want me to do something or say something, you want me. All of me. And I don't know if I've given that to myself yet."

Whoa. Big emotional breakthroughs this weekend.

Since he was in such a sensitive mood, I took another stab. "Well, there's always counseling. If not with Pastor Dre, there are a lot people who could do it. Adrian is even licensed."

Ryan made a sour face. "Yeah: Right. I don't think so. I'm here and my phone's off. Can we start with that?"

"We can. One victory is enough for now. I was starting to think that phone was a part of your body."

He pulled me closer. "It kind of is, but I thought you knew that coming in. I guess working so much and so hard for so long has kind of messed up my social skills. Besides Dana, none of the girls I dated before seemed to care. As long as I gave them presents, they didn't care too much about talking to me, anyway."

I didn't react to that comment, but I stored it away to consider later. We'd talked about his other relationships before, but none of our conversations had given me the complete picture that I'd gotten just now. It explained a lot of things. Slowly I was realizing that everyone in Ryan's life until now, including his mother, had loved him based on what he could do for them. I'd come along with my own business, my own friends, my own money and my own God. If provision was what he was basing his worth on, I could see where my self-sufficiency both attracted and repelled him. Definitely a case for the Sassy Sistahood to work through.

Or not.

Lately, I'd been more and more reluctant to spill the beans to my friends and I felt the same vibe from Dana and Rochelle. We were still close, but some things were just private. Maybe I'd talk to Austin about it. She was newer to the group and didn't have as much baggage to carry. Listening and bringing the right snacks was her gift. She held the spot in the group that had once been mine before I became the tragic newlywed. I didn't begrudge her the position.

"So, it's just you, me and Lily today? I'd better go and call Dana and see when they're coming home from work and who has the baby. I don't hear her downstairs, but she's got to be starving by now."

Ryan sat up in bed and lifted me onto his lap. "She's fine. The last time we were here, Austin's friend had that breast pump and you left the milk in the freezer, remember?"

"Are you serious? That was what, three months ago?"

"Four, but it's good for six months. Apparently, Adrian was too grossed out to touch it and Dana forgot it was there. I guess Adrian has his guy moments after all."

I gave Ryan a sideways look. He and Adrian got along very well, but Ryan told me early on that we all held every guy we met up to Adrian and that no regular guy could deal with that much girl stuff. "It's kind of weird, to be honest," Ryan had finally admitted one weekend when we'd all gone shopping and Adrian had picked out an outfit that was perfect for me.

Adrian's understanding of women made sense to us because of his mother and his first wife, who he'd cared for before she died of lupus. He'd just had a lot of opportunities to observe women in stressful situations, something Ryan's mother was determined that no one see. I also thought it interesting that Ryan would think Adrian's girl powers strange without cluing in on the total weirdness he and his own mother had going on. Human nature, I guess.

"You leave Adrian alone. He had the sense to have Dana's dad call you and tell you to leave your phone at home, didn't he?" I was going out on a limb to see if it had been Adrian's suggestion. Not that it mattered, but I was curious.

"I'll give him that. The guy is never wrong about women. It's just freaky sometimes, you know. Most of the guys I know barely talk to each other, let alone their sisters and their mothers. You all just have a really unique friendship and from the outside, it can be a little intimidating."

So you've told me.

Ryan hadn't always felt that way. It was Dana's beach wedding that kind of messed his mind up. She'd planned to do a dedication ceremony to the Lord, but at the last minute she'd asked the preacher if he could marry her and Adrian. Knowing Dana as he did, Adrian had Ryan help him get an Illinois marriage license since he and Dana had made plans to marry when they got home, anyway. The wedding was amazing, but a little too fairy-tale for Ryan. I'd never thought that he saw me that way too, though. Not until now.

"I'm going to try to get Mom to feed Lily from the milk you pump. I want you to keep nursing the baby, but I see my mother's point about never leaving her. I think if she had more time with the baby, she'd leave us alone. That's my hope, anyway."

I had a lot of hopes, but now wasn't the time.

Ryan went on. "You did mess me up taking the excursion, though. My laptop was in the backseat and I was going crazy looking for it."

That made me laugh. "Same here. About halfway through the trip, I reached back to get mine to put some more songs on my iPod and realized that I had your car. I almost fired up your laptop to take some of your songs—"

"Did you? Use my laptop, I mean?" His lip twitched a little. What was that about?

"Never got around to it. You know how they are here. By the time they were done grilling me, Dad already had you on the way."

Ryan gave me a funny look at me calling Dana's father Dad. "He's not your father, Tracey."

I paused for a moment, not sure what he was talking about. "Oh, I know. He's Dana's dad. It's just what we all call him. For me, it's about the same. He's the closest thing to a daddy I've ever had. Same for Adrian and Rochelle, too, I guess."

Ryan went to the closet and grabbed one of Adrian's robes. "Yeah, well, again, it's weird." He pulled the belt tight. "Adrian does know how to shop, though. This is nice. I'm going to have to get me one of these."

I shook my head. "You're a trip."

"Hey, I just call 'em like I see 'em. Weird is weird and nice is nice."

And fine is fine…just like Mark Johnson.

Where did *that* come from? I whisked that thought away and got out of bed, too. "And silly is silly."

He grabbed me around the waist, lifted me up and squeezed. "Don't get mad, babe. You know I have to tease you and your little black 90210 crew. I'm not hating on what y'all have. It's nice, actually. I'm thankful for Adrian and Dana's dad. They are part of who you are and I love who you are."

He put me down and turned back toward the closet, reaching up for a towel. "Besides, if it wasn't for them, you might have turned out like me."

It wasn't even a whisper, but I heard it.

"What did you say?"

Ryan started for the door, but stopped in front of the full-length mirror. For the first time, I noticed something that he did while stroking his goatee and checking for razor bumps.

He frowned.

"Nothing, babe. I didn't say anything important. I'm heading for the shower. You coming?"

I nodded and grabbed a towel, too, but not before wondering whose mirrors my husband had been looking into. I wished he could see his reflection in my eyes. It was nothing to frown at.

Chapter Seven

159.

Whatever. Though I'd been happy to see that last week, I was about to cry now. I was so sick of that scale I could have screamed. I was trying to grease up my finger with the coconut oil I used on my hair so that I could pry off my wedding ring. I'd had Chinese food last night and I must have swelled up or something, because my ring was so tight I felt as if I'd have to go to the emergency room to get it cut off.

I'd let it go until later, but right now it was hurting so bad that I couldn't type, which was not acceptable since my whole life existed in cyberspace. Wasn't that sad? I was sad just thinking it. I loved computers but I really had to work on maintaining more human contact. Maybe I'd invite some of the moms from the church over for lunch. Maybe not.

I took only thirty minutes for lunch. No extra. No

chitchat time, no nothing. Just colors on the calendar waiting to be removed. I had to finish as much work as possible before Lily got home if it was a day-care (blue) day or before she woke up if it was a stay-home (pink) day. Then there was exercise (green), shopping (red, don't spend too much!), errands, bookkeeping… I didn't even have enough time to have lunch with myself!

After watching Ryan melt down lately I was thinking of closing my client list for a while and slowing down some, especially if I took the church Web site account. (I wasn't sure if I wanted to, though; too close to home, if you know what I mean.)

I had another online friend who was a Web designer and she'd begged me not to take the job. She'd been doing the site for her church for years and she said they tapped her shoulder right during service and asked her to take a look at things. That would stink. Big-time. Still, I did want to serve my church and I knew it would make Ryan proud…who knew? For now, I needed to get this ring off before I had to get it cut off my greasy fingers. This coconut oil smelled up my whole bathroom.

I checked the clock: 10:42. Three minutes before I had to start my workout. That was it, maybe I could sweat my ring off….

For the next twenty-seven minutes, I punched and kicked in my sports bra and spandex (hey, these are the benefits of working out at home). Every time I shot out my left hand, I gave it a little more oomph, hoping to push the ring down some. After a while, I was too into the workout to think about it, but when I did think about it, I realized that while the ring wasn't off, it had moved.

Ready to do this thing now and really get rid of both the ring and some body fat, I approached the last segment of my workout like a madwoman, doing jumping jacks so fast that my chest boomeranged and did an extra rep of its own, almost knocking me down. Though I was glad no one was around to see, my chest-jack was just the trick for the ring, which dislodged itself and came totally free, flew across the room and…

Hit Ryan square in the forehead before dropping into his palm.

Good catch, I thought, though my body froze in a punching stance. One thought about how I must have looked and I burst out laughing. "I didn't hear you come in."

He shook my ring in his hand like a pair of dice. "I meant for you not to hear me. I deactivated the alarm. I thought I'd find you typing furiously or rushing out the door." He checked his watch. "I'll have to make a note to stop home at this hour as much as possible." He walked toward me with open arms.

"I'm sweaty." I backed into a chair, wishing the lady on the video would be quiet. She was quite inspiring when I was alone. Now, with Ryan here, I just felt silly.

He sat down on the bed and clicked off the remote, then inspected his now-open palm. It was greasy and smelled of coconut. "What in the world? What are you testing now for Dana, elbow grease?"

No, but that'd make a great product for men. *Mental note.*

"My ring was stuck. I guess that Chinese food last night made me swell or something. I see your ring isn't…" My words hung in the air as I stared at my husband's ring finger.

It was bare.

All of a sudden I wanted him to leave the room so that I could turn back to my DVD and pound out a few more kicks and punches. Why wasn't he wearing his ring? What did that mean? I was too afraid to ask. I asked anyway. "Where is it?"

He started to answer while I was asking. Maybe we were starting to know one another. "My ring? Is that what you're looking for? Yeah. I lost it. Sorry I forgot to tell you. I called in about another one, but I figured you might want to get another set or something. Or is that taboo? I don't know about these things. It's not like it's that big of a deal, anyway. The ring doesn't make the marriage, the people do."

Uh-huh. I wasn't one of those cosmopolitan girls who'd had enough relationships to see trouble coming, but this looked like a red light to me for sure. The problem? I could feel us speeding past it already. "Well, I do today's work tonight and we could go in right now and get you fitted for another one. You're already here anyway, right?"

Wrong. "Nah. I don't have time now. Not for that, anyway. I left some files here, some contact information. That's all. We'll talk about this later. We can even pick a new wedding set if you want. God knows you deserve it. See you later." With that, he kissed my cheek and slipped my ring onto my pinkie finger. "Drop that off to get sized when you can. I'll have someone pick it up and courier it over if need be."

"Sure." I stood still for a long time, until even after I heard the door shut and the alarm beep into "away" mode. He'd coded the house as though no one were home even though I was there. I thought for a second about how he could have lost his ring. It wasn't like he had to do any dishes. He hadn't offered any explanation, either. He'd just left and plugged in the code that suited him best: away.

I slid the ring off my pinkie and tucked it into my top drawer. Maybe it was time for me to get away, too.

163.

Sometimes a girl just can't get a break, especially on the scale. Despite my daily punching and kicking, the numbers continued to rise. Since my doctor didn't want me cutting back on food, I was trying to increase my exercise, but I had to do it in a way that wouldn't deplete my milk stores, either. Being a mother, I realized, was like being a scientist, CEO, secretary, teacher…and that's just during the first year!

I sat next to some ladies from the Mother-to-Mother

ministry on Sunday and they suggested I pick up an herb called fenugreek from the health-food store. They were sisters-in-law and known for their grueling walking schedule. I called them the Stroller Sisters, but their names were Susan and Rainy. Yes, Rainy, one of those throwback names from the eighties when people were naming their kids after the seasons and the elements. She was pretty sunny, though.

Anyway, back to the fenugreek. I was shocked such a thing existed with a name like that, but it did and it actually helped with my milk supply. I was on my way over to Susan's place this morning to meet up with them for a walk around their subdivision which was just a few neighborhoods away from mine (minus the gate and the guard). Brenna chuckled a little when I agreed to walk with them and she wished me good luck when I talked to her on the phone last night. I wasn't sure what that meant, but it was a pink day (Lily was at home) and we were heading out for Soccer-Mom Land!

A few minutes and miles later, I arrived in my new friends' subdivision and realized that it was a much scarier place than I'd thought. There seemed to be people everywhere, pushing strollers, walking dogs, washing cars… Didn't these people have jobs? Goodness. As much as I enjoyed working at home, if the whole neighborhood was home with me every day it might be a little unnerving. Or not. I guess it would be nice to have someone to talk to during the day.

Not that talk paid any bills. Ryan had things well in

hand, of course, but my grandmother's teachings about being an independent woman hadn't worn off quite yet. Maybe if I'd sold my business and become a stay-at-home mom like Liz suggested I wouldn't be gaining weight and losing my mind. Oh well. I was who I was.

After scanning the addresses of two identical stucco houses, one peach and the other periwinkle, I realized I was in the right place. Next-door neighbors. The two ladies hadn't mentioned that they lived that close—

"There you are!" Susan wheeled out first, her shoulder-length relaxed hair back in a ponytail and pulled through a ball cap.

Her double stroller, complete with two smiling children, a drink holder, key-chain clasp and cell-phone tray almost made my mouth bulge open. My Graco basic paled in comparison. I smiled anyway. "Good morning."

"Same to you," Susan said, surveying my attire and kidware as though I was definitely in need of an upgrade. I could tell by the look on her face that she was thinking what most people thought when they saw me: "Didn't somebody say that her husband had money?" Ryan did have money, but not as much disposable cash as people might think. He had a lot of investments, developing projects and employees who depended on him for a paycheck. Though I was thankful that Lily wouldn't have to worry about money for college, my goal wasn't to suck my husband dry. Giving was what I wanted to teach my daughter, all while learning it myself.

Rainy Moore exited the house next door in one fluid

movement, all arms and teeth. "Tracey! You made it. We're so glad." She did the same up-and-down double take that her sister-in-law had done, but with much more grace and flair. Rainy hailed from Cairo, Georgia, and was a Southern belle to the core, despite having being transplanted to Illinois. Her stroller had three seats for her adoring toddlers, aged one, two and three. I'd been shocked to learn that they were all hers. She looked so cute and so…sane. One kid had me about at the end of my rope.

There was a bit more chitchat and retying of laces and then, like two maniacs, the Stroller Sisters took off down the road, talking and walking at what seemed a hundred miles an hour. They looked back after about a quarter mile, realizing that though I'd kept up at first, Lily and I had fallen out of rhythm with their grueling pace. Though I was a kickboxing fool, I hadn't walked this fast since, I don't know, high school? My pace was the dog-walking-look-at-the-moon-isn't-that-a-pretty-yard sort of speed. These girls could try out for the Olympics. And they could do it without me.

Just as they were about to turn the corner out of sight so that I could slip back to my car and ride away in shame, Rainy shielded her pink visor with a deeply-veined hand. "Tracey, honey? Are you okay back there? Let's slow down, Sue, and talk to our company. We don't often get guests so we forget that our warm-up can be a little intense."

Warm-up? Were they for real? Or was I going to wake up any minute in a pool of sweat? I pinched myself. Nope, definitely real, though from the looks of things I might just get that sweat after all. "Don't slow down on my account. I was just going to wheel back to my car for my iPod. That should help me pick up my pace a little."

The two women, now dubbed Grim and Slim in my warped mind, slowed down and closed in, each taking my arm.

"iPod, schmi-Pod. We'll give you all the tempo you need," said Rainy.

"Follow us and you'll have that weight off before you know it," said Susan, with a smile that looked more like a grimace.

What had I gotten myself into? I thought as they released me and we set off up what looked like Mount Everest. I thought I was out for a relaxing walk with some moms from church, but this was like some kind of motherhood boot camp. Despite being nominated for the Air Force Academy, I never enlisted in the armed services. I loved my country enough to stay out of that arena. Rochelle, on the other hand, would have made the best drill sergeant ever. And these ladies could have been her next in command.

"Pick up those knees, honey. That's where the power is, in the lower body. Dig into this hill. Push that baby up, just like you did to get Lily out. Think of it every time you go up here, believe it sticks in your mind the next time you're in labor. It's the little things that get you over, right, Sue?"

"Right as rain, honey!" That produced a giggling fit from both of them that was a little too over the top. Even their children, silent until now and adoring the daily routine, broke out into laughter. Lily, on the other hand, started to cry.

I'm with you, honey. This is a little sickening.

As we crested the hill, relief washed over me until the next hill, just as formidable, came into view. My chest started to tighten. I felt dizzy. How far back was the car? "How many of these hills are there in your neighborhood?"

"Six!" Rainy said with enthusiasm, blasting down the straightaway toward the next hill. "These first two are the hardest, just like contractions. Every day as I cover this trail, I remember that. This walk is bringing me health just like those contractions brought my beautiful babies!"

Right, that's what I was thinking.

Not.

Her babies were beautiful, though. That much I had to admit. I just couldn't imagine three of them so close together. By the time I recovered from Lily, I might be too old to have another child. Not to mention that with the way things were going with Ryan, we might have our hands full just staying married.

A few huffs and I pushed myself to keep up as we started up the next hill. I pushed up through my feet for power as Rainy suggested. It worked! I wasn't so sure about the labor thing, but hey, I took what I could use and left the rest. "That pushing deal is really okay. I'm not so into the labor concept, though. I'm not sure that Ryan and I will have any more children. We'd planned to wait several years before starting a family, but I got pregnant on our honeymoon."

Susan and Rainy exchanged a glance, the kind of look that teachers share just before addressing young, dumb students. I could tell that they chose their words carefully, realizing my obvious stupidity.

"Honey, getting pregnant on your honeymoon is the best thing that could have happened to you, don't you see that? God designed marriage to produce Godly seed. You are a blessed woman. So many women today deny God the right to their bodies. He wants to use you to bring righteous children into the earth. You just stick with us, sweetie. I'll give you some scriptures and books when we get back to the house. It's a process, accepting God's plan for Christian womanhood, but it's the best thing that you can do, both for yourself and your marriage. When we get in place, the husbands take their place as well."

Susan nodded as though she couldn't have said it any better herself. I wiped my brow and took a deep breath. Wow. Could that be the problem? Me being out of place, out of order? I didn't want to do anything to disobey God. Faith had been so much simpler before I got married: love God, love people. The golden rule and all that. Now there were marriage rules, mama rules…and big hills to learn it all on.

"Thanks. I guess I'll look at the books—" I paused

to take a breath as the incline increased. Why did I choose now to talk? Wasn't that some sort of indication of whether you're working too hard in cardio, whether you could talk? The talk test. Well, I was definitely failing. "It's just that, to be quite honest, I'm not sure that my husband really wants any more children, now or ever. And since I'm the one who has to do most of the child care, I don't know if having another baby is what God wants us to focus on right now. And of course, there's my weight and everything."

I staggered on huffing and puffing like the Big Bad Wolf with no house to blow down and feeling more and more like one of the Three Little Pigs. Make that One Little Pig. These ladies were long and lean, more like turkey bacon.

Over the next three miles, Slim and Grim gave me a short course in the ills of birth control and its ravages on the Christian family. Some of what they said made a lot of sense, considering my own body's reactions to the different types of birth control we'd tried since having Lily. Hair loss, weight gain, mood swings…lots of weirdness. It probably had something to do with my fluctuating weight, as well, but what's a girl to do? Triple strollers just aren't in my future. Still, I dug in my heels and did the hills. I listened and I prayed.

Once we got back to the house, the Stroller Sisters (I'd stopped calling them Slim and Grim by then) loaded me down with books on Christian womanhood, marriage and family. They looked quite satisfied with themselves as I pulled off. Me? I felt confused. Again. It seemed that every woman I met had another answer to all of my problems, something else that I needed to do to earn the favor of God.

It's not only what you do, Tracey. It's who you are.

It was my mother's voice in my head and it brought tears with it. I thought I'd forgotten what she sounded like, but these words, something she'd said to me from the time I was born, always seemed to come back to me at the right time. I gripped the wheel and prayed that God would show me who He wanted me to be and what He wanted me to do.

Chapter Eight

"What is this mess?" Ryan held up one of the books Rainy had loaned me and waved it in the air. "Did you read this?"

"Well, uh, yeah. I did read it. Not all of it, but some. I especially wanted you to read that part that I marked, one of the reasons the whole birth control movement began was to cut down on the black population. They even used black churches to spread the message. Can you believe that?"

He nodded. "Now, that does get to me. I can't lie. And yes, I do believe it. The black church has always been a pawn in politics. It's not like it once was, though. When my father was alive…" He looked away for a moment, then refocused on the stack of periodicals in his hand. "I'm going to have to do some more research on that point. It seems that I recall hearing it before. The issue is complicated though, Tracey. It's not as cut-and-dried as these people make it seem. What I want to know is what's up with this?" He lifted up a home-school catalog with a lovely blond girl in a pink dress flanked by sisters in matching costumes on the cover.

I was confused. Sure the scene was a bit *Little House on the Prairie,* but I sort of dug that show. What was my husband's problem now? "What about that? I sort of flipped through, then Lily started crying. Is something wrong?"

Ryan scratched the side of his face, which sported a shadow I rarely saw. He looked tired, strained even, but he'd taken the time to listen to me read to him from some of the books the Stroller Sisters had given me. When I told him about the issues of race in birth control, he'd grabbed a stack and headed for the bathroom. Usually he took his time reading, making meticulous notes for further research. He was a detail man to the core. Now something in the details of this catalog had him riled. I was getting a little testy myself.

"I really thought seriously about us teaching Lily at home, but reading through some of these materials, I don't think it's going to work. Look at this, the books for manhood are all about Civil War heroes. One book even refers to John Brown and other abolitionists as communists. Can you believe that? I don't know if we'll ever have a son, but I would never subject him to that kind of mess. And the thing is, one of my favorite ministries puts that catalog out. I don't know what to think."

Me neither. So I didn't think, I stood up and walked

over to my husband, rubbed his shoulders and scratched his back. "Baby, I'm sorry. I know that it's important to you that Lily lives in a diverse culture while knowing her history at the same time. It's important to me, too. I guess working at home now, I'm not faced with the same 'isms' you are, but I'm learning that there are new ways for women to discriminate against each other outside of color as well. We all just need to cut each other some slack."

He turned to me, kissed my fingers. "You're so right. You always give me the benefit of the doubt, baby. I'm sorry for jumping all over you. Things aren't going so well with the company right now. I didn't want to say anything because I don't want you to worry. I made a bit of an investment that I shouldn't have and now some of the people that I've worked with since the beginning are starting to give me the cold shoulder. Not returning my calls, that sort of thing. It's been wearing on me. I should have told you sooner. But this stuff, this family stuff, it's important to me, too. I hope you know that."

"I know." At least I used to know, but tonight was a start. A drop in a very empty, very tall bucket. A bucket that might require a lot of long nights and rainy days to fill.

Rainy. She'd been e-mailing me every day now with new links and articles, calling to offer more scripture to back up what she'd told me in the previous call. Though it was nice to have someone to talk to, I got the feeling that our continued conversations depended on my be-coming her newest disciple. While I was always trying to learn something new, about God and about life, the days of me blindly following friends were long gone. I appreciated her input, but I realized then, with my head on Ryan's chest, that it was really his friendship that I craved right now more than anything.

Tell him that. Right now.

Ryan's phone buzzed at him. He pulled away, holding up his this-will-only-take-a-second finger.

I turned away, having learned long ago just how long a second lasted when my husband was on the phone.

Oh well, so much for that.

Maybe next time.

160.

Even my purple bathroom didn't make me feel any better. I tried to forget what I'd just seen on the scale. At least it smelled good in here. I'd infused some sesame oil with lavender buds a month ago and opened it up this morning. Very nice.

The rest of my life, however, sort of stunk. Between my weigh-ins and my e-mail box there were plenty of opportunities to feel bad about myself. Pamela Brooks, one of the women from the Cry Room, had sent an e-mail invitation to lunch. In her P.S., she'd asked if I'd made Lily's "darling" dress from the previous Sunday. I'd read Pamela Brooks's e-mail so many times before going to bed I think I'd almost memorized it. Did I make Lily's dress? I wasn't sure if that was a compliment or a jab.

True enough, I was pretty handy with a sewing machine, but what about my daughter's dress had made her say such a thing? Or was this all in my head? These days I couldn't tell. I was too busy trying to sit up straight, concentrate on not chewing off my lip gloss and staying awake despite the quiet darkness in the Cry Room. I was actually starting to have nightmares about the place.

She'd written, "E-mail is such a time sucker. Don't bother to reply unless you can't make it." Not having to RSVP Pamela was both refreshing and creepy. What kind of person didn't even want to get a "thanks" e-mail back to acknowledge that the communication had been received? Why, a busy woman, of course, someone who was actually getting work done instead of fretting over not having enough time to do it. Someone who was a confident, strong woman instead of a needy loser….

Stop it. Speak gently to yourself.

I stepped off the scale and blew out a breath. One of the last women's conferences I'd gone to at my old church had been about building a life of blessing, starting with ourselves. Each day during the conference, we'd written our own blessings, and our homework each evening and morning was to recite our blessings in the mirror before coming to the opening session. It was amazing the transformation that had taken place in the course of those days. By the second evening, women were going out and buying makeup and new panty hose. Others lined up in the fitness center or crowded the gift shop for swimsuits to wear into the hotel pool.

My wedding had been months away then and my mind was more on Ryan than on God, but writing my blessing had done something to me, too. Even now, with everything that had gone on, I still remembered it. I rubbed a circle in the steamed bathroom mirror so that I could see my face. Though the image wasn't clear, it made me smile all the same. So did the sound of my voice.

"Tracey Janelle Blackman, you are a wonder, a blessing. You were born to answer a question that no one else can answer. You are an Andrew sistah, introducing people to Jesus everywhere you go. You are a peacemaker, a pain taker, a hardworking, beautiful woman inside and out. You are strong enough to be weak. You are powerful enough to be meek. You are kind enough to risk love. Go out today and bless the world."

I stood there, dripping wet, with tears in my eyes. It had been so long since I spoke something good, something strong over myself. It felt good enough to make me cry, to make me fight for my life, for my marriage, for my purpose. God was doing something, something that wasn't in any marriage or parenting book, something that I'd have to follow him close to experience, let alone understand. And yet, there I was, shaking every bush for an answer, for a mentor, for a method. Maybe sometimes the paths of others curl up behind them and the only road left to follow leads to a rugged, bloody cross.

With a shake of my hair, a handful of coconut oil and some finger combing, I was ready to face the day. Even

Rainy and Susan's hill couldn't get the best of me this morning. There was nothing—

"Ma…meeeee!"

Well, nothing except that. I could feel my cheeks tighten into a smile as I went for my sweet girl. She called me for the first time. No matter what I weighed, I felt on top of the world.

Nobody answered.

Though Sue and Rainy were usually halfway down the block "warming up" by the time I pulled up, this morning there was silence from both houses. No lights. Nothing.

I rang Rainy's bell again. Had they gone out of town and forgotten to tell me? No. Rainy had hugged me at church yesterday morning, saying that they'd look forward to seeing me on Monday. Today.

Finally, Sue came to the door. She looked as though she hadn't slept. A TV, something I'd previously doubted that either of them owned, blared in the background. She held a hand up to her mouth. "Tracey! Oh, goodness. I forgot to call you to cancel. I'm so sorry. Rainy isn't feeling well and I'm over here watching all the kids, so…" She looked around as though someone or something might uncoil at any moment.

Weird. "Okay, sure. Sorry to hear that Rainy is sick. Is it a cold? I'm sure that spring in Illinois is a lot different than in Georgia. I can't believe how cold it is today. Last week it was so warm."

Weather chitchat was my specialty, but Susan wasn't

going for it. And I wasn't going for this ruse, whatever it was. Any other time, I would have said okay and walked away, but something told me that things were not okay. Still, I didn't want to pry….

"Okay then, tell Rainy I hope she feels better. I'll call her later and see if she needs anything."

Susan leaned forward and looked right and left as though she were about to cross the street. "Oh no, that won't be necessary. It's not a body sickness. It's a sickness of the heart. She's just having a low time. Sometimes things can get overwhelming all of a sudden and she just needs to rest. You know what I mean."

I didn't know what she meant, really, but I just nodded my head. In my crew of friends we spoke plainly about such things. It was never "a low time," it was, "Stop calling me. I'm going to bed for a month." I was usually the one on ice cream and shower duty during those times, but we'd all been single and stressed. It hadn't occurred to me that married women went through things to the same extent. I guess I'd thought that once you got a husband, he helped you through those kinds of times, not your girlfriends.

My foot pressed the stroller out of park so we could head down the driveway. I waved. "Okay, well, I know that Ryan will probably see Steve at the ministerial meeting. I'll be sure and tell him to ask how Rainy is feeling."

Susan froze. "Please don't do that. Rainy and I keep our little low times to ourselves. The men, well, they don't always understand and we don't want to trouble them. I'll cook double dinner tonight and she'll be up to serve it. Steve's world keeps rolling, but us girls…we take care of each other, right?"

"Um, I suppose. We'll talk soon," I said, though I doubted that we would. This was beyond freaky. What if Rainy was having a breakdown or something? Shouldn't she let her own husband know what was going on? What kind of marriage was that? So much for Christian Womanhood 101. If this was the graduate class, you could count me out, I thought as I pushed my stroller up hill number one, which I'd named Herbert. (Hey, I was here, wasn't I? No use wasting the walk. I had my mind set for it.)

The kicker was that every time I'd mentioned Brenna to Rainy, she'd given me a disparaging look. "Some women just sort of lose their way. You have to be careful in associating with them. You become like your teachers, you know. Your friends, too. The Bible says it in the Psalms." I crested the first hill and broke a sweat. The memory of Rainy's tone and the cold March air gave me a bit of a chill.

We become our friends. Looking at Dana, Rochelle and I, the truth could easily be seen. Over time, though, we'd all become individual women who made space for others to be themselves. Well, most of us anyway. Rochelle was still working on that. Now, seeing Rainy and Sue's strange codependence, I could see the truth in the theory. What I didn't get was what Brenna had done to make everyone talk about her in the past tense, as if she'd once been a good person, but somehow fallen from grace. She seemed like the sanest person around the place to me.

But appearances, I was learning, could be very deceiving.

After a night of the sniffles thanks to my walk yesterday, I skipped my morning weigh-in. My jeans told me pretty much all I needed to know, anyway. Or should I say all I wanted to know. I'd been working out more than ever before and everything seemed to be tighter in the waist despite my efforts. Friends tried to give me the "you're building muscle" excuse, but even that didn't make sense. As I sped through my morning e-mail check, I dropped myself an e-note to call Dr. Thomson sometime this week. As much as I wanted to nurse Lily for a whole year, something (namely my girth) had to give. With the quickness.

As I thought that, my screen went blank, turning an ominous shade of blue. I rested my head on the keyboard. The blue screen of death. Why today? Sure I had a Linux partition on my hard drive, but those CDs were somewhere in a box…or something. Meanwhile, I had site updates for CurlyDivas.com, Dana's Made of Honor Web store and the church site, which has somehow been assigned to me even though I never officially agreed to do it. (I made a mental note to address that with someone before the week was out. Church or not, that wasn't cool.)

I'd uploaded last night's work before going to bed, but the old blue screen would still cost me a couple hours of design work that I'd done this morning for Dana's labels for her new mom-and-baby line. The new honeysuckle samples she'd sent me were right on the money of the scent I'd described to her after one of my walks. The label fit it perfectly. I'd even thought of a new name for that line: Sunny Hunny. With calendula flowers, arnica and marshmallow root, the soaps, lotions and balms all made me smile. Until I got the blue screen, that is.

With the clock ticking down to my lunch with Pamela, I had two choices: rummage through the guest room for the right CD case to reboot with Linux or borrow Ryan's laptop, which he had somehow managed to forget without so much as one call home to inquire about it. Maybe if I worked quickly, I could get my work done before he returned to retrieve it. Yeah, that was the plan.

I clicked on Ryan's computer and sifted through the files for his graphics program, a free, non-Windows-based version of the Photoshop program I often used. I could work with either, but it would take a few Google searches to brush up. I clicked the shortcut to the Internet and chose "restore session" since Ryan had Google as his home page. What came up—a woman's smiling face and her svelte body—threw me for a loop. Beneath it was an e-mail greeting to my husband.

Thanks for the lunch, Ryan. Looking forward to seeing your assets. I'm hoping that this transaction will be to both our benefit.

Kisses,

Sierra

Sierra. I'd considered naming Lily that, but Dana had said it sounded too much like the truck by the same name. Right now, I couldn't agree more. Sierra had just flattened my heart like a monster truck. My faith was running pretty low, too. It had been years since a curse word had graced my vocabulary, but the phrases came back easily. Too easily. The bad thing was, I wasn't sure who to be mad at, Ryan or this corny woman. (Looking forward to seeing your assets? Come on.) Taken at face value, the woman's words seemed innocent, but underneath them was enough innuendo to start some serious mess, not to mention the photo. The picture left little room for doubt.

Ryan had mentioned his concerns about his business and its holdings. Would he go as far as flirting to keep the Blackman Software ship afloat? Was I, like so many other wives I'd known over the years, supposed to accept that this kind of thing was just part of the business world?

No way. I closed Ryan's laptop and headed for the guest room for my CDs. Whatever else might be on his machine wasn't anything I wanted to run across by accident. Whatever was going on, if anything at all, needed to come from his own mouth, not by my prying.

By the time I found what I needed and restored my hard drive, it was time to head out for Pamela's house. In the days since I'd received her e-mail invitation, I'd thought many times about writing back to say that I couldn't come, but I'd done enough of that, too. If we didn't click or like one another enough to be friends, at

least I'd know her better. It was time for me to deal with
the fact that Promised Land Worship Center was my home
church now. Ryan's people had to become my people.

And if I had my way, his cell phone and his computer might have to become mine, too. As I drove the
winding road around the corner to Pamela's, I tried
Ryan's number several times with no answer. What I
had to say I didn't want to leave on voice mail, so I said
nothing at all. He'd see my number when he checked
his missed calls. For now, I just needed to eat something and stay calm. Maybe it had been God's timing
that I accept Pamela's invitation after all. There's no
telling what I might have done or said otherwise. I can
just hear Dana now. She'd have had me pitching a fit
for sure.

Pamela Brooks, standing at the top of her driveway
in a gold-and-cream pantsuit too dressy for everyday
wear unless you were trying to impress someone, did not
look as if she threw fits. Ever. If anything, she might
make some other folks throw a fit, but not her. The house
surprised me, though; it was much smaller than the huge
image Pamela had projected. The smallest house on the
block, in fact. I had a feeling though that the inside
decor would make up for that. The yard certainly did. It
was jam-packed with fountains and animal-shaped
shrubs. Peter Rabbit might jump out at any moment.

"I see you found me," she said in a lower pitch than
I remembered. "Your hair looks good. Highlights?"

I bit my lip. "Sun-In. You know, in the bottle? I just wanted to try it."

Her eyebrows knitted together. "O-kay. You're something else. Sun-In. Do they still make that? I haven't seen it since high school."

"Right." I followed her inside, realizing that Pamela wasn't someone who valued honesty. She was a girl who only wanted to hear the right answer, even if it wasn't the true one. Those types of people made me tired. Not to mention that Ryan's little e-friend was weighing heavy on my mind.

"Come on in," she said, winding through a maze of knickknacks and curio cabinets. I could hear Rochelle's words in my head, whispering, "Less really is more. Really. Trust me on it." Maybe the whole becoming-like-your-friends thing was true, but I heartily agreed with Rochelle's decorating philosophy when looking at this house—or should I say museum.

My loafers skimmed the carpet while Pamela's pumps sank right in. High heels during the day? With no one at home? That was so over my head. "You have such an interesting home, Pamela." I didn't want to lie and say that it was beautiful. It was interesting, however. A little too interesting.

"Thanks. Call me, Pam. I was so excited to meet you, since you have your own business. Most of the women at church don't understand what being a helpmeet really means—helping your husband meet the bills. I've tried to talk to many of them about my Melaleuca and

Pampered Chef business opportunities, but they're just too lazy most of them. Hiding behind their diapers. I can't even get the scrapbook club to sign up as Stamp It Up consultants. Tell me if that makes any sense."

I didn't tell Pam a thing. I was too busy silently lamenting the fact that I'd fallen into another "be my disciple" trap. Didn't anyone just genuinely want to be my friend? Probably not. The main thing I'd gotten out of college was that people crave commonality, even if what they have in common is false. Instead of sharing that with "Pam" like I wanted to, I scanned her house for any evidence of the diapers she accused others of hiding behind. Though she sat in the Cry Room, I'd never actually seen Pam's children. I guess they knew better than to actually cry. I found the family photo quickly enough, a picture of Pam and her husband, Damon, at the beach with four perfect-looking little children in matching outfits. The older ones were probably at school, but what about the smaller ones?

She must have read my expression. "The kids? Oh, they're all down in their rooms until 2:00 p.m. Quiet time. They've had their lunch and time with Mommy. Now it's Mommy's time. Don't worry. They love it." She walked over to a long black sword next to one of the curio cabinets. "Look at this. We got this on our trip to Japan," she said, sliding a long sword out of its sheath. "Damon says it's his sword of the Spirit. Isn't that cute?"

Another big fake smile from yours truly. How could I answer this one without lying? It was cute to her, I guess. To me, it was just…interesting. And I told her so, but in a nice way. "Again, you all are such an interesting couple."

A few cups of tea later, I found out just how interesting they were. Damon, it turned out, was a sex addict with a pornography addiction that surpassed my affinity for M&Ms. Scary. I tried to act interested in hearing the gory details of my new friend's intimate life, but there are some things you just need to work up to, you know?

By the time we'd had our grilled-chicken salad (I should have known) and chocolate cake (that was a surprise), Pam laid the real reason for my invitation on the line. "You're good with computers, right?"

Here we go. "You could say that. What are you trying to do?"

Pam leaned forward a little in her chair and whispered in the same weird way Susan had done when telling me about Rainy. I scanned the room for possible hidden cameras. You could never tell these days and this was all getting way too strange. Still, I couldn't help wondering what Pam was going to say.

She didn't disappoint. "The hidden files," she whispered while tenting a cloth napkin over her mouth.

It was all I could do not to scream. Instead, I pressed a hand against my belly to physically suppress the silliness bubbling into a howling giggle. Though I found all this strangely amusing, it really wasn't funny. This was someone's life, someone's marriage. Perhaps this was about me as much as Pam. "What hidden files?"

She gave me a sharp look. I must have been talking too loud. Were the hidden children listening in? Maybe whatever was in the secret files was even more alarming and personal than what she'd already told me.

I hoped not. I was starting to feel sick in the I-gotta-run-home sort of way.

"You know, the hidden files, where the guys hide their Web history. They're so smart now with all these little programs, but Damon can't fool me. I can always tell when he's into his stuff. He acts different. I just want to see for sure. I just want my ammunition."

Whoa. Cyber-bullets. Not so nice. "Are you sure? Shouldn't he be accountable to someone else? One of the other men at the church maybe? It just seems like a lot of pressure to put on yourself, trying to keep a grown man from doing something. I don't think it's really about you—"

Pam covered her mouth with both hands. "You're serious, aren't you? Oh, goodness. I'm so sorry. You look older than you must be."

Thanks again, Pam. You're killing me here.

She wiped her eyes and took another look at me. "How long have you been married to Ryan again?"

"A year. Almost two." I smiled like a Girl Scout selling cookies. I have no idea why.

Pam dissolved into a heap of laughter. "Oh my. What was I thinking? I saw you talking to Brenna and you seemed a lot like her. She's the one who told me you were a computer person. She used to come over and help me with all this, finding the hidden files and stuff. She always told me she couldn't find anything, but I know she did. She just didn't want to hurt me. I get like this every now and then, a little crazy. I'm so sorry. It's just that once you've been taken advantage of, you never want to let it happen again, you know? I was so stupid for so long. I missed all the signs."

She reached over to the cake dish and cut two more slices, both twice as big as the ones we'd had at first. "Cake?" Pam asked as she plopped the whopping piece on my plate.

Realizing that I was about to have a meltdown of my own, I shoved the plate away just in time. To be sure, I poured a little water on it, like I often had to do to stop eating a bag of potato chips.

Pam gave an eyes-wide-open look. "Ooh. Water on the food. That's ingenious. I'll have to try it. Now that I've spilled my guts and probably totally scared you off of ever coming here again, you might as well spill whatever is eating you."

She swooped a forkful of cake into her mouth and remained silent, waiting for me to follow in her tradition of verbal explosions.

Unfortunately, I did just that, with lots of crying in between. "There weren't any hidden files. Well, I really don't know if there are. It's probably not anything, but there's this woman sending him e-mails. A business associate—"

"Oh, honey. I'm so sorry. The online affairs are the

worst. Even Damon isn't that far gone yet." She hugged me, smearing chocolate across my shirt. It may as well have been blood for the way I felt at the moment. "Don't you worry about a thing, now. We'll get this all straightened out. That's what friends are for."

I sighed. That's what I had always thought that friends were for, too, when I was single. Now I was confused about the whole thing. One thing I did know, though. Pam's confident and creepy tone scared me almost as much as that woman's pretty smile on my husband's computer.

Almost.

Chapter Nine

"Tracey, what did you do?"

It was my husband's voice, low and wounded, like an animal on the wrong end of a hunting expedition. He was coming into our kitchen. If I didn't know better, I'd say that he'd been crying.

So had I.

"Do? Well, not much today, I'm afraid. I had lunch with a lady from church. Pam Brooks, do you know her?" I could feel the urge to nervously ramble kicking in, so I cut it off and went back to trying to calculate the Weight Watchers points in the pot of spaghetti I was making. Where was that pasta box?

Ryan stormed out of the kitchen and plopped down on the couch. I usually would have followed him, but there was something big in the room, sucking out the air. There didn't seem to be room for me and Ryan in the same space. Something had really rattled his cage. Something I had done.

Before I could contemplate following him any further, he was back, leaning over the granite counter, resting his head on the cabinet. "I got a call from Pastor Dre today. He asked me point-blank if I was having an online affair…among other things."

The spaghetti box drifted to the floor. I closed my eyes and swallowed hard, vowing never to tell Pamela (she was so not Pam) Brooks anything more than the date and time ever again. Still, since the elephant in the room was up and walking, I might as well jump on it and take a ride. "Well, are you? Having an online affair, I mean. Or any kind. Of affair." That sounded so much better in my head.

My husband lifted his head and looked at me as though he wanted to do me bodily harm. "Tracey, what on God's green, clean earth are you talking about? I'm saying that you started some rumor and the pastor is calling me because our business that isn't even our business is all over the church and you are going to ask me some mess like that? What is going on with you? Are you having an affair? I saw you with that guy at the restaurant that day you ran home to your friends. Unlike you, however, I chose to think the best of you."

Oh no you don't. This isn't about me.

My dinner pot was set to warm and I waved Ryan over to the table where he'd put down his things. Without a word, I fired up his laptop and opened his e-mail, right where he had left it. My finger traced the woman's face and then the curve of her hip. Next, I pointed to her words. "That's what's going on with me, Ryan. That. Who is that woman and what assets is she talking about? Because it sure doesn't sound like she means your business. Perhaps if you'd answered your phone the twenty times I called you this morning, we could have avoided this whole thing."

He folded his arms and shook his head, not willing to give me even an inch. "No, Tracey, if you had used the common sense God gave you we could have avoided this whole thing. How could you talk to Pam? She's always starting some mess. That's why I married you instead of her."

My breath caught in my throat. I thought I might choke to death by the time I managed to speak. "You— you dated Pamela?"

Ryan nodded. "Yes. A long time ago, long before I met you. She was Queen Elizabeth's first pick. Still is, probably. I just couldn't deal with all the drama. We were even talking marriage at one point. Her biggest goal was for me to become one of the ministers so that she could run with the pastors' wives. That girl has issues. No wonder Damon acts a fool like he does."

The sickness I thought I'd felt at Pamela's house came on now for real and in full force. I took small breaths. "So…you know about him? Damon, I mean."

"Come on, Tracey. Think about it. You had lunch with Pam and it ended up with me getting a call from the pastor. How do you think she does things with her husband? The same way. Only she does it sneaky with him——prayer requests."

I slid down onto the couch and lowered my head between my knees. Prayer requests. Have mercy. It was Adrian who said that sometimes it was hard to tell the prayer hotline from the gossip grapevine. What a mess. "But still, Ryan. You haven't told me anything. Who is this woman and why is she writing you like this? I'm sorry for jumping to conclusions, but my laptop died and I was trying to do some work, so I used yours. Then I couldn't get you and I was at Pam's and she's going through all this drama about hidden files and being stupid and then I remembered how you asked me at Dana's if I'd used your laptop that day I took the Excursion. It all started sounding very, very wrong."

He sat down next to me just as Lily woke up from her nap. She didn't cry today, though. She just stayed in her crib, playing quietly as though she knew something was going down.

Ryan sat down beside me and pulled me into his arms. "She's a flirt, Tracey, okay? Some women just do business like that. They think it gives them power. I just do what I have to do as far as business is concerned and keep going on. Right now, there's no one else in my corner on this business thing and it looks like we might lose everything. There, I said it. I've been putting up with that woman so that I can keep *this* woman." He took my hand. "You. Can you forgive me?"

My stomach tumbled again. My bones creaked as I

stretched my arms over my head. This was sounding way too much like a soap opera.

Help me, Lord. Help me.

I kissed the top of Ryan's hand. "I wish you would have just showed me that e-mail from the beginning and told me what was going on. I mean, you're walking around without your wedding band on, acting strange, being distant. What am I supposed to think? And as for Pamela, I don't know why she felt the need to call Pastor Dre. That story wasn't hers to tell. I wonder, though, why it had to get that far. I need you to talk to me, Ryan."

He stood. "By the time I get home, Tracey, I don't always feel like talking. I'm tired and I just want something to be easy. Simple. Why can't you ever let things be easy? The rest of my life is hard enough. You had your own friends, your own business, your own faith. That's what made me love you, even though they sometimes intimidated me. Don't let these Promised Land women get you turned around. I want you to make friends, but don't forget who you are. Who we are. And don't think I haven't noticed that you're not wearing your ring. What's that about? I told you I'm getting another one."

I didn't have an answer, so I didn't offer one. I didn't offer anything, except salad, bread sticks and some slightly mushy spaghetti.

We didn't say a lot more that night. I got the baby up and finished dinner. We ate, cleaned up and watched TV.

Lily went back to sleep for longer than usual. The moon was high and full when Ryan reached for me. It was hours later, while watching the sunrise through the fingers spread over my face that I realized I'd never answered Ryan's plea for forgiveness. Usually, I was nodding before he got the words out.

Some people vowed that time healed all wounds. I was starting to wonder if time wasn't just another shade of makeup, covering over all the scars from before. That worried me because even I knew that scars needed open air to heal. I knew now that for some people, especially couples, healing meant hiding. That wasn't for me. I'd been hidden away behind my fat all my life. There was no going back now.

Hear ye, hear ye! Now welcome Queen Tracey....
Lily's hair tickled my ears, jerking me out of my dream, bringing me back to my nightmare—real life. The radio, which had supplied the gospel music that carried me to la-la land, now grated against my ears.

"Don't forget, now. Today's the day. Spring forward. Fall back," said the woman on the radio.

The female deejay with the perfect enunciation could have saved some of her spit and shine for someone else. I'd sprung forward and fallen back every day this year. The only difference today would be having less time to recover from it. After last night's debacle, I'd curled up and just about died inside, but there was my Lily, looking at me with those wise eyes, cooing at me with her angel voice.

After a few times of getting up and down with Lily, I'd let her stay in bed with me, since Ryan had taken the couch for the night. At first, I'd despaired that it might be a permanent arrangement, but with another Sunday morning bearing down on me, I was starting to wonder if it made a difference, anyway.

You don't mean that.

Didn't I? I'd already had a call from my royal mother-in-law this morning stating that she'd be waiting to speak to me at church about an important matter. Never mind that she had me on the phone (though I did point that out). She was out for blood, mine specifically. That was evident in her tone. What she didn't realize was that I was way ahead of her, rolling back my sleeves to offer a vein.

Maybe I'd just stay home from church today. After all, it wasn't like anyone would miss me. Ryan had come to say good-morning and offer some halfhearted apology, but we both knew that damage had been done, on both sides.

And my damage required brightly colored pieces of chocolate candy with "M" on them, not the prying eyes and disapproving looks of a roomful of church ladies.

What you need is Jesus.

Well, duh. Of course I needed Jesus. That was understood, wasn't it? Could I invite Jesus to my pity party? Probably not. Hmm…I'm pulling a Dana, here. Need to get it together.

Lily farted on my elbow and gave me a huge smile. I

smiled right back, then started laughing…and laughing. Though I tried, I couldn't stop. Pretty soon, my baby girl was laughing with me. When I looked up, Ryan was leaning against the door frame watching us, tightening his tie, one I didn't remember seeing before. Not that my lack of recognition meant anything. Ryan could wear a different tie every day and never repeat. Why he married three-shoes-and-two-skirts me I have no clue.

He came over the bed with us and climbed in, without even trying to keep his clothes unwrinkled like he usually does. He hoisted Lily up over his head. She giggled and proceeded to throw up…right in his eye. Ryan closed his mouth just in time. My baby thought this was funny, too, and gave me a big smile as if awaiting applause. To his credit, Ryan put her down slowly and calmly, chuckling a bit himself.

"I guess I pretty much deserved that," he said as I wiped his eye with a clean cloth diaper hanging from the exercise bike next to the bed. "You put her up to that, didn't you?"

I shook my head and continued to wipe, though I knew Ryan well enough to know he'd be heading for the shower. One fleck of baby fluids and the man considered himself contaminated. Mothers didn't have such luxuries. I can remember one lady's advice at my baby shower: "Wear prints. All the baby vomit blends in when you're in a hurry and have to do a spot wash." I had almost thrown up when she said that, but I'd since learned what she meant. Motherhood wasn't for the faint of heart or the faint of stomach.

"Again, I'm sorry, Tracey. About everything. I can see how I let this whole thing get out of hand. I should have talked to you about all this in the first place."

"Yes, you should have. We still need to talk about these business problems. You seem so stressed about them. Is there a way to sell and get out without losing everything? Can we sell the house? The—"

His jaw tightened as he undid the last of his shirt buttons. "No. Naperville is our home. This was the house you chose. I'll keep you in it, no matter what."

The determination that I saw in his eyes had once inspired me, even attracted me. Now, it only scared me. Why did things have to be all or nothing with Ryan? Sure, I liked this house, loved it even, but it was just…a house. It was Ryan and Lily that made it special.

We could have just as much fun in another, smaller place. I mean, how many bathrooms did two adults and a baby need, anyway? Six, according to Queen Liz, who'd been sold on the number of bathrooms. One never knew how many might come for company, according to her. The fact that her own home had one and a half baths and she never had *us* over, much less anyone else, totally escaped her. Not unlike most things.

Ryan gave me a quick kiss and headed for the shower while I fought with myself about going to church at all. It wasn't something I'd thought about in a very long time, whether to go to church or not, but today, I didn't want to be false, smiling and shaking hands like some crooked politician. Everyone would already know (or thought they knew) that something was going on and my job would be to act as if none of it ever happened.

Before I could get too caught up in my mental gymnastics, the doorbell rang. My shoulders tensed. The Queen probably couldn't wait until we got to church to break me down. I tugged at the pink robe Rochelle had given me for Christmas, scooped Lily up and headed for the door. With each step, I thought up and threw out a witty retort to whatever my mother-in-law would have to say. In the end, I turned the knob, resolved to accept whatever verbal tirade Liz would launch at me without defending myself. It would make the candy comfort so much sweeter later.

Tracey Blackman, mother and martyr. Ha!

It would have been funny only it wasn't Liz at the door. It was Brenna and she'd come bearing flowers. Roses, even.

"Here, hon," she said, planting a kiss on Lily's cheek and giving me a big hug. "Just wanted to stop by and give you a little something on our way to the church."

I hugged the bouquet to my chest, trying not to cry. "Thank you. I—I—"

She shook her head and reached in her pocket for a fun-size pack of M&Ms. "I hope I'm not ruining your breakfast, but hey, sometimes a girl's gotta do what a girl's gotta do."

A horn blared out front, likely one of Brenna's teenage sons. She shouted something before returning to me. "You know what? How about I go and drop off my guys so they can set up for youth worship and then I swing back by for you and Lily? That way, Ryan can just get dressed and roll out."

My chocolate-filled cheeks puckered. "Um, I wasn't planning on going to service today, actually. I was just thinking that maybe—"

"I know. I do. I can't make you come, but I think it'd be better to get it over with. And if you come in with me, they may well forget whatever it is, anyway. Being annoyed with me keeps most everyone busy these days."

Ain't that the truth. "Why is that? That people are annoyed with you, I mean. What did you do? There's so much underlying stuff going on that I'm totally out of the loop on."

The horn blared again. "Be grateful that you don't know, hon. You aren't missing anything. Just sheep biting sheep. That's never pretty. You get ready now, okay? I'll be back for you in a few minutes."

I shut the door and rested my forehead against it.

Spring forward. Fall back.

Too bad I couldn't set my clock forward a few extra hours and skip the whole service….

Brenna came back for me just in time. Thirty more seconds and I'd have been back in my pajamas and under my covers. Ryan seemed a little shocked I'd left with Brenna, maybe a little worried. I couldn't blame him. Look what my attempts at friendship so far had brought. Nothing but trouble.

I'd expected an interrogation on the ride to church. It's definitely what my friends would have done. Brenna wasn't one of my friends, though. Not yet, anyway. She played praise music full blast instead, songs I'd never heard mixed with some of my favorites, as well.

When we got to church, everyone seemed cheerful and my mother-in-law was nowhere in sight. Pam Brooks gave me a tense smile as she passed by us to get water for her classroom, but she didn't say a word to me.

Amazing.

"Watch out for that one," I heard Brenna say through her teeth. Must be something they taught at those women's ministry meetings. Definitely a useful skill. "She's got a good heart and she doesn't mean to hurt people, but she's hurting, and without realizing it, she spreads her hurt. I've been there. It's a dangerous place to be, both for the person and for everyone around them. You just may not need to be around her right now. Give her some time. Pam really is a gifted and giving woman."

You think? I sure hadn't seen any of that in her. "Brenna, do you always see the best in people? I used to, but I think I'm becoming cynical or something." We stopped at the nursery and dropped off her baby, a month or so older than Lily. The attendant looked as surprised as I was when Brenna handed over a bottle and bottle warmer and took a number for her young son.

Maybe I'd imagined it though. Brenna didn't seem fazed at all. She smiled as we entered the Cry Room, which to my surprise was totally empty.

"Wow." It looked so much bigger with no one in it.

Brenna smiled. "Something told me to come to the early service today and swing by and pick you up. Thought you might want to talk." She patted the seat next to her. "Or to just be quiet. That's harder than talking, you know. For me, anyway."

Wasn't that the truth? There was a lot to be said for silence, I was learning. I put Lily in the baby swing and sat down. I'd brought one of Brenna's roses in my diaper bag. I picked it up now and twirled it between my palms. "Quiet is good. I really don't know what I have to say except that things aren't the best right now, not in any area of my life."

Brenna crossed and then uncrossed her legs. "And trying to make friends here at Promised Land has only made things worse, is that right?"

I leaned forward, perched my elbow on one knee. "Well, I guess I hadn't thought about it in those terms exactly, but yes, it's definitely been confusing. Each woman I meet here seems to think she has the answer to what kind of wife, mother or woman I should be. My mother-in-law definitely thinks she has things figured out. It seems like the harder I try to listen to them, the more trouble I get into in my marriage and everything else."

"So, are you ready to give up on us? Have you had enough of our meddling and confusion?" She ran a hand through her hair.

My other elbow placed on a knee, as well. My hands cupped my chin. I considered it for a second, what

Brenna had said. Should I just give up on these weird women and go it alone? Or did each of them offer some element of truth, of hope, of something that I could learn? As silly as it seemed, considering my results so far, I decided that each of these women did have something to give me and that maybe I had something to give them, too. For whatever reason, this was where God had planted me. My job was to get rooted and grounded and despite inclement conditions, manage to bloom. This conversation felt like a handful of fertilizer.

"No. I'm not ready to give up on you. Maybe I don't understand all the books and tapes and seminars. Maybe I'll never fit exactly into any one group. I still want to know all of you, learn from you, be friends with you. I still want to grow here. I have to."

Brenna pressed her lips together. Tears formed at the corners of her eyes. She leaned over and gave me a big hug. She patted my back at the end. "Good. I'm so glad. We can be a little crazy sometimes here, but at heart, we're good people. Don't give up on us or you'll always regret it. I did. I still do."

What was this, an estrogen party? Now I was crying, too, and I wasn't sure why. I definitely didn't get what Brenna meant, but now seemed like a good time to practice my newfound power of silence. If she wanted to tell me more, she would.

She did. "Being a musician, Bo has always had women attracted to him. I thought—silly me—that when we got saved, that would stop. I thought that church was a safe place for my husband, for my family. And in a million ways, it was a safe place. It can also be a place for bad things to breed, when someone has a nice voice or a pretty face. In Bo's case, he had both. Nobody cared much back then about who he was. It was all about what he did. And what he did was sing like a bird. Even I can't dispute that." She pressed her thumb to the corner of her eye.

The gifts of God are without repentance.

How many times had my grandmother said that when I came home gushing about how well someone sang or preached at church? A million, probably. Nana wasn't impressed by the things that came easy to people. She wanted to know what you struggled with and where you were with that thing today, not ten years ago. She believed that every day should bring a testimony of what Jesus had done, what He had spoken. It seemed a long time since I had thought of my own faith in those terms.

It was my turn to pat Brenna's back. I didn't speak, though, just touched. Sometimes that could be more powerful than words. I offered her a Kleenex, as well.

"Thanks. Sorry I'm bawling like this. I guess I haven't really said these things out loud much. Everyone here already knows my story. Or at least they think they do. I don't really care anymore. Anyway, Bo had fans in the congregation, women who saw more Jesus in my Bo than they did in their own husbands. Women who gave themselves to my husband. And he received them. All of them. And the women in this church, the women who will soon fill this room… They knew about it and didn't tell me."

The music started in the sanctuary. I looked through the glass at Brenna's husband, so clean-cut and bright-eyed. His suit today was the color of the mosaic tile behind my stove, gold mixed with a smidge of green.

My new friend shook her head. "Don't look at him like that. I don't tell you this tale for that reason, to make you see him differently. I tell you this so that you can see me and know from whence I've come, where I'm trying to go. You see, what he did was nothing compared to where I ended up."

I got nervous then. Nothing? How could anything be worse than what her husband had done to her? I dug into my purse. I was going to need chocolate for this.

"When I found out what had been going on, who it had been going on with, I was devastated. I went to my friends, some of the same women you've been spending time with, and they gave me all the reasons it had been my fault. All the things I could have done better—prayed more, been sexier, everything they could think of. Only none of it made sense to me. Against their advice, I confronted my husband, who not only admitted to what I knew, but told me what I didn't know—that my friends had known his secrets all along. That broke me. I felt like this church, my marriage, my friendships and even my God had been a lie. As much as I hate to say it, for a short while, I didn't even feel the same about my children. It was a dangerous place to be, especially alone." She paused for a moment, unable to go on.

Another song started, one that Brenna had just played in the car on the ride over. Holding hands, we sang praises to God, Brenna and I. Lily wasn't swinging anymore, but she wasn't crying, either. Still, I wanted to hold her. When I looked over again, she was asleep. I got her up and put her in the portable crib at the other end of the room. Usually there were so many women that I couldn't even get to this side.

Brenna followed me, helping me replace the blanket with my own.

I smiled at her as Pastor Dre started teaching. "You don't have to tell me any more. Really. It won't make a difference in how I see you."

"It will. I want to tell you my story. And when you're ready, I want to hear yours, too. I don't want to play friends anymore or to play church. Things are too crucial at this point. Everything I do, everyone I love, it all has to be real. God won't let it be any other way. Neither will I. I know now what happens when people play games with one another. Everyone loses."

You could say that again. My marriage to Ryan was starting to feel like a bad game of Monopoly, only neither of us owned any prime real estate. We just kept pulling the bad cards.

"I went to the pastor." She raised a hand toward the window. "Not Dre."

"His father? Reverend Redding?"

Brenna shook her head. "No. Ryan's father. Brother Blackman was the interim pastor then. I went to him and told him what Bo had done…but he didn't believe me. In fact, he refused to even listen to me. He told me to go home and be a better wife and these types of things wouldn't be a concern. He said that a good wife wouldn't be slandering her husband's name to the pastor and that none of this was any of his business."

What? "Are you serious? What about church discipline as outlined in the Bible? What about Matthew 18? You went to Bo alone first. Sure, maybe you could have taken it to some of the deacons or something next, but ultimately you weren't wrong. I am so sorry. I never knew Ryan's father, but I had no idea…."

Queen Liz came to mind. This might explain a lot about her sometimes abrasive personality. Might explain some of why my husband frowned at himself in the mirror, too. Maybe not. Maybe my father-in-law just hadn't wanted to be bothered with counseling his congregants. And in his defense, there were crazy women making allegations in pastors' offices all the time, only to go back and claim that the pastor had tried something with them, as well. Brenna just didn't strike me as that kind of woman, though. He had to have known there was some merit to what she was saying. The only other explanation was that he just didn't care.

Brenna laughed a little. "Don't apologize to me yet, honey. There's more. After that meeting with the pastor, I guess, looking back, I just sort of lost it. A psychotic break or something. I don't know and it doesn't really matter now, but basically I stood up during the testimony time—which we no longer have, probably for this reason—and testified everything."

I closed my eyes then opened them, looking out into the sanctuary. There would have been hundreds of people. Promised Land had always been packed at every service, to hear Ryan tell it. "You didn't."

"I did. I pointed out the women, every last one of them. I pointed out the pastor for not listening to me. And when he told me to sit down and stop lying, that such things didn't go on in our church, I pointed out all of my friends and their messes, too."

A quick breath sucked into my mouth as it seemed as though all the oxygen had been evacuated from the room. Finally, I found my words. "No. You didn't. You called them all out? Right there in the church? What did they do? The men, I mean?"

"It was a mixed bag. A lot of the husbands of the women involved already knew. Some knew that it was going on, but they didn't know who. Bo started crying but nobody wanted to hear that either. It was hard for me to do and I knew that I'd probably lose Liz as a friend because of it, but that's just how it went."

My eyes went big. "Liz who?"

She gave me a smirk. "Liz you know who. Yes, we were friends once. She was the one person whose secrets I didn't tell. Not that it mattered. When I looked at my friends on the way out of that church that day, I knew that it was over. I thought that I could never come back, not to this church and not to God. So I left."

By now, I was on the edge of my seat. "You left Bo? Your children?"

"Yes."

"Where did you go?" Immediately I regretted asking, and tried to take it back, but Brenna patted my hand.

"It's okay. I was going to tell you anyway. I went to stay with family for a while out of state, but they were asking too many questions and making not-so-subtle hints about me going home. I got a job. Met a man. We moved in together."

"You didn't." I could hardly breathe.

"I did. Bo was the only man I had ever been with in my life. I had read all those books Rainy and them are going to give you, if they haven't already. I'd gone to the all the Christian-womanhood seminars. I thought that I had done everything right, although my daddy told me that I'd regret marrying a music man. He said it was trouble. He was right, only what he and I didn't know was that I knew how to be trouble, too."

Time seemed to stop in the room for a moment. I felt a little dizzy. Still, I needed to hear this. I knew that I did. This was what lurked under the awkward silences when the room was full of women, practiced and pre-tending. Even if it was ugly, I needed to know, to see why I needed to fight on my knees for my marriage and for my own relationship with Christ. The Devil didn't just want to play house with me. Destruction was his plan.

"One day I woke up and realized that no matter what Bo had done, no matter what people at the church had done, this was really between me and God. Could He be trusted or not? That was the question I had to face. I decided that without Jesus I couldn't live. I told the man I was sorry and asked him to forgive me. I called Bo, not to ask to come home, but to ask his forgiveness for what I had done. He only wanted to know two things— where I was and when he could come get me. I came home that day and slept in the spare bedroom, crying myself to sleep. The next day I missed my period."

"A baby?" This was straight out of a movie. Whoever said church people didn't have drama just didn't know the truth of it.

Brenna nodded. "Yes. A baby. We lost her, but it was a baby just the same. And my husband would have raised her with the rest of them. By that time, Pastor Redding had come, and his first focus was on bringing accountability to the men. Unfortunately, the brokenness among the women remains and since I broke it, I'm not the one to fix it. You, however, might be just what we need."

"Me?" I swallowed hard. "Oh, I don't think so. I'm on the outside looking in. Besides what you just told me, I don't know the truth about anybody."

Brenna sighed with satisfaction. "Exactly. That's why people feel comfortable enough to try to shape you into themselves. You don't know the truth about them."

Maybe not, but I was starting to see and I wasn't sure I liked what I saw. And I'd thought the Sassy Sistahood was work. Getting to know these women in a real way could take a lifetime.

It's a good thing that you have that long.

It sounded like they were playing the benediction song, signaling the end of the service, but that was impossible. We hadn't been talking that long, had we? Now I wanted to talk to Brenna about what was going on with me and Ryan, see what she thought. As fast as I thought it, though, I realized that might not have been what God intended at all. My old pastor had always taught that for every New Testament principle, there's an Old Testament story. My job when I got home would be to ask God what I was to learn from Brenna's story. I was already getting some possible ideas.

"I just want to thank you for being real with me today," I said. "Some of the other people I've met with have told me things, but the stories seemed more about them than about me. I feel as if you gave me something this morning. Something that I needed to hear. Thank you for that. And thank you for not adding in the details of the other people. You easily could have."

"No. I know how much that can hurt," Brenna told her. "It's not my job to tell you anyone else's tale. I can only pray that those women will get up the courage to be honest with you themselves. Though they see me as an enemy to their belief system, I only see them as sisters in Christ. I pray for each of them every day and regret that I turned my mouth against them."

Before I knew it, both our husbands were banging on

the door. I gathered up Lily and gave Brenna another hug, and the second-service crowd started to file in. If she made half as good a friend as an enemy, we'd be doing great.

Chapter Ten

"I am so sorry." Ryan took the diaper bag from me and shifted Lily onto his other hip. "Here it is that Brenna came to pick you up and then I got caught up talking and you were in that room all that time. I know you hate it in there."

I shrugged. "Today it wasn't so bad. I guess I'll get used to it, like you said."

"Maybe. You don't have to get used to anything, though. I called Dre this morning when you left and we met for a quick minute before the service. I told him that I may have to step down from this minister thing. And you know what? It turns out that Pam didn't tell him anything after all. The questions he asked me are part of a list that he asks all his ministers on a weekly basis. Evidently his father does the same thing with him. Isn't that bugged out?"

Brenna's story came back to me. No, I didn't think

the pastor's accountability strategies were silly at all. What didn't make sense was how happy Ryan seemed now that he thought no one knew anything about him. "Wow. I mean I'm glad that rumors aren't flying all over the church, but I'm sad, too, that things even got that far. I think it's great that Dre is going to be checking in with you every week. Maybe you and I should do that, too."

Ryan turned to the side to squeeze past someone in the hall. He certainly seemed to be in a hurry, probably trying to avoid his mother. I'd have to remind him that she wanted to talk to me. Even though the whole church might not know, I had a feeling that Queen Liz didn't miss a thing.

Once we made it through the swarm of people trying to get down the hallway to children's church, Ryan gave me a funny look. "You and me? What would we do? Ask each other those same questions? I don't think that's necessary. You find some women—anyone but Pam will do—that you can trust and I'll try to keep in touch with these fellas and we'll see how that works."

"But—"

"Just trust me, Tracey. It's not as bad as I thought. We can work this out. Now let's go home and thank the Lord for each other. It's been awhile and you're looking mighty good in that skirt."

Was he serious? The only thing I wanted to do right now was go home and get on my face before God. This was past knees only. I was going to have to lay before God. Things were getting serious right about now and

Ryan wanted to choose now to try to get with me when he'd been ignoring me for what seemed like forever? (Okay, so it was eight days. Same difference!)

Still, I had managed to hear some of Pastor Dre's sermon this morning, a passage from Corinthians about a man's body belonging to his wife and vice versa. Though I didn't think that Ryan was interested in any of the women in the church who always hunted him down for a hug, there was no use starting problems in the one area of our marriage where there weren't any. "Sure, baby. Let's go home."

We made it to the car, but Queen Liz cut us off, parking right behind us. Just when things were getting good…. I should have known that this whole scene was too good to be true.

Liz got out of the car and over to us as fast as her peach-colored pumps would carry her. "Where are you all going? Tracey, I told you I needed to talk to you." She seemed nervous, which made me even more nervous. Since I knew now that Liz probably didn't know about the whole e-mail fiasco with Ryan, I wondered what this was about.

"A friend brought me to the early service." I tried to relax. "Brenna Ross," I added, remembering that they had once been friends. I knew better than to say any more.

My mother-in-law looked stricken. She waved Ryan on to the car, then closed in on me. "About that. Someone told me that you and Brenna were becoming friends. I just wanted to caution you about getting too close with her. She's nice enough, but she's not someone that you can trust. You're a minister's wife now and people like Brenna are dangerous to you. Do you understand what I'm saying?"

I didn't. Not at all. It seemed to me that the Queen herself posed the biggest danger in my life. Her and the woman on my husband's computer. I had something for her, too, though. All this mess was getting on my nerves. "Queen, I really don't know what you're saying. I don't know Brenna very well, but to be honest, she's shown me a lot more kindness than you have in all the time I've been with Ryan. I go by what people do, not just what they say."

For once, the Queen looked stumped, as though she didn't know what to say. Then, as always, the dart came back to her, resting right on the tip of her tongue. "You know, I was right about you. You're just a selfish, lazy little fat girl who tricked my son into marrying her. You think I believe that pregnant-on-the-honeymoon mess? You could have done a lot better than that. Well, don't worry, because that woman you told Pamela about is just the beginning. Ryan is his father's son. You think you're better than me now, but we'll see how you feel after sleeping in my bed for a few years. It's a hard place." Her eyes settled in on my bare ring finger before she turned away. I'd meant to put my ring back on this morning. Ryan still hadn't replaced his.

She'd spoken this last bit of venom too softly for Ryan to hear, but he knew it wasn't good. He took my hand. Liz was right. I was feeling it. The bed I'd made was hard. Maybe too hard.

There is nothing too hard for the Lord.

With a wave to Ryan, my mother-in-law got back into her car, eased away from our space and to my surprise, drove totally out of the church parking lot. Ryan looked surprised by his mother's exit from the church property, but he had the good sense not to ask for a recap of the conversation he'd missed. "Everything okay?" he asked.

I rested back in my seat, wondering why it seemed like all the people who I'd thought were in my corner turned out to be fighting on the other side. Or was it me who was out of place? I was too tired, too hurt to care. "Everything will be all right, boo. Let's just go home."

The next week flew by as I caught up on all the Web work I'd slacked off on while my laptop and my love life was offline. Things were better between Ryan and I in the bedroom (not that they had ever been bad), but I couldn't help thinking about what I'd said to Liz the last time I'd seen her: It wasn't just what people said that mattered, but what they did. After praying about it, I'd considered wearing my wedding band again, whether Ryan got another one or not.

And though I'd laughed at Pamela about the "hidden files," it was all I could do to keep from snooping in Ryan's files every time I saw his laptop lying around. (Which wasn't very much anymore. He left it in his truck now mostly. I didn't know what to make of that.)

What I did know for sure was that Ryan had not con-fronted this woman about her behavior in any way. Nor did he plan to. He'd told me as much.

Though my husband reassured me that he loved me, sometimes I didn't know what to believe. One thing was for sure, though, as much as I loved my girlfriends, old and new, there were some things that Jesus alone can get you through. I'd been reading back through the vows that Dana had written for her "Married to my Maker" ceremony a couple years back. Though she ended up marrying Adrian that day, the sentiment holds true. I had a husband long before I met Ryan and He's never been unfaithful or let me down. Jesus is my provider, the lover of my soul. As much as I'd like to pin my every hope and emotional need on Ryan, I could see now that doing so was not only foolish, but dangerous.

He was just a man. I realized now that as a single woman, I gave Ryan and all the men like him too much power in my life. I wanted somebody to want me then, and to be honest, I wanted the same thing now. I just didn't want to want it. Okay, I was confusing myself.

Anyway, the days flipped by with me riding through drive-thrus like a maniac and saying those dreaded words that I thought I'd never say again—Supersize me! After almost a week of that, everything I owned was tight. I wouldn't be buying another scale until something I owned loosened up around the waist. I wasn't sure I wanted to know how bad I'd blown it. I kept thinking about that woman's picture and how slim—no, skinny—

she was. And those breasts? Well, they weren't serving
up three meals a day, that's for sure. That stuff looked sur-
gically enhanced like the women I saw everywhere these
days. From sidebars on my e-mails to commercials for
coffee and condiments, there they were. And Ryan saw
them, too.

What's a regular woman, a wife and mother, to do?

If I'd been surprised by Pamela's invitation to lunch,
the linen invitation from the First Lady to her luncheon
for friends and other ministry wives had stunned me. I'd
picked up the book Hyacynth had chosen, scanned it and
hoped the luncheon would be better. Now I stood in my
bathroom on Saturday morning, preparing for the First
Lady and Friends Society luncheon when a scripture from
last Sunday morning returned to my mind, my heart.
Instead of continuing the appraisal of my body (too big
here, too little there), I began an appraisal of my God.

On my knees, I used my scale as a kneeling stone
instead of the rock of my esteem. "You are altogether
lovely, Lord. Altogether wonderful. Thank you for being
my counselor when folks think I'm crazy. For being my
husband when mine won't act right. I might not be
going over or around like I thought I would, but I thank
you for taking me through. Just don't leave me. That's
all that I ask. I can't do anything if you leave me."

Sobs shook my shoulders as all the pains I'd stuffed
away, the hurts I'd saved for later, came tumbling down.
A cry came from somewhere deep inside me. The kind

of cry that only God can understand. In that moment, I heard all the hurtful words that had been spoken, felt all my inadequacies, my insecurities.

And then, in my spirit, I felt God's healing. I spoke a new blessing, one I'd written the night before.

You are enough, Beloved. You, daughter, are far above rubies, redeemed with the value of the world. Rise up, daughter, and walk. Rise up, daughter, and follow Jesus. Do not trust your eyes. Trust His word.

These were the kind of deep spiritual moments that happened to my friends. Though I'd been in a serious frame of mind, these words, this love, made me happy. Made me stand to my feet and look at myself in the mirror.

And smile.

As my grandmother had always told me, "You've got to know how to make your own love. Some folks just don't have it to give." I hadn't really understood that back then, but I got it now.

After singing myself a song, I toweled off and laid out my clothes, cooked Ryan brunch. Instead of fighting with my prepregnancy wardrobe to find something to stuff myself into, I opened the trunk at the back of my closet, with the only clothes I had left from before the baby, the tens and twelves I'd been saving for Dana but always forgot to take when we went to visit. I pulled out a bright yellow suit and matching pumps. I took a sunflower from the kitchen table and tucked it in my hair. I dressed Lily quickly and headed for the door.

On the way out, I heard a sound in the kitchen that I hadn't heard in months.

I heard my husband praying.

"You look like sunshine, baby. Now, that's what I like to see. That's what I'm talking about. Come on in here. That suit fits you so well." Mother Redding couldn't stop complimenting me as I entered the annex where the luncheon was to be held. Evidently, I was the first to arrive.

Without knowing it, I'd dressed to match the table, a lush garden cloth with bursts of gold streaking through the fabric like rays of light. Along the table were several centerpieces of sunflowers and yellow daisies. The tables were covered in green silk tiebacks. I could see now why the hospitality committee had chosen this side of the building. The light streamed in the windows, beaming me a second welcome. Even Lily raised her hand as if to say hello.

Mother Redding worked quickly with the other women, most of whom I hadn't met except for seeing them up on the two front rows. I tried to help set the table but they shook their heads and shooed me away. Before I knew it, the empty room had filled with women. Susan, Rainy, Brenna, Pam, even Sister Hawkins. She looked as surprised and unnerved as me to be there. Maybe this was her first time, too. I smiled, remembering how she'd said that the ministers' wives would eat me alive. Perhaps she'd been voicing her own fears.

After all the hugs and introductions, we were led

back to the long table. The name cards by each chair were hand-written in calligraphy. Rochelle would have loved this. I felt silly allowing the older women to pull out my chair for me, but they insisted.

At the top of the table sat First Lady Hyacynth, in a handkerchief dress with a royal blue and gold swirl print. She wore a matching scarf around the sea of braids cascading over her shoulders. Those braids had inspired the only negative comment I'd ever heard from Queen Liz toward the new pastor's wife. "Totally inappropriate." Again, I found that ridiculous, but I'd kept my mouth shut.

Today, I opened my mouth in a wide smile. There was power in this room and not only the power of strong women or good men, but the power of God. As Mother Redding lifted Lily from my arms, I felt myself relax, felt quiet growing in my soul. It might not last, but it was a beginning.

We shared a short prayer time, with people speaking out individually around the table as they felt the urge. Though it was comforting, I didn't jump in. The luncheon, a delicious shrimp-salad croissant with grapes and red onions, a garden salad and fresh blueberries, came complete with a nutritional information card to take home for later. Where had these women been all my life?

Right here. They've been right here waiting for you.

It felt good to feel as though I was in the right place. That someone had wanted me to be there. Even for a moment, an hour. It felt good.

As we ate, Sister 'Cynt, as Hyacynth was evidently known to her close friends, opened the book that had been chosen and began to read.

"'Women are not meant to be doormats, but instead they are like sturdy furniture, undergirding the home with virtue and strength. The man is like a knight, braving the uncertainties of the world to provide for his family—'"

"What is that mess you're reading?" It was Mother Redding, now up from her chair, with Lily clinging to her hip.

'Cynt looked aggravated. "It's our study book for this quarter, *Mother. Ministry and Marriage: Seven Secrets to Serving Successfully with Your Husband* is the title."

Mother Redding began to laugh. "A man wrote that, didn't he?"

Even 'Cynt had to smile. "Yes, Mother. The author is a man, but he's a pastor to a large church. He and his wife—"

"So, are all of you looking to marry him? Is his wife dying? Your husbands, too?"

We all shook our heads.

Mother Redding began to pace around the table. "Okay, I'm not understanding then. All that man can tell you are seven secrets to serving with him. And since you're not his wife, I don't see where that's really going to benefit you. Don't get me wrong, the gentleman probably has a lot of good insights about relationships, but you all are starting off wrong from the get-go."

Hyacynth slammed the book shut and straightened

her shoulders. She steepled her hands until all her fingertips were touching. "Mother obviously has some things she'd like to say, so I'm going to turn today's message over to her." She sat back with a look that made me know she thought she'd fixed her mother-in-law good. After all, wasn't it she, Hyacynth, who preached with Dre at the conferences? Wasn't it she who'd taught at numerous retreats? Mother Redding and her friends hadn't done any more when they ran the church than they did now, sitting on the front row and blocking people's view with those ridiculous hats.

The first lady's expression said it all, as clear as if she'd spoken aloud. I rubbed my palms together. Things were heating up. I didn't know Mother Redding well, but I knew that whatever this woman had to say was going to be better than anything in a book written by some stranger. (Though I was still going to read that one later, just to be sure I wasn't missing anything.) The books were almost sold out when I'd gotten mine.

Mother Redding made it to my chair and set Lily back into my waiting arms. "Sugar, I'm not trying to get in the way of your meeting. I know that there's only room on those thrones you and my son have erected for one woman, especially with my thighs."

No, she didn't go there with the thrones. I love this woman.

Restrained laughter trickled around the room.

Mother Redding waved a hand, flashing her rings in the sunlight. "Go ahead and laugh. Those chairs are ridiculous. Y'all know it. I don't fault Dre and 'Cynt alone for it, though. I fault y'all, too. You are supposed to pray for these folk and tell the truth when they're wrong. In love, of course, but the truth has to be told. That's why folks are dying in the pews now. But I'm getting ahead of myself. I apologize for interrupting your teaching, baby girl. I was just here to serve you ladies, not get in anybody's business."

Get in my business, lady, I thought. This was the time for us to do it. Not in the middle of a service like Brenna'd had to do. Even though we were all saved, we were still human. We hurt. And as Rochelle would say, every good woman needs a safe place to bleed and a good friend to point her to Jesus when the bleeding is done.

Hyacynth began to cry. "Now see, this wasn't supposed to happen in front of you all. I'm supposed to be perfect, strong and beautiful. The preacher's wife who does everything right. Well, the truth is, I don't always do things right. In fact, sometimes I don't know what to do at all. When I was preparing this month's luncheon, the Lord told me to let Mother speak, but I rebelled against that because I thought that this book and my "resources" were what you needed. I realize now that what you need, what we all need, is to be willing and obedient to hear God's call. I pray that you will forgive me."

Nods came quickly all around the table.

The first lady spoke again. "Mother, I ask that you forgive me, too, and that you will share with us. Whatever God puts on your heart to say."

Mother Redding went to Hyacynth and kissed the top of her head. "Nothing to forgive, baby girl. Nothing at all. We're just doing the best we can. Now back to this book. First of all, the Bible says that the older women are to teach the younger women how to love their husbands and their families. I'm not going to tell you about training your husband for ministry, because that's not my job. It's not yours, either. God will give the call to your husband. You have to focus on not resenting the call or the man. But that's ahead again. For starters, give me those books."

Everyone but me looked surprised. Some even looked a little annoyed.

The older woman gripped the back of her daughter-in-law's chair. She signaled to the friends she'd brought along, the ladies from the front row of the church. "Sisters, collect those books for me, please."

The women complied, moving much faster than I would have thought they were able.

"You can have those books back when I'm done today, but I don't want you leafing through them while I'm talking. I need you to hear me now because these things are basic but important. I could get up here and give you seven things or seventy things to do to please your husband, but none of them would work permanently. You know why? The Bible says that every man is to have his own wife. You are the answer to one man's prayers. You need to study him the way you did when you dated him. Take that thing back to the root. Uh-huh.

When he fixes that car, go out there and bring him lemonade. Stop trying to be your husband's mother and learn how to be his wife!"

There was a collective gasp around the room. Most of that air had come out of me. Someone at the end of the table started moaning, crying from the gut like I'd done in my bathroom this morning. I was surprised to see that it was Sister Hawkins.

Brenna took a cloth napkin from the table and began to fan her.

"Leave her go, baby. She's going to have to cry this one out. That's just how it is sometimes. We don't have enough time today to make it pretty. Just fix your makeup before you go back home." Moving almost to the beat of her words, the six older women in aprons who'd come with Mother Redding emerged from the room where they'd taken the books with several boxes of Kleenex. They set a box on the table in front of Sister Hawkins.

"Thank you, sisters," Mother Redding said. "Before I go on, let me introduce you to my sisters. This is Gertrude, Charlene, Barbara Jean, Betty Lou and Donna Lee. You all probably know them from their seats in the front with me, but I need you to know that though we didn't send out invitations or have computers in my day, we did this same thing. These are the women who sat at my table, who held up my hands for these thirty years that my family has been in the ministry. And I've done the same for them. We still come and clean this church every Friday night, praying as we go."

Hyacynth twisted in her chair. "That's where you go? I thought—"

Mother Redding patted the top of the chair. "Turn around, baby, you're messing up them plaits. Now listen, I didn't tell you that so you could think well of us, because in truth, that's a fraction of what we do. Here's the first secret I'm going to pass on to you about serving with your husband. Serve and stop trying to be seen! Everybody wants a throne and a microphone, but nobody wants to clean the toilets. And believe me, I know!"

It was Hyacynth's turn to cry this time. She kept trying to get up, to apologize to her mother-in-law, but Mother Redding wasn't having it. "Just cry it out, baby. We don't have long." As if she knew her work with Hyacynth was done, she began to walk around the table, pausing at different places. "Some of you all have forgotten what it means to be real. You've forgotten how to be friends. You're worried that somebody is going to tell your mess. Well, baby, we already know!"

There was a shout across from me. Rainy, this time. She tried to get up. She tried to run out of the room....

"Baby, just sit down. You ain't going to make it."

And she didn't make it, either. Rainy fell slap-out about ten feet from the entrance, calling for Jesus at the top of her lungs. Susan jumped from her seat.

Mother Redding sat her right back down, but not before waving her prayer warriors in Rainy's direction. She turned back to Susan. "No, no, sister-in-law. You can't cover this. See, you've been covering and lying long enough. You don't have to do it anymore. You know why? Look around this table. These are not your enemies. These are your sisters. They are going to pray for you. They are going to come in the dark of night, in the dim of morning. You, woman of God, need to tend to your own husband and let us take care of sister girl here. All right?"

Susan sat on the edge of her chair, rocking like a baby. She managed to nod before wiping out right into her plate. I snatched it away before her face hit the china.

"Good catch, baby. Y'all see that? That girl has quick hands. How many of you know we need some quick hands up in this church? The men, now, they have things sewed up, but we're too busy being cute trying to act like it ain't our men over there every week in the other room, telling the truth about themselves, that they're sinners. We don't want to admit that, because if we do, we'll have to say that we're sinners, too, that no matter how prosperous we get or how blessed we get, we still get it wrong."

Preach, lady. Just preach.

Baby Lily clapped her hands as though she knew this was some good stuff. I felt tears coming, but I held them back. I didn't want to miss one word of this.

Mother Redding came to my chair. Took Lily from my lap. "See now, this baby knows a good word when it goes forth. That's how we have to be. Like babies. We can't fight them by trying to be prettier...though you need to do what you can, don't get me wrong. Stop thinking that you'll keep him if you starve yourself or do what you think other women are doing. He married you! A man who finds a wife finds a good thing. Let me hear y'all say, 'I am a good thing!'"

The words choked out of my mouth. I couldn't hold my tears back any longer. As we said those words together, whatever tension, whatever pride was left, came tumbling down. Though I couldn't see past my tears, I reached out and grabbed somebody's hand on both sides of me. They held on to me as we said it over and over again, all of us crying, all of us praying.

When we were done, tear-soaked and mascara-streaked, Mother Redding took her seat. "I think my work is done here, ladies. Anyone ready for dessert?"

Chapter Eleven

It'd been three weeks and I was still coming down from Mother Redding's talk at the First Lady and Friends Society luncheon. I was horrified when Brenna told me that the luncheon was only held once a quarter. Today, I was having a luncheon of my own to try to come up with some way to keep the fellowship that we'd had that Saturday going throughout the year.

The day was brisk, still moist from an April shower the day before. It was my first time having a gathering outside since my housewarming party more than a year ago, but I'd opened the double French doors anyway and filled the living room with toys so that the children could go in and out as they pleased. I'd never liked those outdoor parties where it was clear no one could go inside. I'd always end up shifting from one foot to the other at those things, then running to the bathroom inside and heading next to my car.

No, even though the first lady and Mother Redding were coming, I had to be me. I'd been to Hyacynth's house once with its high ceilings and twenty-foot windows (with drapes the same length). Though my home was bigger than anyplace I'd ever lived, I'd kept the same simple, cozy decorating style I'd always had. Today's get-together would reflect that, too. Though Easter was a week away, I told the ladies not to wear the white gloves and pretty dresses someone told me they'd worn to Hyacynth's garden party last spring. No, sir. We were having a barbecue and Dana's father had even driven over from his restaurant to do the honors.

I hope no one bites off their fingers. I should have warned them.

My girls Rochelle and Dana were coming, too, bringing goodies of their own and helping me keep from melting down. Unable to be quite as flexible as Dana or as rigid as Rochelle, I did hand-paint each lady's name onto ceramic pots this week when I should have been sleeping. But as my husband said, sometimes I just don't know when to quit. He was right about that, of course, but that this be a special day was really important to me. It was also cool to think of my old friends meeting my new ones.

New ones? Yes, that's just what they are. My new friends.

I hoped that Austin, one of our more recent sassy sistahs, would be able to wrap up the edits from the morning news and come along too….

"This looks nice, baby. Look how you did their names on the flowerpots. I saw some piggy banks like that at the mall. Those are pretty flowers in the center-piece, too. Who picked them? Who did the balloons?" Ryan asked me.

Me, me and, yes, me.

"I did them, sweetheart." I refolded one of the napkins on top of the nearest place setting. One more favor still needed to be set at each place, but I didn't really want to do it in front of my husband if I didn't have to. That he seemed proud of what I'd done so far really made me feel good, though. I made a mental note to try to find some-thing to praise him for before the day was over.

Ryan took my face in his hands and kissed me. His lips were soft and sweet. They tasted like mangoes. Definitely praiseworthy.

I wrapped both arms around him, pressed one hand between his shoulder blades. "So, you've been using my lip gloss, huh?" I asked, already knowing the answer. I'd have to run him a bath and put in some of those bath oils for him, too. Not to mention Dana's new body gloss. Umph. I had to focus before all the churchwomen arrived to find me indisposed.

He kissed me again, this time right below my ear. "I couldn't find my lip stuff. I think I left it at the gym. At first I was tripping because yours was all fruity, but if it's going to get that kind of reaction from you, I think I might have to call Dana up and order myself some, too."

"No need," someone called from the kitchen. Dana appeared a second later, her natural braids now swinging past her shoulders. She had a tan fresh from whatever trip Adrian had whisked her off to and sunglasses that matched her nail polish. She'd come a long way from the awkward Dana I once knew, but she'd only become what I'd seen inside her all along. A good love can grow you in many ways. I gave my husband one more squeeze as my friend approached.

He shook his head. "Just go on with your friends. You know you want to."

I sure did want to. I gave him one more kiss and ran across the living room and toward the stainless-steel wonderland also known as my kitchen. Dana stood just outside of it, now balancing Lily on her hip.

Not having talked for a week or so, we embraced fiercely. I took in her new sun-kissed beauty and beautiful accessories first, then tipped her chin up so that I could get a clear look at her eyes. She opened them wide for me before turning away. She'd kept them open long enough for me to see the disappointment, the sadness. There was no need for me to ask if they were still trying to have a baby or how things were going. They were trying, but this month had brought them another no. I could see that and other things that we'd have to talk about later in her eyes.

"Daddy's coming in with his things. I told him that you have a state-of-the-art grill back there, but he insisted on strapping that fifty-gallon drum from his backyard onto the back of the car. I'm shamed for you, girl. Maybe we can set up some bamboo to hide it or something."

Lily shifted in Dana's arms until she was released and set down on the floor. She clung to my leg for a moment before crawling away. Dana and I walked over to one of the many couches in the room and fell into it, both laughing about her father's makeshift grill. Ryan passed us on his way outside to help the other men get everything inside.

"Girl, there's no sense trying to hide your daddy with any bamboo. He'll catch that mess on fire just for spite. It's all good. Living in Naperville in this big house hasn't changed who I am. I still know how to throw down like we're back on the block. Did Shan happen to have any sweet sauce? I know that it was short notice. Ryan was the one who thought of it. He's addicted to that mess. I think he'd drink it if he could."

Dana cracked up laughing. "Ryan, too? Adrian will hurt himself with it if I don't stop him. Reflux. He is so pitiful. He's on this diet kick again, but he cannot do anything with Sunday dinner. Between Daddy and Shan, he's done for."

I nodded. Nutrition kick? Maybe something to do with the infertility thing. Dana looked as if she had dropped a few more pounds, too. We were nearly the same size now. "I see that you're losing, too. You look great. Walking around looking like that, you'll be pregnant before you know it."

Did I really say that?

The sadness I'd seen clouding Dana's gaze earlier gathered in the corners of her eyes. She wiped her tears away as quickly as they'd come, adding a smile for good measure. "I sure hope so."

I can be so stupid sometimes.

While I apologized, the men passed in front of us with enough food and equipment to feed a small nation, let alone a few churchwomen. I turned to Dana in surprise as we both stood up to go and help. "What is all that? I didn't invite that many people. And the ones I did invite are women."

Dana's father clapped his hands against his knees and took a breath on his way back to the car. "Exactly. Everybody knows that churchwomen know how to eat. They know how to cook, too. I can't just throw them a chicken leg. No, these are God's women, the women of your church. You're as much a daughter to me as Dana or any of the rest of 'em. I have to show these women that we raised you right, that we know how to do things."

Though we hadn't eaten anything yet, I felt full off those words alone. "Thank you." Among family, that's all that needs to be said.

Ryan, who'd been watching from the kitchen, walked toward us and took Dana's father's arm. "You sit. We've got it, Dad."

I tried not to cry at the sight of them, the care which my husband took in leading the man who'd served as my father for most of my life to the best recliner and handing him the remote.

The old man handed it back to him. "No, thanks, young man. I'm much too busy for television. I have too many things going through my mind, questions, like why a good man like you isn't wearing his wedding ring."

It started with a phone call.

"Tracey, is it okay if my husband comes? I hate to ask, but I let it slip that the owner of Rose Barbecue would be doing the catering personally and he insists on coming over to meet him. I told him I'd just bring him a plate but—"

"Pastor Dre is more than welcome here anytime, Sister Hyacynth. Anytime." Anytime but now, of course, with my table covered in tiaras and toffee candy. This was going to be interesting. "He could even share a word if he'd like. I'd prepared something to say, but I'd love it if he would like to do it."

The first lady laughed. "The only word he wants to share is 'pass the sauce,' believe me. And you prepared something to say? Girl, you are really something. It takes me all year to get that luncheon together and you see that Mother had to do the talking for me even then. Are you sure I shouldn't dress up? You're making me think that this is really going to be a big deal."

Rochelle's husband, Shan, passed me, balancing a gallon of sauce in each hand. "No, Sister Hyacynth. Dress down and bring an empty stomach. We've got wet wipes here. It's that kind of party."

She laughed again. "Okay. Now, one more thing."

"Yes?" I clicked my pen in case it was something I would forget.

"Stop calling me Sister Hyacynth like we're both ninety years old. Call me 'Cynt, okay? I like you. A lot. Just treat me like you do your friends."

I looked over at Rochelle and Dana, fighting over the best kind of potato salad. I'd have to settle the argument like always, by voting for German. It's all about the mustard. "I'll try and treat you a little better than the way I do my friends. At least for now. But only slightly better."

"Promise?"

"Promise."

That call was the first of many. For some reason, the husbands, brothers and sons of every woman I invited all wanted to come, too. The young boys wanted to hang out with Ryan since he'd been working with them for the past month or so in Sunday school. It'd come as a shock to both of us when they all began to follow him around the church, even starting to wear suits like his, with cubic-zirconium cuff links to match his diamond ones.

One of the reasons I hadn't had many people over was that I didn't want them to get the wrong idea about us or about me based on the house we lived in. Many of the people who'd come today might still go away with the wrong idea about my family, but knowing that we're just a few cell phone calls from losing it all brings perspective. It also makes it much easier to open this house up and let people have the run of it. This time next year, we'll probably be holed up in an apartment some-where. Ryan's just too headstrong to face the real pos-sibilities. He hasn't learned that sometimes failure is the option that keeps you alive to fight another battle on another day.

Though the morning had been bright and chilly, the noon sun bathed my yard in light and warmth, just in time for the stampede. Even with the calls I'd received, I'd felt bad about Dana's father bringing so much food, until my neighbors started to arrive, that is. One by one, the quiet couples who inhabited the pristine houses around us with the bright green lawns appeared, their eyes unsure, their stomachs ready.

"Um, we were just coming over to say that you can use our driveway if you need more parking…."

"I saw the truck. Rose Barbecue. Is that the real one, from down in Leverhill? I just wondered."

"My son saw the little boys and wanted to come over and see if anyone wants to come to our house to play. I hope I'm not interrupting…."

And on it went like that until everyone on the street was in my backyard: husbands clustered around my husband, children swinging from the swings, women shaking hands with the women from Promised Land. White, black, brown, fat, tall, slim, rich and the not-so-rich mixed together into a beautiful scene. We all had one thing in common—dirty fingers.

"Mommy, can I have a crown, too?" A little girl from down the street wound her hair around her thumb instead of sucking it like I'd seen her do many times before.

"Sweetie, I think that's for something else. When we go out later I'll—"

"Nooooooo! I want one of those. The ones at the store break too easy. Those look real."

I picked up the one from my place and put it down on her little head. "Here you go. You can have it, but you have to promise me that you'll remember to act like a princess and treat Mommy like a queen."

The little girl looked at me hard and even, like I'd made a tall order. "Act like a princess? All the time or just when I've got on my crown?"

"All the time." I waved her over closer. "You see, God gave you a crown when you were born. We all have one. We just have to accept it. So when you're not wearing this one, just put your hand on your head to remind yourself that the other one is still there."

She nodded as though that made perfect sense. "Can a princess climb trees?"

"Absolutely," I said.

"Deal." She shook my hand and went on her way, but her mother, who'd been silent throughout the exchange, stayed behind. "I love the crown thing. Do you have a minute to explain that again?"

I didn't have a minute. All my guests were seated at their table and finishing their meals. Dana was passing out their goody bags full of her new Motherly Love line, and Rochelle was instructing them on how to best preserve their tiaras. Still, I gave Dana a signal and led the woman into the house. There were some things that just took precedence over my plans—God's plans—and this seemed to be part of them.

We walked a while without finding a spot that wasn't full of people. Finally, I gave up and led my neighbor down a back hall behind the piano that no one ever played and into the princess potty, my regal bathroom. "Don't laugh, okay?" I said as I unlocked the door. "It's a long story, but I can't think of a better place to talk about the crowns God has for us."

She didn't laugh. She screamed. "Oh my goodness! Look at this! It's fabulous. And all this bath stuff. Made of Honor? They did my friend's bridal shower. And the gold toilet and towels…" She looked as if she would burst.

"Don't tell a soul. Now sit down." I offered her my throne, while I sat on the edge of the tub. I'd eaten too much and stayed up too late, but somehow I managed to review the goodness, that Jesus died, was buried and resurrected to buy her (Lynn) a ticket to heaven. He had some plans for her on earth, too. Jesus wanted to love her, to guide her and to be King in her life.

It wasn't the best delivery, but I don't consider myself the evangelist type. I'm more of a hug-and-run sort of person, the one who plants seeds and says, "God bless you." Well, in spite of me, Lynn reached out for the Jesus in my jumbled words and rededicated her life and her heart to Christ.

When we both stopped crying, she began to laugh. "You know why I really came over here?"

"Why?"

"To count your bathrooms. We have four and I really thought that was something until your next-door neighbor said that you had six. I wouldn't believe it and neither would my husband. When we saw her coming over, we came, too. But once I got inside, I forgot all about it. Now, I see what I was really here for. To hear this. To reunite with the Jesus I'd loved as a child. And I have to say that both He and you are beautiful."

I was as shocked as her. The neighbors were counting our bathrooms? We all have issues. "Hey, I thought I was just having a girlie luncheon for some ladies from my church. I had no idea it'd turn into some kind of block party."

Lynn shook her head. "Block party? Are you kidding me? There's a revival going on down there. I saw my husband following yours somewhere with a Bible in his hand. And the man who made my rib sandwich prayed for me, too."

I almost told her that she'd met my father, but I didn't. He wasn't my father. Not exactly.

There was a knock on the door. "Can you let me in? I need to use the restroom. All the others are full."

Lynn got up to open the door, but I grabbed her wrist.

"What's wrong?" she whispered. "Who is it?"

"My mother-in-law," I said softly. "The Queen herself."

* * *

To say that I didn't want to open the door would be an understatement. It was more like I wanted to climb out the window and run for my life. Unfortunately, even that wouldn't work. The window was too small.

"Tra-cey! I know you're in here. Now open up, hon. Queen needs the facilities."

"Tracey, should I open it? Are you ready?" Lynn said, looking at her new friend with unsteady eyes.

Ready? I wasn't, but sometimes you just have to fake it till you make it. I found my feet and thanked Lynn with a smile before opening the door myself. "Come in, Mom. Sorry. You startled me. We were in here talking about J—"

"Will you look at this!" Queen Liz, arrayed in a bronze sundress and metallic sandals, covered her mouth with both hands. She took it all in, the purple velveteen shower curtain with gold tassels, the gilded picture frames from Finger Hut, the crown resting on its pillow on the back of my throne…. Though I'd been worried about Lynn's reaction, the look on Liz's face just made me mad. I'd hoped that she'd recognize my fake throne room for the joke it was. Instead, the joke was on me.

She giggled into her palms, still covering her mouth, then replaced her hands at her sides. "Who knew that little Miss Need-Nothing fancies herself a queen? You tried hard, baby, you really did. Just know that's all it was, trying. This can be Lily's bathroom, though, when she gets bigger. She really is a princess. You just don't have what it takes to be a queen."

With that, she pivoted and opened the door all the way in a gesture that meant for us to leave. I couldn't get out of there fast enough. In fact, I broke into a jog to keep from making all the clever retorts that kept coming to my mind. If being a queen meant talking crazy like that to people, then maybe the whole thing was overrated.

As we walked back to the crowd, Lynn touched my arm. "Are you all right?"

I smiled and it wasn't fake this time. "Yes. I'm fine. I'm sorry you had to see all that. My mother-in-law is just—"

"Insecure? Rude? Crazy?"

And then some, but I wasn't about to say it to this stranger. Liz was all the mother I had. "I wouldn't put it quite that way. She's different. She's hurt because she didn't know about my bathroom and in truth, I suppose it is a little satire on her. You see, she's the Queen to everyone else and sometimes it seems like my life is where she gets to rule. So for a little while each week, I get to be Queen."

Lynn nodded. "You don't have to explain. For me, it's my mother. Her name isn't Queen, but it could be. It should be."

We made it through the kitchen and back into the noise and bustle of our neighbors and friends. I gave Lynn a hug. "Hey, don't worry about me. I'll be fine."

My neighbor hugged me back and waved to her

husband, who was holding her daughter and talking animatedly with Ryan. I stepped outside to the sight of all my lady friends seated around the table, wearing crowns on their heads and looking very happy.

I walked toward them with a mouthful of excuses. "I am so sorry, ladies. My neighbor wanted to talk. And then my mother-in-law—"

"Shh." It was Dana, up from her chair and nudging my side. "Hush, girl. Things worked out perfect. Just sit down and be quiet."

Mother Redding nodded at the head of the table. "You can say that again, baby. This thing here was something real. This was the best church I've had in a while."

There were amens all around. I nodded like a fool, still not quite getting it. "Well, things didn't go quite as planned, but I did want to talk more about ways for us women to get together more regularly, to get to know one another and all."

'Cynt, who sat next to her mother looking as though she would burst, leaned forward in her chair. "Girl, you don't get it, do you? Look around. We've been here studying and sharing. The children are playing and some people have naturally taken over that area. The men are ministering to one another. The youth are listening and learning. Y'all are having backyard church today. This is way bigger than some ladies' luncheon."

I swallowed hard and looked around. Since my time in the bathroom with Lynn, it looked as though ten more families had arrived, most of them from the next street over. I still didn't know who had called my mother-in-law since she wasn't on my invite list (another faux pas on my part). Back in Leverhill, my friends' husbands, Rochelle's grown son, Jericho, and some other men met in a group called Keepers of the Door. I could see now that Adrian and Shan were passing out cards with their Web site on it and instructing the men on how to e-mail their virtual prayer line.

Not knowing what to say about it, I shrugged. "Maybe you're right. Maybe this thing does have some potential. I just wanted to be a blessing to all of you. I tried not to overthink it. I figure God will show up and change the program around anyway."

"I know that's right," someone said.

"Well, programs are still nice to have," Rochelle said, making everyone laugh. Obviously they'd gotten to know her a bit in the short time I'd been away. She held up the little itinerary that I'd printed out and set at each place. "We've each shared a prayer, eaten a good meal. Now, what about this scripture that you were going to bring?"

"I—"

"Speaking of that, let's praise the Lord before we begin." The voice, now quiet and unassuming, came from my mother-in-law's body. I turned around in my chair to be sure, but I knew it was her.

Now, isn't that something? You have to give the lady a few points, for nerve alone. Funny, though, no one responded, not even when she started slowly clapping her hands. I felt something break open inside me the way it had that day at the restaurant. I did all I could to hold it in.

"Though most of you already know her, this is my mother-in-law, Queen Elizabeth."

"*Queen Elizabeth?* I thought she was white," I heard a little girl at the next table say as she squinted at Ryan's mother. "She looked much different on TV."

Tell me about it.

Just as I was about to tell everyone about it, about how my mother-in-law must be a descendant of Jezebel and Athaliah, the evil queens from the Bible who tried to manipulate their husbands and sons…I saw someone standing apart from the others, waving at me.

He came closer and gave me a wink before disappearing through the bushes with a plate of barbecue.

Mark Johnson.

Chapter Twelve

"'A wife of noble character who can find? She is worth far more than rubies. She watches over the affairs of her household and does not eat the bread of idleness. Her children arise and call her blessed, her husband also, and he praises her…'"

My voice cracked as I read the verses I'd copied down in my notebook. Easter had come and gone without incident. The women from my church were meeting weekly, both for fellowship and to help Mother Redding and her sisters clean the church. The cleaning day had turned into a morning out of sorts, with some of the older women watching the children after the church sparkled, while the rest of us learned to sew, cook and make Web pages. Guess who contributed that skill?

Me. I'd always been proud of my computer savvy, but the more that I went and saw what the other women knew how to do, things that I'd like to learn more about, my virtual reality had started to seem a little silly. Though things with Ryan and I seemed to have gotten worse after the luncheon instead of better, I felt more determined than ever to do my part in making our marriage work. For starters, I was trying to cut "the bread of idleness" from my life's diet.

After writing down what I do every thirty minutes at one of the other women's suggestion, I was shocked to see how much time I spent surfing the Internet for nefarious details about…well, nothing important. My time on the phone was another shocker. Did I really need to chat with Dana and e-mail at the same time? Probably not. And if we did need to talk, couldn't we schedule it to certain times and keep our concerns until then? Of course. TV? Well, don't even get me started.

Taking stock of my time made me realize a lot about myself and about my family. Ryan and I had a lot to say about what we believed when all our neighbors and friends came to visit, but when it came down to it, our lives didn't really look a whole lot different than the other folks' on our block. It was easy enough to tell someone that Jesus would make the difference in their lives, but harder to show that reality every day. And believe me, people were watching.

Especially Lynn.

The doorbell rang. Probably her. Though Rainy was still having her ups and downs and being tended to by different women from the church (next Thursday was my day), I'd resumed my walking schedule, only this time in my own neighborhood. Lynn joined me, leaving some more of her story with me with each mile that we covered. Today, though, walking wasn't on my mind. I had a different agenda.

Reciting my verses on the way, I went to answer the door. Lynn came right in, all hair and hands. "Hey. What's that you've got on? It's walking time, girl. The eye of the tiger, baby!" She put two fingers up to her eyes and pulled them away, adding a nod.

I laughed. "Yeah, I'm right there with you, just not today. I'm having a garage sale." I cut through the laundry room and into the garage, where I'd laid everything out the night before. I hadn't really wanted Lynn to see, or anyone in the neighborhood, for that matter, but sometimes you just gotta do what you gotta do. I wasn't even sure people in this neighborhood had garage sales.

Lynn gasped when she descended the stairs leading to the garage. "The royal throne room? You didn't."

My shoulders shrugged. "I did." Maybe it was the look on my mother-in-law's face or the fact that I'd been embarrassed about it, but I wasn't feeling that bathroom anymore.

Laid out on the tables between us were all my royal implements. (I'd restrained from offering my gold lacquer toilet seat for sale, though it would have brought a good price from someone with a wry sense of humor.) My thousand-thread-count towels, gold vanity, purple rugs, gilded picture frames and more than a few of my tiaras.

Ryan was out of town and had been reluctant to agree to the idea. "Those people are going to think we're broke. Or crazy!"

My response? "We're both."

That hadn't been the best answer, but each day brought it a little closer to becoming true. The way things were going with Ryan's business, I'd be driving our pots and pans to some swap meet in Indianapolis or something soon. I'd tried to talk to Ryan about folding what money we had into another venture or trying to get him a job with Adrian or Shan until things blew over, but he wouldn't hear of it.

"Those kids in the youth group are really starting to open up to me. I remember being where they are. It's important to me that I help them. I can't do that if I'm broke. Nobody wants to hear what you have to say if they don't see you pulling up in a nice car or wearing good shoes. I wish it wasn't like that, but it just is."

I'd disagreed. I still did. Did society care about appearances? Sure. Kids did, too. Yet in the end, it was about who showed up, who listened, who did the work, who was willing to sacrifice something. In this case, it looked like it was going to be me. It was this or become a personal trainer as Mark had suggested in an e-mail. He'd even offered me free training for Mother's Day. I hadn't responded. Besides that idea being laughable, I wasn't so sure if it was wise. Sure, he was some gorgeous guy being nice to me because of his business, but it was still unnerving, especially when Ryan only came to bed a few nights a week now. I was starting to wonder if his all-nighters were about saving the business or destroying our marriage.

"What's this?" Lynn asked, picking up a bar of soap and bringing it to her nose. I watched her lips curl into a smile at the scent of it. I matched it with a smile of my own.

"Oh that? Some soap I made. My friend Dana—the one who did the bath stuff for your friend's bridal shower—well, I've been working with her on a baby line and that stuff was some idea I tried and we decided against. That one is shea butter and lemongrass. I grew the lemongrass in the backyard, believe it or not—"

"And this?" Lynn had an armful of products now, snatching up bottles and boxes off each pile.

More shrugging from me. What was her problem? "Oh, that's Boo-Boo Balm, an herbal stick for kids. It's also a natural insect repellent. You know, no DDT or yucky stuff. It has sunscreen in it, too. I was just playing around. It's a beeswax base."

As a swarm of morning walkers, each of whom looked a lot like Lynn, approached, my new friend waved both hands. "Spa sale!" she screamed at the top of her lungs. "Soap, lotion, natural sunscreen and bug repellent…." She paused to pick up other items and wave them in the air. "Is this calendula salve?" she asked in a whisper.

I nodded. "Yeah. It came out too yellow for Dana."

Her eyes widened. "Calendula salve for diaper rash. Looks like some—"

The walkers, or should I say stalkers, from the looks

on their faces, were upon us like a pack of mama bears. Others ran full speed back to their houses for money. They approached, talking a mile a minute, asking questions about each item.

"So, are there chemicals in this? Fragrance?"

I shook my head. "No, not that one. That's just aloe and almond oil. Some of the items have essential oils. Lavender, tea tree, lemongrass, that sort of thing. They're all marked. No chemicals, though. They're from a mom-and-baby line. All herbal. My friend—"

"Make a line here!" Lynn cut me off with a glaring look. She took a stack of empty paint cans from the corner and passed them down the row. "Fifty bucks fills your can. Ready, set, go!"

And to my shock, they went. Soap, lotion, body butter, Boo-Boo Balm... Even the soy candles that I'd made during my last shift in Adrian's workshop disappeared.

This stuff was serious business. "Do you have any coconut soap? You know, from straight coconut oil? I have really oily skin and I used to order it from Hawaii. I lost the contact and never could get any again."

What was this, Bath & Body Works? Goodness. It's a garage sale, lady. Still, I knew that I had what she wanted. Being curious, I often deviated from Dana's proven soap recipe of several blended oils and created batches from single oils to understand their properties better. Coconut was one of my favorites, next to olive. I went back into the house for a box in the laundry room that I hadn't thought to bring out.

"Here," I said, plopping the box down on the table. With reservations, I produced the odd-shaped soaps that I'd attempted to make in a section of rain gutter from the hardware store. I'd almost killed myself getting it out of there. That'd been during one of Ryan's long trips last winter. The soap, made with organic virgin coconut oil and coconut cream, had been pale then. Now it was a warm tan and smelled like paradise.

The woman pulled out a one-hundred-dollar bill and pulled the whole box across the table. "I'll take it."

My eyes widened. "All of it? They're not pretty. Sort of deformed-looking. I could—"

Lynn bumped me over with her hip and took the money. "Isn't this incredible, Brooke? I mean really. We're all going to have to get together and have a spa party. You know, some mom time."

Or some mom thyme. A garden party would seem like child's play after that barbecue. I thought it, but I didn't say it. Though I liked Lynn, I was still getting to know most of these people. I knew my husband well enough to know that now wasn't the time for me to be planning another party without talking to him first. Still, he was gone most of the day. "I'll just schedule some free time during Tuesday nap time. It won't be for a few weeks, but maybe you all could come over and we'll make something."

The chitchat stopped. Everyone focused on me.

So what am I, E. F. Hutton?

Lynn spoke first. "You would do that, Tracey? You'd teach us how to make these things for ourselves?"

"Sure. Why not? Maybe we can all take turns teaching each other things. It might be fun."

Lynn's eyes sparkled. "Oh, honey, you don't know us well at all, do you? Those are famous last words."

I watched as Ryan's SUV slowed at the end of the driveway, saw him watching our neighbors walk away with tiaras on their heads and paint cans in their hands. Each woman waved to him as they cleared the way for him to pull in. I could see him taking off his sunglasses from where I stood. My husband was home early and he did not look amused. Further inspection revealed a passenger I didn't expect.

My mother-in-law.

Lynn received my last smile for the day before I bid her goodbye.

Famous last words indeed.

"Do you go out of your way to try to embarrass us? Here it is that Ryan has worked himself to death so that you can live out here and you have to go and act like some kind of slave girl selling off your bathroom items. Why, Tracey? Please tell me why. Do you hate me?"

With that, my mother-in-law started to cry real tears, equal in fervor to those her granddaughter was pouring down my shoulder. I patted Lily's back and eyed my husband, trying to hold on to what was left of my mind. He shook his head slowly, almost imperceptibly. That meant that I could not, would not, tell Queen Liz the state of our affairs, either marital or financial.

That meant that once again, I was going to have to be the one to suck it up and take the punches while Ryan looked on.

You have a good role model for that. Depend on Him.

I tried. "Mom, of course I don't hate you. I'm very thankful for you and for Ryan. I'm just practical. If there's something I can't use, I see no use in holding on to it. What's left here I'll donate to the women's shelter. I took a carload of things over there already. The sale went very well, actually."

Very well. The Queen's screaming kept interrupting my count, so I couldn't be sure exactly how much I'd sold, but I knew five hundred dollars when I saw it. Not bad considering that most of my bathroom stuff was still there. Only the bath-and-body stuff and the tiaras had really sold. The women had stopped at the table of bathroom things, though, some of them whispering and nodding. One had even pulled out her phone and taken a picture. She'd asked me where I'd gotten some of the items and tapped the Web sites into her phone as well.

Technology sure was something. As someone who spent much of her life chained to her computer, I was still awed by the incredible advantage and intrusiveness of it all.

Ryan said nothing, extending his arms to take our now whimpering baby. As he did, he handed me the mail and mouthed "I'm sorry" before going to put Lily down for her nap. Using my mother-in-law's words as background noise, I opened the letter on top, emblazoned with the familiar Promised Land Worship Center logo that I had designed.

Queen Elizabeth quieted. She'd seen the logo, too.

Evidently she hadn't noticed that the letter was addressed to me and not to Ryan.

Dear Tracey,

I'm pleased to inform you that First Lady Hyacynth and the other members of the Women's Ministry Committee are interested in your service in our new Kingdom Builders family ministry. Since your husband is already serving the youth, we would like you to join him in serving the women and children of our congregation as well. Please pray about this and talk to your husband and get back to us in the next thirty days. All families who serve together at Promised Land are required to attend twelve weeks of counseling and attend regular accountability sessions with other ministry workers.

We are so blessed to have your family with us. If this position is for any reason unacceptable to you, don't worry, we have other plans for you, as well.

Blessings,

The Promised Land Ministry Team

As I tried to recover my breath, I heard an unfamiliar sound from my mother-in-law.

Silence.

* * *

"I think you should keep it."

I turned to Ryan with surprise as he held fast to the last box of the things from my royally crazy bathroom. I tried to pull the box away from him, but he held firm.

"Seriously, babe. I'm doing everything I can to keep you in this house and in your bathroom." He kissed my hand. "No matter what my mother or anyone else says, you'll always be my queen." He took a bow. "I'm sorry if I don't always treat you like one."

Before I could answer, Ryan pulled me close to him. I tried without success not to melt against him. We'd had our ups and downs but when we touched, so much of that fell away. I noticed, too, that since that talk with Dana's father at the barbecue, Ryan had a new wedding band. I ran my finger across it now.

He ran a hand down the curve of my arm, which had grown quite muscular over the past few months. Though the scale often betrayed me and my waistband refused to give way, my arms, shoulders, thighs and calves bore the marks of my stepped-up strength and cardio routine. I thought of a lot of things to say about why I didn't need my throne room anymore, but Ryan's kisses confused me.

When he leaned over and scooped me into his arms and carried me into the house, I forgot the conversation altogether. Lynn was watching Lily for a few hours while I carried off the last of my garage-sale stash (though she begged me to keep the bath-and-body stuff I had left for a special spa day). I hoped that she wouldn't look outside and see that my fully packed car hadn't so much as backed out of the driveway.

If she was as good a friend as it looked like she was going to be, she would never say a thing. I sure wasn't going to. Or at least I didn't think so, until I looked over Ryan's shoulder at the carpet in the downstairs hall.

It was covered with roses. My heart flipped for a few seconds, then dollar signs began to accumulate in my head. I appreciated the thought, but maybe carnations...

"How much were those? I—"

Ryan kissed away my objections. "Hush. You said that the garage-sale money was mine to do with as I liked. This was what I liked. I like you. Besides, five hundred dollars isn't going to solve any problem that we have. That won't even pay the electricity bill, sweetheart. I have some savings that I think I can keep from being touched if everything falls through. Today, though, it's all about you."

A few months ago, I would have been delighted to have something, anything, be all about me. Now, though, I wasn't so sure if that was something to strive for. I was a little sick of me lately. I don't know how those TV people do it.

As I purged my self-indulgence, my husband turned into our bedroom, or should I say the room formerly known as our bedroom. Tulle flowed from the light fixture over our bed in a canopy. The roses from the hall swept over the room in a wash of peach and crimson. Candles of every height and width lined the windows and the hardwood floors, infusing the room with the scent of jasmine and mango. Strawberries and grapes filled a glass bowl from downstairs, the one I usually filled with ornaments at Christmas. As I slid down my husband's chest and found my feet, I held a hand to my mouth.

"Ryan…"

He didn't answer. Instead, he turned away and walked into our bedroom closet. When he returned, I felt the press of combs against my scalp as he pressed something onto my head. I walked to the mirror and smiled. My tiara, the best of the bunch. I'd bought it for our wedding, but chickened out at the last minute. It just seemed a little over the top for me. Here, though, now, it seemed fitting.

Fitting, I thought as my husband kissed the bridge of my nose. It was afternoon and despite the low light on this side of the house, I'd been surviving with the help of a good girdle and the toned look of the rest of my body.

I crossed my arms.

Too bad this tiara didn't have abdominal-suppressing powers.

He held me again. "What's wrong?"

What isn't? "Nothing. You just—just surprised me, that's all. It's beautiful. Did someone help you? Did you—"

He frowned. "Call Adrian or Dana? No. I didn't call any of your friends for help. I figure it's time for me to do some of this stuff by myself. So I just thought about all the things I love about you. You're delicate like a flower, but sweet and strong, too. You cover people in your love and throw yourself at Jesus' feet. Even when I'm not right, you still love me. I wanted to show you today that I know things have been hard and I'm going to try to do better."

With that, he lifted me again (is he going to throw his back out?) and carried me to the bed. The satin sheets felt smooth beneath me and made me want to giggle. When we'd received them from Mother Holloway, an older woman at my old church, Ryan had rolled his eyes. He'd wanted to take them back, but I'd insisted on keeping them. Ryan had obviously changed his mind and I was glad.

Ryan lay on his side next to me. He rubbed the undefined area once known as my stomach. I tried not to cringe. It wasn't like I wasn't trying. I'd crunched, lifted, walked…and nothing. It had gotten firmer at least, but no smaller. Bigger, if anything. Maybe motherhood had expanded my horizons for good. From the goofy look on my husband's face, he didn't seem to mind.

I tried not to, either.

Then it happened. Ryan's hand jerked under my shirt. I looked at him like he was crazy. "What are you trying to do, hand sit-ups? I'm telling you, I'm trying—"

"That. Wasn't. Me." Ryan looked faint. Sick, even. I was still mad. I totally wasn't getting it.

"What do you mean it wasn't you? Sure it was. Sure, I ate some curry chicken for breakfast, but there's nothing in my belly that would…"

The world slowed down. My breath came in short gasps. There was no way.

Ryan's hand jerked again.

And once more just so that we'd be certain.

He moved his hand away slowly and brought it to his head. We stared at each other in disbelief, united in our distress. Everything passed in front of me, my dizziness, occasional stomachaches, Lily's not wanting to nurse… and of course, my disobedient scale. But still, I couldn't be pregnant, could I? And not far enough along for a baby to kick.

I gripped his hand. "It's impossible."

He turned away. "That's what you said last time."

Chapter Thirteen

If I didn't know better, I would think Dr. Thomson was laughing at me. His eyes were definitely twinkling like the black Santa Claus that Queen Liz keeps on her mantel year-round. Since I was looking for him to confirm that I was not pregnant, this was not a good sign. Dr. Thomson loves babies. I do, too, just not for me, just not now.

After examining me, Dr. Thomson took my hand. "Well, Mama, you pulled one over on me this time. No wonder Miss Lily didn't want the milk. It was skim and probably sour. Not only are you pregnant, but you're very pregnant. Sixteen weeks and four days to be exact."

My hand slipped from his. Though I'd been hurt when Ryan stayed home from the appointment, now I was grateful. I wouldn't want him to see me cry. It seemed obvious that he blamed this on me. As if I could get pregnant by myself. Still, I didn't get it. After Lily,

I'd made sure that we were good in the family planning department.

"But how?" It was all I could manage through my tears.

Dr. Thomson, who had nine children, could have easily grown annoyed with me, but he didn't. He patted my hand instead. "It happens, sweetheart. None of that matters now, what matters now is continuing to take good care of yourself. You've done great so far. Only eight pounds over your weight from your last postpartum checkup."

My tears turned into sobs. In one weekend, I'd gone from Maddy Midsection to Patty Pregnant. I wasn't sure which one was worse. Even thinking that made me feel guilty as I remembered Dana's tears over the phone as we talked a few days before. It was becoming more and more apparent that they might never have a child of their own. And here I was, Miss Fertility, and too ungrateful to appreciate it.

Lord, forgive me. I love Lily. I know that I'll love this baby, too. I just wanted our next child to be planned so that I'd know that Ryan wanted it, too. If he's going to be mean to me from now on, I don't know if I can take it.

The other thought, the question of how big I'd get this time, of whether loneliness and stress would finally poof me back into my old fat self, was left out of my prayers. I wished that I could leave it out of my thoughts, too.

I took the prenatal vitamins and congratulations pack from Dr. Thomson and waited for him to leave the room. I dressed slowly, not wanting to think about what Queen

Liz would have to say. I would rather not tell her at all, but I was so far along that it would already be insulting to tell her now. Never mind that I hadn't even known. Who would believe that? I was, after all, a grown woman, right?

Wrong. As I walked back to the lobby where Brenna, Lynn and Hyacynth were waiting for me, I wondered if I wasn't still that little orphan girl, sitting on the curb waiting for a mother who would never come home, never teach her how to be a woman. Maybe I was still that girl, but I'd have to trust God to take care of the rest, because I was having a baby.

Again.

In the lobby to Dr. Thomson's office, my new friends sat in a cluster, whispering way too loud and hashing out my possibilities. I smiled. It was annoying but comforting to have people trying to run my life again.

Though Lynn was newest to my little circle, she was the most insistent for information also, both in Bible study and times like this. She shook her hands as if trying to dry her nails. "Well?"

"It's positive. Sixteen weeks." I allowed myself a sigh before slumping into a chair between them.

Lynn and Brenna, the other mothers in our party, looked surprised. Brenna was downright shocked. "Are you serious? That far? I always know the next day. I wake up, roll over and laugh. I think to myself, "I'm knocked up again."

Hyacynth shook her head, sending her spiral curled

braids flying. "Don't say 'knocked up,' Bren. You make it sound so vulgar. Being pregnant is a blessing. I can't wait until my turn."

We all stopped our chattering and gave Hyacynth a "riiiiight" look. Brenna spoke first. "Well, honey, I suppose it might sound vulgar to some, but I'm just telling it like it is. Some people get pregnant. Others get blessed. I get knocked up."

Tell me about it.

We all dissolved into laughter, even our prim first lady. Lynn didn't laugh long, though. She was already calculating due dates, planning baby showers and choosing nursery colors. That subject brought up the question that I'd forgotten to ask during the quick ultrasound. The jelly had been so cold on my stomach and I'd been so traumatized to even be getting the procedure that I'd bypassed Dr. Thomson's offer to tell me the gender of the baby.

"So, is it a boy or a girl?"

"I don't know." I stared blankly back at all of them, wishing now that I'd found out. At the time, I'd been doing good to make it back to the lobby without passing out. "I'll find out next time, okay?"

They seemed disappointed at the thought of waiting a whole month to find out if I was having a boy or a girl, but to be honest it was going to take me that long to get used to the fact that I was having another child at all. It'd take me about the same amount of time to get over the number I'd seen on Dr. Thomson's scale at the start of the visit.

167.

While gaining only eight pounds was great, the other gazillion pounds still hanging around from the last baby sort of negated my joy about this news. That and the fact that now that I knew about the baby, I ate like it. (Last time, there was a seven-day stretch now known only as "cookie week.") I'd hardly known anyone at church then, though. Maybe cultivating my new friendships and accepting the ministry position I'd been offered (would I have to change my mind about this now with the baby? I hoped not), I'd be able to hold things together.

Who was I kidding? I couldn't even deal with this doctor's appointment. I'd brought three grown women with me just to help me accept the news. God, who'd been doing a great job holding up the universe and everything, would have to be the duct tape for my fractured mind. Not to mention my raggedy marriage. People always make it seem as if children bring couples closer together. Ryan must not have gotten to that chapter in Relationships 101.

If only there was such a class….

As my friends and I walked to the window to pay my outlandish copayment (What was the point of insurance, again? Shouldn't it actually cover all of something?), a nurse ran out of the same door I'd come out of.

"You forgot your ultrasound photos," she said, beaming. "I know you didn't mean to leave them. The first shots are always so exciting."

Everyone looked at me sternly. I cleared my throat and thanked the nurse, asking how she could read the odd shapes and if she could tell me the baby's sex.

"It's a boy. See?" She traced the picture with her finger. Her words and the room melted away. For the first time in my life, I thought I might faint, though I wasn't sure why. A boy, huh? So much for the tiara collection. The tears I'd been holding back broke free. Maybe now Ryan would be happy.

Lynn crossed her arms beside me as we left the doctor's office. Anger flashed behind her tight smile.

I stopped walking, causing Brenna and 'Cynt to almost pile up behind me. "What? Why are you looking at me like that?"

My neighbor shifted from one foot to the other, licking her lips as if measuring every word. "It's just that—I don't know. I guess I don't get it. You seem so sad."

Lynn was right and I knew it. What had happened to me? Wasn't this everything I'd prayed for? Hadn't I gone to sleep for the past ten years longing for a family? And I'd been a hundred pounds heavier then. Why did getting what I'd prayed for make everything so confusing?

I took Lynn's hand as we approached her car. She'd offered to drive me when she heard what was going on and now I was glad of it. "We'll talk in the car. Thanks, 'Cynt. Thanks to both of you. I'll see you at Ladies' Day. I'm on cleanup this week."

My friends smiled and went off, shouting a few more congrats for good measure while we headed for Lynn's sunny-yellow two-seater Porsche. It looked much smaller now that I knew what I weighed. I hoped that I could still fit in the seat. I shook my head as if to shake the thought away.

Lynn smiled and put the top down. Soon, we were moving down the road like two carefree friends on a road trip. The ties from my head scarf blew in the wind.

I asked her to slow down so that she could hear me. "I'm sorry that I haven't necessarily been the model of Christian motherhood today. Life is a blessing. Thank you for reminding me of that. Don't always look at what I do or say. Read your Bible. Follow God. And tell me the truth like you did today. I need that."

She pulled over into a gas station, despite her full tank. Lynn got out, rounded the car and opened the door to give me a big, tight hug. "I think you need this, too. I guess it's good to know that you're human. I was starting to think that you and Ryan were too good to be true."

Me, too, I thought as I wiped another tear away. *Me, too.*

At least he was consistent. That much I could say about my husband for sure. He loved me when I was two hundred and sixty pounds. He loved me now. He wasn't happy when he felt the baby kick. He was not happy now that he knew the kicker might be a linebacker, his first son. In fact, I thought it made things even worse, made him worry more than ever about his business and our future.

When I put the ultrasound pictures down on the table between him and his mother, Ryan looked at them and gave no reaction, the huge pastel blue "It's a Boy" sticker that Lynn had bought at the gas station notwithstanding. Ryan's mother gave me an amused look, disdain settling into the laugh lines around her mouth. Today, as on other occasions, I wondered again how she had gotten those. I'd only ever seen her laugh at me, never with me. I thought then of Ryan's brother, whom I'd only seen at our wedding. He never wrote. Never called. Maybe Liz had laughed at him, too. I hoped my son and I would be different.

Queen Liz just happening to stop by and make Ryan lunch didn't make things any better. Though I tried to think the best of my mother-in-law, sometimes it seemed as though her presence poisoned things, like she deliberately turned my husband against me.

Duh. You think?

There I went with that again. The weapons of my warfare were not carnal, not human. This was the enemy's work, worming though my marriage since our wedding day, whispering doubts, planting confusion. Well, I'd been reaping the harvest of that bitterness for the past year and a half and I was sick of it. Right now, I needed to pull up some peace.

Dr. Thomson's voice came to me in a surge of warmth and strength. I'd pushed him back when he'd tried to protect me from Liz that day in his office. Perhaps that had been my mistake. Family was important to me, but

I saw now that it was my family I was going to have to start fighting to keep together, not Ryan's.

"Ah, there you are," Liz had said coolly. "There's a salad for you in the fridge," she said with a dismissive wave as she removed the crust from Ryan's triple-decker Reuben sandwich. His favorite.

I took a deep breath, thankful that Lynn had dropped me off instead of coming in like she usually did. She, at least, had the decency to realize that Ryan and I needed to talk, that we needed to pray. My mother-in-law, unfortunately, was neither decent nor respectful today and though it went against everything inside me, I was going to have to put my foot down. I was tired of exploding and running away. Liz might be a queen, but she was messing with my castle today.

Before taking action, I paused a minute to look at my husband, to see if he had anything to say. He was hunched over his plate like a kid avoiding his mother. Avoiding me. Only when I pulled his plate back did he look up at me.

When I took Liz's plate away, he started to choke. He opened his mouth as our eyes met, watched as I held my hands over my head, adjusting my invisible tiara. That made him smile, reminding him of the way he put on the armor of God every morning. To complete the reminder, I mimicked his final motion before leaving our bedroom each day. I reached across my waist and held my hand high as if brandishing a blade.

Ryan closed his eyes.

Liz opened her mouth, speaking in a pitch high

enough to endanger our chandelier. "I know you didn't just touch my plate, Tracey. I know that you have no home training and no—"

"Mom, I'm going to have to ask you to leave now. Perhaps I can come over to your house next week." Though my husband was speaking to his mother, his eyes were on me, watching as I put my purse on the floor and sank to my knees.

Liz was watching, too, too stunned for a moment to speak. As always, though, she managed to find her words. "What is Tracey doing now? Is she...praying?" she asked in an uneasy voice.

Was I praying? Oh yeah, I was. Praying like I hadn't done in a long time. It started in my head, but at some point the words started flowing out of my mouth. "Father, you said that your word is like a sword, able to cut through all my intentions. Forgive me, Father, for my selfishness, for my willfulness. Thank you for my son, and daughter, Lord God. Thank you for my husband. I plead the blood of Jesus over my house, over my marriage! May no weapon formed against us come to prosper. Help me, Jes-us, help me!"

The force and volume of my words surprised even me. It wasn't a pious prayer, but a needy one, the kind that dying folks and prostitutes pray in church, not caring who's looking. I realized then that though I'd wanted God in my life, perhaps I hadn't truly needed Him, not the way I needed Him now. My scarf caught on my fingers as I lifted my hands. One earring clanged against the kitchen tile. I knew I looked a mess, sounded crazy…but I didn't care. Something had to give and it had to give today.

I went on, praying through the promises of God, asking forgiveness and healing for my heart and home. I had no more strength to fight. No more resources to be good enough, pretty enough, thin enough… And yet, God was more than enough. He was my wonderful counselor, my mighty God, my ever-present help in times of trouble. And now, right now, I was too tired for this trouble. My stomach lurched like I was on a ship's deck and my back hurt all over.

I was just plain tired.

Ryan's voice lowered to a whisper. The door to the garage opened and shut. I was alone now, cried out, prayed out and laid out on my back against the ceramic tile of our kitchen floor. I looked up at the ceiling, pondering silly things like whether I should have gone with the hardwood that Ryan had preferred in here instead of the tile. It might have been more comfortable to lie on.

My breathing adjusted to the rhythm of the fan purring over my oven. Scents of sautéed onions, melted cheese and roast beef swirled between my remaining prayers, now whispered silently in the recesses of my mind. My soul went quiet. A car started outside and drove away. The door Ryan went out of didn't open again.

I put an arm over my eyes and tried not to cry. What had I been thinking to get down and dirty with God in front of company in the middle of my kitchen? It was me and God now. He would be my husband, my baby's Father, just as He'd been my Father for all these years. Though I'd gotten the husband I prayed for, the babies, I'd never felt more alone.

"Lord, you are enough. You will never leave me. You will never forsake me."

"Neither will I." My husband's hand slid under my back. His hand down the front of my sundress, resting on the curve of my stomach.

I struggled to sit up, but he held me firm, so close that I could almost taste the cloves in his cologne. It smelled to me like Christmas. "But—but—your mother. I thought you'd gone."

He shook his head. Something wet landed in the hollow of my neck. Ryan cleared his throat. "No, I went to the backyard for a minute, to pray and try to get myself together before I came in here to apologize." He looked from my face to my belly. "To both of you."

More tears, this time from both of us. I thought back, wondering if I'd ever seen Ryan cry like this. No, not even at our wedding. I pulled him close to me, kissing his eyes, his ears…

"Baby, I am so sorry. Can you ever forgive me? I have let this stuff with the business change me. I am happy, so happy. So thankful. I'm just scared, Tracey. I don't want to be my father. I can't be him. When I felt that baby kick, it was like the weight of everything kicked me, too, right in the gut. Today, though, I remembered that I am not the provider. God is."

"Yes. Yes," I said, stilling my sobs. Though I'd waited so long to hear these words, all I could do was agree.

Ryan pushed up my dress and kissed my belly with a kiss so tender that it made me start crying all over again.

"Hello, son," he said softly. "I am sorry for not greeting you the first time. I pray that every moment of your life is lived in grace and truth, that you will always be a man of honor, a keeper of the door. May your every breath be in God's hands."

With that, we collapsed against our underused, overpriced kitchen floor and made love.

Chapter Fourteen

Morning sickness. What a joke. If it was only the mornings, I could totally deal. Instead, it was every-minute-of-the-day sickness with a few breaks in between. The sight of raw meat made me want to walk in front of a car, and seasoning chicken was like torture. In the past week, it'd gotten better, but I now knew the layout of each of my six bathrooms very, very well. Ryan joked that he was going to start putting buckets in every room so that I wouldn't have to sprint around the house like a maniac.

It was insane and yet, somehow I was happy. Sleepy, but happy. Lily had cut down to her night feeding only, but she wasn't ready to give that up without a fight. Ryan had a meeting this morning with his lawyers, so I gave in and nursed her. That child of mine looked like she'd just seen a glimpse of heaven as she floated off to sleep.

I should have followed suit, but I stayed up instead, finishing up projects that I'd put off in the past few weeks. A long walk with Lynn last night kept my dinner down, so I was now wondering if my body wasn't missing my exercise. Who knew? I might have just had to take Mark up on his free training offer. At least I didn't have to worry about him hitting on me now that I was expanding by the day. Soon I'd have a belly that only a husband could love. And from the way Ryan had been looking at me lately, he loved it indeed.

My queasy life was good even though I'd had to go no mail on the Sassy Sistahood list. Hyacynth and I were working on a similar list for the women's ministry. I'd thrown out lots of names, but we settled on the Hallelujah Club. Now if I could get the list up and running and get the Mother's Day brunch squared away. It was 1:03 and ticking until my next retching episode. Lynn would show up soon. She had to.

The doorbell rang once. I made a run for it so Lily wouldn't wake up. What was Lynn thinking? Surely she knew by now not to ring the doorbell during my only feel-good time of the day....

It wasn't Lynn. It was Mark Johnson, looking handsome despite being totally sweaty. Willow paced beside him looking as though she hadn't broken a sweat at all. Her stomach was as flat as mine was round. She didn't say anything, but Mark flashed his smile for good measure. He handed me a flyer for his services. "I was just going to leave this in the door. I wasn't sure if this was the right house or not. They're all just sort of..."

"Big?" I'd felt the same way the first time I'd pulled

into the neighborhood. It reminded me of a place I'd lived in just outside D.C. when my parents were alive. Reminded me and frightened me, too.

Willow rolled her eyes.

I bit my lip. I hadn't meant to sound prideful. It was more house than I could deal with, especially now. I'd just been trying to break the very thick, very dangerous layer of ice covering this conversation. The question I hadn't asked rested safely at the bottom of the pond, shifting awkwardly between us: What in the world are you doing at my house?

"Exactly. Big. I feel like a fool that I didn't even know this was your place when I came here for that barbecue." He turned to Willow. "I e-mailed her, like, 'I saw you at that party. It was a nice house, right?' I saw something about your husband and his business on the news and I recognized him as the guy who owned the house. Someone had pointed him out to me. You never told me you had it like that."

Probably because I don't.

I prayed that Ryan wouldn't come home from the lawyers' today with a bankruptcy verdict. I tried not to even think about it. *Be Thou our provision,* that's what Ryan and I prayed together every morning. His business, this baby, our church involvement…every part of our life was in God's hands.

Especially sweaty, sexy Mark Johnson standing on my porch. Even almost five months pregnant, I wanted to slam the door in his face. He just had a way of looking at me, that trainer look he probably gave every woman he met, that just didn't seem safe. Willow's piercing stare didn't make me feel too good, either. For some reason, that chick just couldn't stand me. Or at least that's how it seemed. Maybe I was making it all up in my head.

"Oh yeah. That software guy. That's your man?" Willow began to chuckle. "I guess you won't be in this big house much longer."

Maybe it wasn't all in my head. Mark gave her a pointed look. I sighed with relief as Lynn came bounding up the driveway with a wicker basket full of treats in each hand.

It was my turn to chuckle. That woman had perfect timing. She skipped right up between Mark and I, walking over and patting my stomach. "Hello," she said, waving to my two guests before whispering a greeting to the baby in my belly. "Hi, little guy. This is Miss Lynn. I have cranberry scones. Apple-pecan muffins, too. You have to kick for me, though."

She turned and held up both baskets to Willow and Mark. With hearty thanks, Mark took a muffin and a scone, while Willow backed up so far that she almost fell off the porch.

She slipped a strip of some kind of gel from under the iPod band constricting her arm. "I only eat foods that require a fork. Refined carbohydrates are not part of my destiny," she proclaimed loudly, as though she was trying to convince herself more than us. She swallowed hard and jogged off the porch. "Come on, Mark. Let's go. We have clients in an hour."

Lynn and I watched with gaping mouths as Mark shoved a muffin in his mouth and started off behind his low-carb queen.

"Thanks. This is delicious. And congrats. Look at the flyer. Call me." He licked his lips.

And then his fingers.

One by one.

More nodding, a thumbs-up and then he was gone.

Lynn stood on the porch fanning herself with the towel that had covered the basket of muffins. "I may not know much about the Bible, but I know trouble when I see it. That's the guy from the barbecue, isn't it? I had to give him a muffin. He looked like he was going to eat you up if I didn't."

I waved my neighbor off as we went inside. "Girl, please. Mark was just running through. You saw his girlfriend." I pointed to my now-definitely-showing stomach. "Look at me. I am the antithesis of hotness, okay? You are totally confused." I bit into a muffin and tried not to scream. It was past delicious.

Please Lord, let me keep this down!

With a cranberry scone in hand, Lynn dragged me to the kitchen and plopped me down on one of the high-backed stools around our stainless-steel kitchen island. "Honey, you are the one who's confused. Sure, some guys don't dig babies, but there are ones who *really* do. And Charles Atlas out there thinks you and your belly are hot, honey. You can mark that down."

I stared at the crumpled paper in my hand, the flyer

for my old trainer's new Mom Muscle program. Though I hadn't noticed at first, there was a phone number scribbled on the back. I paused to read the words underneath.

Call me. Anytime.

Mark that down indeed.

Lynn spread news faster than the *Chicago Tribune*. I didn't know what she said or who she said it to, but after our day of scones, muffins and party planning, my voice mail was blowing up like I owned a record label.

"Yes, this is Judge Williams, from over on Treblebrook? Yes, well, I caught the end of your last gathering and even drove out to your church last Sunday. I know that you don't know me, but I'm new to this area, and you and your friends remind me of the town in Ohio where I grew up. I'm rambling. Just call me…"

"Tracey, this is Adrian. Dre and Ryan mentioned your Mother's Day event on the Keepers of the Door list. I'm just calling to say that I am so happy to see you walking with God in all the gifts and strength He has given you. Dana and I would love to donate some gift packs for the mothers. Remember that honeysuckle you described to me? It came out glorious. I think you'll be pleased. Take care of the babies!"

"Uh, Tracey? Hey, this is Pam. Pam Brooks? Well, I know we didn't get off to a very good start, but I just wanted to tell you congratulations on your pregnancy. I'd love to lunch again soon…oh, and if you need

anything for the Mother's Day brunch, let me know. I'd
love to help."

It went on and on like that for days and days, with
messages from Sister Hawkins, Brenna, even Mother
Redding herself. I thought I'd heard it all until I pressed
play on my machine for the final time of the afternoon.

"Tracey, it's me, your mother-in-law. I just called to
say that I'll be coming to the Mother's Day brunch
today. Thank you very, very much for inviting me. Oh,
and you did a good job on the invitations. The paper was
just right."

Just right? That anything I did or said could be considered acceptable by Ryan's mother had become a
long-lost dream. A few months ago, I would have been
digitally recording that message for posterity, just to
prove that for at least once in my life I'd done something
to make that woman happy. Today was a new day,
though. I deleted the message and returned to the ladies
in my living room, the eclectic group known as my
Mother's Day Committee.

It'd been awkward at first, these meetings, especially
since many of the ladies were from my neighborhood
and had only attended Promised Land once or twice. I'd
suggested having the brunch at the church to keep things
simple, but everyone had objected, especially Hyacynth.

"No, Tracey. You're teaching us something, that the
church is bigger than the building and that it can't be
closed in by walls. You're bringing Jesus to your Jeru-
salem, your neighborhood. More people received Christ

at your last barbecue than in all three of our Sunday services on a regular week. We'll do the work, you just lead the way."

Lead the way? That seemed like a cruel joke as I half waddled back to the couch to hammer out the last of the details before the mothers arrived. The honeysuckle candle and bath sets had all been wrapped in gold tulle and tied with bows worthy of a wedding gown, all done by a seamstress from the next street over.

Some of the ladies from Promised Land had expressed concern about so many new people being involved with the planning, but first lady 'Cynt had given me the go-ahead. "None of them were interested when I was begging for people to help. Now that they see all these new folks doing it up, they 'shamed. Girl, you know I'm not up for that. Do you—do you hear me?"

I did hear her and I did me and then some. The colors were cranberry, gold and cream. Adrian's honeysuckle scent burned throughout the house in candles, incense and diffusers, making the air almost sweet enough to eat. Sweet Honey in the Rock, a woman's a cappella group that I'd seen in college and had been listening to ever since, sang "Balm in Gilead" softly in the background.

Mother Redding and her faithful five instructed the younger ladies armed with cameras at the door. Each woman would receive a photo of themselves to commemorate the day's event. The scripture for the day was

Proverbs 16:24: "Pleasant words are a honeycomb, sweet to the soul and healing to the bones."

Mother Redding had been an easy choice for the speaker (we couldn't get enough of her), but though she accepted the job, she added that she'd have some of her friends say a few words, as well. I wasn't worried. I'd heard several of the sisters who were friends with Mother Redding speak on other occasions. I just didn't want the affair to go on too long....

My stomach was already pushing it three hours ahead of schedule as it was. I wanted to keep my lunch down and my energy up. "Let's get started," I said, waving the women through the house and into the backyard where chairs fanned out under a gold gazebo. I paused to see if the speakers were working, satisfied when the song played just as gently as it had inside. The last gift was placed under the last chair when the doorbell began to ring.

And ring.

And ring.

After five minutes, I gave the signal for the photographers to move into the front yard and instruct the ladies to come around the house. The seamstress who'd made the bows ran to her car and returned with a huge bolt of tulle, which she promptly made into a Yellow Brick Road to the backyard. That reminded me of the trail of roses Ryan had made to our bedroom weeks before. I grabbed one of the centerpieces that had been left over and began pulling off the rosebuds. Way ahead of me, Lynn was already sprinkling petals by the handful onto the ground. We shared a knowing smile. Perhaps Lynn's husband wasn't as quiet as I thought.

I watched as the other women followed suit, creating a scene worthy of any wedding. Returning to the backyard, I turned and watched as the women who'd arrived alone and lonely locked arms and walked to one of the tables, giggling over the pictures they'd been given. Sister Hawkins came alone, with a fistful of rose petals pressed to her face. She stopped to listen to the music and started to cry.

So did I, though I'd determined not to. As I started back to the front yard again, one of Mother Redding's saintly sisters pressed me down into the nearest chair and pushed a nearby stool underneath my feet.

"You've done enough," the sister said. Charlene, I think. She smelled like lilac and wore a beautiful silver choker and matching earrings. She reminded me of my nana. They all did today. I'd lived through many Mother's Days since losing my mother, but all of a sudden I felt the loss as if for the first time.

I buried my face in my hands, just for a few seconds. I didn't want anyone to think that I was sad. The tears were full of joy, too. For so many years I'd accepted my place in the Sassy Sistahood, the fat one, the young one. The one that everyone else needed to tell what to do. The one with no real family. My girlfriends had become my family. Then, I'd married Ryan and felt as if I would never fit in again. Now, in some way that didn't quite make sense, Ryan and I seemed to have found our place.

Things felt so right that when my mother-in-law sat next to me in a gold St. John's knit suit, I didn't even flinch. Not then, anyway. When she reached out and took my hand under the table, I felt a little weak in the knees.

We passed the meal quietly, listening to Rainy and Susan singing "Mama May Have," a poem on motherhood recited by Sister Hawkins, a praise dance performed by Brenna. Ever the pageant queen, Hyacynth delighted us by playing "Amazing Grace" on the violin.

The mild morning whispered along the tables, tugging at the oversize hats and long scarves, teasing the flames of the honeysuckle candles sweetening the air outside as much as they had inside the house. Liz gave me an occasional smile, but said nothing as she nibbled her scone behind the veil of her hat.

Growing tired myself, I didn't say anything, either. No need in rocking our already wobbly boat. It was a good start today between us, all of us. And for me, that was enough.

Or so I thought.

Mother Redding moved with the quickness of a much younger woman as the first lady equipped her with the small microphone on the lapel of her burgundy suit. The back of the skirt fishtailed into a gold rose appliqué of lace. A matching design adorned the front inset of her jacket and the crown of her hat.

"Well, well, we mothers of Promised Land have come a long way, haven't we? I was asked to speak this morning about the power of our words, how pleasant words are as sweet as the honey in our tea this morning, as healing as the scent hanging in the air out here. As powerful as any prescription that a doctor could give us."

"I know that's right," someone said in one of the front rows.

The older woman smiled. "I know it's right, too. Today, though, I'm not the one to bring the word to you about it. I've asked an old friend to come and share. Most of you know her; in fact, she's part of the family that's hosting us here today. Please welcome Queen Elizabeth Blackman."

My hands were slow to find one another as my mother-in-law rose and met Mother Redding in the center of the backyard. The restless wind seemed to quiet as she approached, as though it knew better than to knock off her hat or ruffle her perfect hair. Though I was the last to join the applause, no one seemed to notice.

Liz took a moment to pray before she began, asking for courage and strength, for the power of God to be with her. I shifted in my seat, not sure what to think. The Queen was famous for her sayings, but usually not in a good way. For a moment, I thought about all the time and work that had gone into planning this day and wondered how many words it would take from my mother-in-law to destroy it.

I took a deep breath, inhaling the honeysuckle fragrance of the candle in front of me, catching a Jesus breeze, as Dana loved to say. Whatever Liz would say would be covered in the blood of Christ, wrapped in His grace. I had to trust that, believe in it. Brenna reached forward from the table behind me and patted my shoulder as Liz began.

"Before I got married I was a runway model, so you have to excuse my slight change in topic. I wasn't allowed to eat honey for the first twenty-five years of my life and haven't eaten much of it since then, so it was a little hard to center a talk around."

Laughter came easily, like water flowing down a hill. No chuckle came from my mouth, though. I saw where this was going. I stared down at my feet, swelling like sausages. Maybe I'd have to run for the bathroom before she got around to making a fool of me. Maybe. Probably not.

She continued. "So, I kept the color gold and stayed within the same book. I hope that counts. Here we go. 'A word aptly spoken is like apples of gold in settings of silver.' Proverbs twenty-five, verse eleven. Those of you who know me here, know that I can focus better on jewelry than food. Still, the point is the same. Words have power."

That much, I had to agree, was true. The message of the power of words was taught over and over in church. Speak life, people said. Create your own wealth, your own wellness. Create a life where nothing bad happens, where nothing hurts. And yet, things hurt. Bad things happened. And in my own life, it was most often the words said during the bad times, after the unthinkable happened, that had the most power.

Your mother isn't dead, Tracey. She's sleeping. Sleeping with Jesus.

It'd taken me five years to realize that Mama and Daddy weren't having a slumber party in the church basement in those boxes they'd been lying in. It'd taken a lifetime for me to trust people again, to trust God again.

"As mothers, we often focus on using our words to iron out problems, to speak the obvious today to keep our children from trouble tomorrow, the way we wished someone had done for us. Or in my case, the way people did for me but I didn't listen. Amen."

Amens echoed across the yard.

"It's easy to condemn when they come to us hurting and bleeding. We're quick to remind them that if they'd listened to us, they could have avoided this. Our mother love wants to protect, but instead our words hold court and proclaim our children guilty, even though God has erased the same bill for us. Well, for me anyway; some of you all are righteous ladies, you probably don't have this problem."

"Have mercy," someone whispered behind me.

Tears burned my eyes as I thought of my husband, months before, frowning at himself in the mirror. I closed my eyes and remembered the sound of him pacing on the top floor of our home the night before. Up the hall and back again, over and over again. Trying to make it work. Trying to keep it together.

Queen Liz left her place and started down the middle of the tables, her gaze in my direction. My breath caught in my throat as she called my name, asked me to come and stand beside her.

My stomach lurched. I tried to breathe, praying not to be sick. I thought of my mother and peace came over me. I felt as if she was there, helping me take every step.

"Ladies, I wasn't very happy when Sister Irene asked me to speak today. You see, I'd come from my son's house that night, this house, and my daughter Tracey here had done something that evening that cut back the curtain that had been over me for a very long time. I had it in for her that night, sisters. I was going to tell her something about herself. Uh-huh, I admit it. But she had a better, stronger plan than I. A Jesus plan. She didn't fight. She didn't argue. She just got down on her knees in her kitchen and cried out to the Lord for her family. Hear that? *Her* family! Not mine. My son can no longer substitute as my husband. That man is dead and gone and if I'm honest, I'm glad of it."

I gulped. The others gasped.

When Liz reached down and pulled up her skirt, I felt dizzy. She kicked up her rock-hard leg onto the nearest table and pulled the hem up just above her knee. Dark scar tissue circled her leg like a garter of blistered flesh. "This was my reward for wearing a skirt too short for his liking. I couldn't walk for two weeks. I've never been able to wear shorts comfortably since. Perfection in everything was demanded, and becoming pastor of our church was the ultimate goal. We were working for

God's kingdom and my every act brought me closer or further away from becoming his queen."

Something rushed up in my throat. I grabbed some water from a neighbor whose name I couldn't remember and managed to stay on my feet as Liz let her hem fall to the ground. I thought about the circles on Ryan's back, the scars that didn't look like little-boy scratches. My heart broke then, for him and his mother, too.

For the first time, I watched as Liz cried. I put my arm around her and rested my head against her shoulder.

She patted my neck. "This girl here, now, she is a right word, a golden apple. She did what I could never do; she set my son free. And you know what? I got mad at her for it. He was supposed to be chained up with me. When I came to church with an Afro, I got beat for that. Here I am sixty years old and that's honestly what I thought when I saw her. But when she prayed that night, I finally saw me and the spirit of Jezebel and Athaliah that had been growing in me all these years. I was a queen all right, but I was serving the wrong kingdom."

I was squeezing her now, trying to make her be quiet. If she said any more, I thought I might scream.

Liz turned to me and placed her hands on both sides of my face. She began to pray. "Lord, thank you for Tracey, the daughter I wanted but wasn't allowed to have. May her mouth speak pearls of wisdom as she ministers to these women in the days to come, may her speech make pearls of promise instead of the shackles I once gave to her—"

"You don't have to do this," I whispered into her shoulder, but she did not stop praying. Her voice became even stronger.

"Make each of our words as polished as gems as we speak to others. Help us to understand the power of our sweetness, our honey, even when the days are bitter. Help us to consider the shades and shapes of the words we give away from this day forward, knowing that what we speak may be worn by those we love for a lifetime. Make us mothers on a mission, mothers with a ministry in our mouths. In Jesus' name, amen."

With that, she motioned to the five sisters, who started at every edge of the crowd passing velvet cases down the row. I blinked as Mother Redding walked toward us and placed a jewelry box into my mother-in-law's outstretched hands.

"Thank you, Tracey, for being who you are. You've achieved more with your muffins and e-mails than I ever could. I sought to be right. You seek to be good." She clasped a necklace, a strand of pearls interspersed with gold apples and honeycombs, around my neck.

My squeal of delight mixed with those of all the other women as my husband's mother—no, my mother—crossed the yard and passed out of sight. My son, whose name we were still settling on, kicked in my belly. I smiled in agreement. To us, Liz would always be a queen.

Chapter Fifteen

Two weeks after Mother's Day the sea in my stomach was finally calm, just in time for my life to start turning upside down. Despite being worn to the bone, Ryan decided to take the teen boys (about thirty of them) from the youth group on a camping trip with the other men a few weeks before Father's Day. Even more surprising, he came home revived, for a few days at least. Then came the reporters, who kept riding through the neighborhood at all hours, hoping to get a glimpse of Ryan. Trying to get another story.

I kept thinking that maybe if I'd kept a lower profile and not had so many people over the past couple of months, the media wouldn't be trying to put such a bad spin on things, but God knows my heart. Without giving any more details than were already available on the six o'clock news, I asked all my friends and neighbors to pray (and to wave goodbye if they saw us pass by with all our belongings strapped to the Excursion).

Anyway, on the spa day that I promised the ladies of my neighborhood, I thought I'd better get cracking at bagging up all the ingredients. Today we were going to make solid lotion and roll-on perfume. Though I wasn't a big user of chemical fragrances, Adrian did send me some samples for those who wanted to use them. I'd have to give a big speech about precautions for all that, even with the essential oils. If I thought too hard, I'd talk myself out of it, so I tried to remember that I'd assisted Dana with these types of demonstrations a hundred times or more in the years when I was her roommate.

Not that it ended up helping me. In the end, my motley crew of mothers weren't much better than if I'd been working with their kids. The good thing was that they were easy to please and lovers of all things natural. I said "organic" every fifteen minutes or so just to watch all their heads snap in my direction. Quite hilarious. They were so taken by the scent of my unrefined shea and cocoa butter that fragrance never even came up. What did come up, though, were orders. Lots and lots of orders.

"I'm out of that boo-boo stuff you had at the garage sale. I'll need lots for summer. Some spares for friends, too."

"Me, too. That calendula stuff is amazing. We're all out and my cousin is having triplets. How much for a case?"

"Any more honey candles from Mother's Day?"

"What about shaving soap for Father's Day?"

Though I tried to tell them that it was Dana's business and not mine, they just shoved their money and checks into Brenna's hands and wrote their orders on the backs of the instruction sheets I'd given them for their projects. When I finally closed the garage door and collapsed into a lawn chair, Brenna stacked the bills and checks meticulously like the accountant she'd once been.

"Three thousand dollars and seventy-eight cents. Somebody must have calculated tax."

Tax. Great. "That's just it. I'm a Web designer. I'm not set up to take money for this stuff on a regular basis. This isn't my business."

Brenna laughed, holding a handful of money in the air. "I hate to tell you, honey, but this is business. It may not be the business you want, but it's the business you've got. When's the last time you got a new Web design account?"

I scratched behind my ear. "Um, well…" I couldn't remember for sure, but it'd definitely been months before. I had a lot of updates, sure, but recently I'd organized a Web design team for the church, started the Hallelujah Club e-mail list, put together the Mother's Day brunch and attended the weekly women's ministry days at the church.

Though I'd teased Ryan about giving up his job for ministry, I'd pretty much ended up doing the same myself. Though, with the money I'd saved in not paying drop-in day care and other convenience items, we'd pretty much remained the same financially, getting by on Ryan's savings, hoping for something to break through.

Since having Lily and learning of my pregnancy with Christopher (that was his third name so far, but I was-standing by it), I was starting to wonder if a life chained to the computer was really going to work. Being so sick for the past few months had kept me from really pursuing new accounts. It wasn't my forte, anyway. Ryan was the hard-hitter in that area. Every time he picked up the phone for a sales call, his eyes lit up, even though he had an entire department doing it for him. And now, it was quite possible that he would lose all of that.

I'd asked people to pray that God would send an answer, but this definitely wasn't what I was expecting. Wasn't getting pregnant enough of a change? I could only handle one thing at a time.

DO YOU TRUST ME?

Did I trust God? Hmm... I wanted to sound holy and say yes. Absolutely. Of course. At the moment, though, I wasn't so sure. I believed, even tried my best to obey (sometimes I'm slow on that but I'm getting better), but trusting sometimes caught me up short. I didn't have the luxury that a lot of people had of believing that every-thing would turn out all right no matter what. I'd learned young that sometimes things just were what they were and God would get you through it. So yes, I'd like to believe that I trusted God, but I knew that sometimes faith seemed like awful hard work. And yet, I wouldn't have it any other way.

After a call to Dana to make sure she'd be okay with

the idea, she seemed totally relieved. "I never felt comfortable with that mom line, Tracey. Never. I think you should totally go for it. You tweaked most of the recipes, anyway. I'll carry the line in all of our stores and help with anything you need. Just tell me when you're ready."

"Well, I don't know about start-up. We've been living off our savings and I know nothing about the industry. I'd think something like this would require years of research—"

"Which you already did for me, for free. Look, think it over, pray about it, talk to Ryan and get back to me. The best market is always where your heart is. And you know as well as I do that when God is involved, the best thing to do is get out of His way."

Get out of God's way. Why was that so hard? Brenna left me alone to think it over and count my money. Ryan pulled up and gave me a sad look before passing me and my stack of bills right by. He looked as though something had died.

My smile disappeared. "So that's it, then? It's over?"

He nodded. "Pretty much. There are a few long shots, but they might prove more trouble than they're worth."

Sierra.

Ryan didn't have to say it, but I knew. The woman who'd almost driven us apart with an e-mail now had the power to hold our future in her hands.

Wrong again, Queen Mama. God holds your future.

"Well, sorry to hear that, but look! We had spa day today and people made all these orders. Brenna and

Dana seem to think I—we—could make a business out of this. What do you think?"

He thought it was a joke. His eyes gave him away. "A business? You have a bath and baby business? Spa day? I don't know. We'll talk about it later. I'm going to take a nap. I'm tired. Lots on my mind."

As he squeezed past me to go into the house, I took a deep breath and shoved my money into an envelope. When his shirt brushed my face, I froze, paralyzed by the scent of women's perfume. Poison. I'd worn it my freshman year in college. Evidently Sierra had held on to her schoolgirl scents…and her crushes, too.

This time, I didn't cry and I didn't call anybody. I put one hand on my stomach and the other on my heart and prayed for myself, by myself. Sometimes when you've done all you can do, the only thing left to do is stand.

I was surprised to see Queen Liz at the church on cleaning day. She had her hair tied back and wore almost no makeup. The most startling thing of all was what she was wearing. Shorts. They were almost to the knee, with only the edge of her scar showing. The sight of it made me think of Ryan and all the things we still hadn't discussed. I'd tried to broach the subject of his father in the days since, but Ryan always changed the subject. I had the feeling he didn't know about the Queen's Mother's Day talk. Not yet anyway.

She waved at me across the room and came to hug

me and help me with the tons of baby paraphernalia required to keep Lily occupied while I was there.

"You look beautiful," I said, kissing her cheek.

"You think?" she said, sounding unsure for the first time since I'd met her. "It's been a long time. It's uncomfortable sometimes, but most of the time I forget about it. Thank you for having that brunch. So many women have come up to me since and shared their stories. Women who I didn't think had any stories to tell. I feel blessed by knowing what other women have been through. Why is it so hard for us to be real with each other?"

I thought it through. There were so many things: fear of rejection, lust for approval, thinking that no one else would understand. Ryan told me all the time that though men had their issues, he didn't think he'd have made it if he'd been born a girl. "You all have too many rules. I'd never be able to keep up."

Queen took Lily to play with the other children and we decided to make a time for the two of us to get together and explore this idea of story-sharing further. "Maybe we could just have a girls-only testimony night. And not those 'nobody knows the troubles I've seen' sort of meetings either. We need to know where you've been, where you are and where God is taking you. That's where the hope is."

I agreed and headed off to check the cleaning schedule. Today was sanctuary day for me and I'd been assigned the pulpit. Since Mother Redding's comments months ago at the First Lady and Friends Society luncheon, the thrones behind the pulpit had been replaced.

The new chairs, made in a sparse Shaker style that appealed to me but probably made Hyacynth want to run out of the church screaming, required only wiping down. Knowing that my first lady probably needed a little something-something, I reached into my goody bag for the purple silk seat pillows I'd made the week before and tied them onto the chairs. (Martha Stewart, watch out! I am woman, hear me snore!)

Hoping that I didn't get in trouble for changing the decor without asking, I started back to the kitchen to find Mother Redding to see if she thought it was too much.

Instead of the chairs being too much, I heard too much, catching more than an earful of the Queen's conversation with Mother Redding.

"Irene, I'm trying to stay out of their business now, but that boy has me worried. He sounds too desperate and he's going to meet that woman. You know how those kinds of women are, especially when they know they've got a good man in a bad way."

Mother Redding agreed. "I know you want to stay out of it, but you and I both know that many a God-fearing woman has had to roll up her sleeves and go get her man."

"Hmmph. Don't I know it. And the way that man used to beat me, I should have left him where he was at. Those were different times then, though. And the church was a different place. I want it to stay different."

"Amen to that. So what do you say, then? Let's tell her?"

Having heard enough, I stepped from behind the door. "Tell me what?"

I didn't want to go after him.

Wasn't the guy supposed to chase the girl? And we were married, for goodness' sake, saved, no less. This was getting ridiculous.

Mother Redding wasn't trying to hear my excuses. "There's a time for everything under heaven, honey, but like my mama used to say, right now, you need to go get your husband. Are you hearing me, baby? Do you get my meaning?"

Oh, I heard what she was saying all right, even knew what she meant, but I still didn't want to do it. If Ryan was willing to get with some woman to save his business then he'd made his choice already. The fact that my mother-in-law had somehow disappeared and Brenna had shown up out of nowhere let me know that this had potential to be a real fiasco. "You know, Mother Redding, I appreciate what you're trying to do, but I have to be honest. I'm tired of running after him, trying to keep him loving me. I don't think that's the way it's meant to be. It wears on a woman."

Brenna, who'd been silent up until then, locked eyes with Mother Redding. They both nodded slowly. She tucked a blond curl behind one ear before opening her arms to receive my big, pregnant body. "Honey, if you think this is wearing on you, wait until you see what happens if you don't go after him. That'll wear on you for real. That'll wear you down. Don't think of it as running after him, you're not. You're running after you, after your family. If you dropped your purse with all your money and someone picked it up and ran, wouldn't you run after them and tell them it was yours?"

"Yes, but…" My words faded as Brenna's illustration hit home. Ryan was mine, joined to me by God. Though I was tired, God never tired of pursuing me, of loving me, of letting me know that He wasn't willing to let me go. I went down to the baby room and kissed Lily. I took my purse out of her diaper bag and shoved it up on my shoulder with determination.

It slid right down, bringing my bra strap with it.

I'm such a joke. What am I doing?

"We'll be praying for you," the two ladies called out from behind me.

"Put some lipstick on. That peachy-colored one." That was Mother Redding, whom I was learning didn't miss a trick, or a shade of lipstick, for that matter.

"Got it…" I shouted back as I left the church and headed for my car. I got in and started driving, only then realizing that I didn't really know where Ryan was. It wasn't like when he was at the office and I could go there and see his car in the lot. He was freelancing now, taking meetings all over Chicago. Most of the time, I didn't know where he was, except for what he told me on the phone or what I heard in the background.

I could call him now and ask him where he was, but I knew that if I did, we wouldn't see each other now. We'd give our apologies, bid our goodbyes and go through another cycle of real problems with fake resolutions. Rose petals, chocolate and good kisses were definitely on my favorites list, but I was tired of playing games and I think God was, too. We could do better, be better. I could, anyway.

I took a left at the next intersection, passing a restaurant we'd once driven to from Leverhill for dinner. There had been nothing too silly or grand to do back then. Nothing too personal to pray about or discuss. And now, here we were, married and acting like we couldn't talk about anything again since this business thing kept getting worse. That was going to stop. Today.

A few more hunting expeditions through my bag produced my peachy lipstick and my cell phone. Not wanting to be one of those makeup-applying and cell-phone-talking drivers who often caused me to almost crash, I thought about pulling over, but there was nowhere to go. At the next red light, I tilted my chin up to the mirror and gave my lips a good coat of coral sun gloss. I peeked at the light. Still red. A second later, a horn blared behind me. So much for my instant makeover.

Lord, help me to not get into an accident.

A few clicks of my phone brought up a map and a feature that I seldom used unless I was lost, but had added to our plan because I thought it was cool—GPS, global positioning system. Both the red and green dots were stationary. The green one was me at the light, the other was Ryan, closer than I thought. Circling the block, I took another turn, darting looks at the phone screen to see where my husband might be.

I saw his car first, parked in the side lot of the restaurant I'd passed, the one where he'd proposed to me, *Amour.* Love. Though it was only the name of a restaurant and it was the middle of the day in the middle of the week, I wondered who my husband would be meeting here besides me. I didn't have to wait long to find out, especially since I had a pretty good idea in the first place.

Wearing a chocolate-colored suit that I didn't remember seeing before, Ryan emerged from the restaurant, holding the door open for a petite, dark-skinned woman in a short, tight dress. Sierra. And she looked even better in person than her picture online. Traffic crawled along and I was thankful. I didn't want to speed past them, but I didn't want to park and watch, either. I wasn't sure if I wanted to be here at all.

You don't want to be here, but you need to be here. It has to end.

My car inched forward as traffic eased, but not enough for them to see me. I, however, could see them both clearly now. I could see them all too well. Ryan straightened his tie and smiled the way he did when he was talking smack. Sierra punched his arm lightly and giggled into her hand. He sobered a little as if remembering something. I wondered if he was remembering me or Lily, maybe even Christopher. If I hadn't been driving, I might have closed my eyes.

Ryan extended his hand to say goodbye, curving from his hip to his shoulder in his sword movement. I wanted to cheer. Sierra grabbed at Ryan's hand as though she knew, but pulled Ryan toward her in an unexpected move. She kissed his cheek, caressed his face, whispered into his ear and walked away, leaving my husband staring after her like a starving man seeing a drumstick for the first time....

Now, if that isn't trifling, I don't know what is.

Though still in traffic, I think I did shut my eyes, just for a moment. Evidently, it was a moment too long. My movements, sluggish and distracted, almost got me into a three-car pileup as the traffic moved forward all of a sudden. Thank God that the driver in front of me had the presence of mind to drive up on the sidewalk. I jerked my steering wheel to the left and went around him.

"Watch out, lady!" the man said with his head half out the window. "You're going to get us all killed driving like that. What's wrong with you?"

He didn't want to know. I told the man I was sorry and stared straight ahead, hoping that the blaring horns and my bad driving hadn't caught my husband's attention. When my passenger door opened and a breathless Ryan jumped in, I gave up on that one.

He looked in the back seat for the baby and then at me. "Girl, you scared the mess out of me! Are you okay? I heard those tires squeal and—"

Pain must have showed in my eyes because he looked back at the front of the restaurant, back at Sierra's legs as she click-clacked back to her car and got in. She drove a red Lexus convertible, one that I'd seen before many times outside his old office and thought it belonged to some middle-aged man. Evidently girls had midlife crises, too.

I stopped looking into the rearview mirror, not wanting to see the woman anymore, not wanting to think about how Ryan had looked at her. It was certainly different from the way he was looking at me now.

Still, he acted totally innocent. "What? Why are you looking at me like that? Is it because of Sierra? We've been through this, remember? She's just an associate, a consultant that I do business with. There's nothing to that. Really. She's just a flirt. I have to deal with it because she's one of the only people left who's willing to give me the money I need to keep the company going. It's nothing, though, really."

I didn't bother to say anything, knowing that if I did, the words would be hurtful, perhaps even final. I didn't say anything because for the first time, I saw a side of my husband and a side of myself that I hadn't wanted to face. Church or not, ministry or not, we were sinners. Sinners who'd thought that love and going to church every Sunday would be enough to hold their marriage together. It wouldn't. It was going to take more. Much more.

Gripping the steering wheel for support, I took a deep breath, long enough to offer up a quick prayer.

Then I turned and pulled into the restaurant parking lot, next to the red Lexus. I got out quickly, without even checking my lipstick, and rounded Sierra's car.

I tapped on her window just as Ryan grabbed my arm, trying to talk over me. I stood strong and pushed him back. One of us might be crazy, but there was still me. There was still God. I extended my hand into the window, now cracked just enough for her to give me a crazy look. I ignored that, too.

"Hi, I'm Tracey, Ryan's wife. I happened to be passing through and wanted to say thank-you for all the business you've been bringing Ryan's way. It's been a blessing to our family. We'd love to have you and your husband over for dinner sometime. Better yet—" I dug into my purse for one of the new cards the church had printed "—here's the card for our church, where my husband is a minister. Please bring your husband and visit this Sunday. I'll be speaking with the pastor this afternoon and I'll have him recognize you and give you a warm welcome." I ended with my best smile, my closer grin, but inside I was crumbling.

Sierra took the card, but fumbled for her words. "Church? Well, I—I mean, my husband and I don't usually attend church. Well, he does, but I don't. Not with him. Well, not at all, really, I—"

Ryan worked around me somehow and faced the woman. "It's okay, Sierra. Though Tracey is trying to be friendly, it's really not necessary for you to visit our church. I understand that church isn't for everyone.

There's no pressure or anything. This is something for me to work out…"

Sierra leaned forward a little, trying to talk to me again instead of Ryan. "No, I'd like to come. I think my husband would like it, too. He was just asking me, begging me, in fact, to come back to the church that we used to attend. I could never go back there, though. Too many wagging tongues. Also, I didn't know that Ryan was a minister. Marquis could use some new minister friends. He's lost most of his old ones…thanks to me."

That shut even Ryan up. He took a step back, resting against our car. I took over from there, taking down Sierra's number and her husband's e-mail address for our senior pastor to contact him later. When she mentioned the name of the church she'd formerly attended, I immediately recognized her husband as a vibrant pastor who'd been on television several days a week when I'd first moved to town. He'd had a good following, even with folks back in Leverhill. Obviously, Sierra's flirting habit that Ryan thought was so innocent had turned into something else. Something that had cost them everything.

When Sierra pulled off, Ryan was still leaning against the car, one hand across his chest and the other elbow resting on his closed fist. In his fingers was a flat piece of plastic. A hotel-room key. He tossed it on the ground.

"I wasn't going to do it. You know that, right? Not for money, not for anything. I called Dre from inside the restaurant and told him everything. You can call him right now. And that kiss? Well, I didn't see it coming."

"That's funny. I did." A snort escaped me.

Ryan's chin was cradled in his right hand. He looked up at me but didn't say anything for a long time. I didn't say anything, either. I'd save that for our session with the pastor this afternoon. I was already on the schedule about the Web design team, but that appointment was going to have to go double duty. Gravel crunched under my shoes as I walked away.

"Tracey?" Ryan called out from behind me.

Even the sound of his voice right now grated on my ears, but I forced myself to turn around. I still loved him, but I was mad at him. Really mad. It didn't have to come to this. "Yeah?"

"Thank you. For coming, I mean. I wasn't going to go out like that and I was sort of embarrassed at first that you came, but it's good to know that you've got my back. I know you're mad, but I do love you. For real. You'd know that if you think about it," Ryan said, before walking around his car and climbing in.

Yeah, I knew it. I just didn't know what I wanted to do with that love. Right now, all I could think of was getting in my car and getting as far away from Ryan as I could.

After talking to Pastor Dre, of course.

Though Queen Liz had fled the scene, my remaining conspirators wanted to know every detail of my humble husband chase. It was almost as hard to tell as it'd been to experience, but I did it anyway. I figured they might as well hear it from me. Gossip got around fast enough. There was no need in starting off with a lie. Lily stayed quiet while I recounted the story. The two women remained quiet, too, with only Brenna's children making noise playing all around us.

Mother Redding began to pace the train-track rug on the floor. When one of Brenna's sons headed toward her foot with a locomotive, I steered her to a much safer alphabet piece of foam. She seemed undaunted by either. Too deep in thought to care.

"Now. Tracey, this is really something, what the Lord is up to, you watch and see. My husband mentored her husband, Marquis, you know…he went to this church as a young man, grew up with my Andre even. We used to be so proud to see him on TV. People would talk about his wife, but I never would hear of it. Instead, I just prayed for her and for Marquis. I haven't thought about them in a while. I guess maybe this old head forgot. God doesn't forget, though. Know that, baby. He doesn't forget."

Brenna nodded. "It sure can seem like it sometimes, though, like He forgets. I know that woman, too, but I didn't know her husband was a minister. She used to do some business with my company when I was working. She seemed nice enough and her work was always in order. She just never had much to say. She got along better with the men."

I frowned. "I'll bet." Lily's small body was warm against me. I held her tight and thought about her being a girl, who would one day become a woman. How could I prepare for what it would take for her to be a good woman? A good wife? I could hardly figure it out myself most days. And today, well, today I was totally through. "I'm going to talk to Pastor about it this afternoon. I'm sick of this mess. We need some help."

Mother Redding made a funny face and sniffed the air before hoisting one of Brenna's sweet-looking but sour-smelling little boys onto the changing table. When she opened his diaper, we all staggered back.

The older woman shook her head. "Prunes. He must have gotten one of mine at breakfast. This boy is something else. Your man is something else, too, Tracey. I'm pleasantly surprised that he decided so quickly to go for counseling. I'm glad too that Andre had a slot open. I'd have gotten y'all worked in somehow if he didn't. These things sometimes require immediate attention." She put the baby down and scrubbed her hands at the sink before walking back toward me.

I chewed my lip for a second then stopped before Mother Redding pinched my cheek the way she'd done another time. She said my lips were one of my best features. Me, the guppy face of fourth grade. Who'd have thought? "Ryan didn't decide to go for counseling, exactly. I did. I have an appointment today about the Web design team and I just decided that—"

Mother Redding shook her head. "Umph umph umph. You avoided one car wreck and now you're heading for another one. You can't march in there and tell my son all that without your husband's knowledge. You're going to make Ryan hate you." Mother checked the clock and walked into the pantry, coming out with a huge can of fruit cocktail and two warehouse-size boxes of graham crackers. Our church had recently started an after-school program and soon it would be time for the summer school children and volunteers, mostly retired teachers, to arrive.

I sat down in one of the child-size chairs. I put Lily on her blanket and hid my face in my hands. This was all too confusing. First I was supposed to run after Ryan and find out what was going on, but now I wasn't allowed to tell anybody? That didn't make sense. "Look, I'm not out to hurt my husband, I'm just trying to protect myself. Dre is my pastor; if I can't talk to him, who can I talk to?"

Brenna took the seat beside her. "Us. You can talk to Mother Redding, me or any of the women you feel comfortable with. And yes, you can talk to Pastor, too, about anything you like. It's just that it can get tangled up. Complicated. First of all, he doesn't speak to women alone about their marriages."

Smart man, though in my case it didn't really apply. This was news. "Really? Why? I can't even keep my *husband* interested in me, if that's what he's worried about." I smoothed my skirt across my knees, feeling the goose bumps underneath. The air conditioner was really kicking. I felt cold, inside and out.

Brenna leaned over, talking softer. "Look, if you feel

like you need to talk to Pastor, do that. I've done it. You just need to be sure that's where it needs to go from here. Is this the last resort? I'm not trying to act like this situation isn't serious. I'm just saying that maybe you and Ryan should face it together. We don't have all the facts. One thing the past few years has taught me is to get the facts."

I laughed then. I didn't mean to, but I couldn't help it. Talk to Ryan? When exactly would I do that? In the six minutes between his morning run and his morning paper? We did good just to get in a goodbye kiss and that was now that his business was going under. Despite our renewed romance, there hadn't been enough of those kisses. Watching another man's wife kiss Ryan and walk away had almost killed me. Maybe that was the key to get him to look at me like that…walking away.

"Tracey? What are you thinking? You're scaring me." Brenna tugged at one of her huge earrings, taking it out before the baby in her arms yanked it again. That made me smile. Lily did the same thing to me all the time.

I got up, checked on my sleeping baby and looked up at the clock. It was almost one o'clock. Mother Redding had said it was okay to leave Lily until three. Maybe I wasn't going to talk to my pastor, but I wasn't going to sit around and watch my life fall apart, either. I might be pregnant, but I wasn't dead or stupid.

"What are you doing?" Brenna asked as I flipped open my phone and clicked on a number that I'd been hesitant to save and thought I'd never dial.

"Shh," I said as a man's voice picked up on the other end.

"Mark Fit Productions, this is Mark."

"Hey, sorry if I interrupted you. This is Tracey. I was just wondering if your offer still stands about the training. I know you're probably booked."

"I have a cancellation in an hour. Can you make it?"

Oh yeah.

"Sure."

"You know where the gym is?"

"I think so."

"Okay. See you then. And Tracey?"

"Yeah?"

"I'm really glad you called."

We said our goodbyes and I clicked my phone shut. My mind went in a million directions as I gave Brenna a hug. How far was the mall from the gym? Where had I seen that cute maternity workout set?

I gave Brenna a small smile on my way out the door. "Sorry for scaring you," I said, trying to be light and funny. Evidently, I was neither, because concern wrinkled Brenna's forehead by the time I got to the exit. She was scared for me and I knew it. I felt it.

I was scared for me, too.

Chapter Sixteen

Going to a training session with a guy you'd once had a crush on, after seeing your husband with a pretty woman, wasn't so smart. Despite my mall run and meticulously applied mineral makeup, the gym, with its hard bodies and loud music, wasn't the place I wanted to be right now.

Though my new accounts were still lacking, I had enough update work to bury myself in for a solid week; however, that wasn't on my mind, either.

Jesus was on my mind.

Jesus and a long bath with some of Dana's Vanilla Smella bath salts. I sniffed my wrists thinking of it, only to remember that I'd put on some of the Hot Mama Mango that Dana had sent me to sample instead of my usual scent. Why had I even bothered? It didn't matter, I was just going to sweat it off, anyway. As if anyone was going to notice some sweaty pregnant woman lumbering around in a roomful of hotties.

Not.

"Hey. Right on time, I see. Just like I remembered." Mark came out of nowhere, touching my arm. I tried to ignore the way his presence, his voice, seemed to jolt me. Maybe it was static cling from the carpet or something.

"Hey, yourself." I turned away quickly, trying not to stare at him. He was thicker now than when he'd trained me before. His body had finally caught up with his hands. He'd always had strong, soft, huge hands. Even when I was two hundred and sixty pounds, he'd been able to pull me up off the floor like a feather. I swallowed hard, trying not to think of it. Trying and failing. "And here you are, too, all fine. Just like I remembered." That stupid statement was followed by nervous laughter. "I'm sorry. Just kidding."

He led the way to a treadmill with a muscled arm. "I hope you're not kidding, because when I say you're looking good today, I mean it." He paused, his eyes burning into me before turning his focus to just in front of me, as though someone were standing between us. "And you're going to feel even better. Come on, let's do your cardio."

I felt self-conscious at first, despite my new coral and cantaloupe workout outfit. Another quick look around let me know that this definitely wasn't my stroller-and-scones crowd. The funny thing was, my husband would have fit right in. I didn't have long to contemplate it, though, because the treadmill program Mark had designed for me was no joke. The first five minutes was an easy walking warm-up, followed by five minutes of fast hill intervals. I was good for the first minute, but by minute two…

"Oooh…" It was all the sound I could get out as I wiped sweat from my forehead. This was just sad. I couldn't even make it for five minutes.

On the treadmill beside me, Mark gave me a quick nod and then a wink. "Face forward, elbows up. Think about what's chasing you, what you're chasing. You are faster, you are better, you are stronger. You are a hot mama. Now let's go!"

He didn't have to tell me twice. It was slow and ugly, but I pitter-patted on and on, flashing through pictures in my mind: the longing look on my husband's face as Sierra walked away; the scar on my mother-in-law's leg; the possibility of losing my house and many of my friends; the reality of having another baby when I hadn't quite recovered from having the first one… It was all unwinding, pulling free and pooling at my feet, when I heard Mark's voice again.

"Now walk easy, let's cool it down."

The speed dwindled and the hills became flat as I cooled down another five minutes. Sweat traced the curve of my face and down my shoulder. Mark's face stayed dry. This was nothing for him. I'd slacked off totally since getting the news about the baby, but I'd done worse on the treadmill than I would have thought. Still, I appreciated the fact that Mark often worked out with me instead of just standing over me and telling me what to do.

When I got off the treadmill, my legs felt like spaghetti. Watching Mark's wide back spread out in front of me as he walked to the circuit area, my heart felt a little like pasta, too. I knew for sure then that I shouldn't have come, that maybe I shouldn't be training with him at all.

What was all this about, anyway? The new outfit, putting on Dana's Hot Mama Mango? Was it about somebody wanting me, even for a minute? Was it about wondering if somebody could still want me? I didn't want to believe that. I'd seen marriages fall apart in the church. Good people, people in ministry, people who'd ended up in each other's beds, who'd broken each other's homes. This wasn't that, was it?

Of course not. You'd never let that happen. This is just a workout. How can you compete with the women Ryan sees every day if you don't do this? You have to do it. It's your reasonable service.

I slid into the exercise machine, closing my eyes as Mark clicked the weights into place and placed his hands on my arms. As my hands found the right position and he moved away, I opened my eyes and stared at the vein trailing his bicep, leading to the curve of his shoulder. There was a scar there, one that I didn't remember from when he'd trained me before. I pushed up the weight, trying to push away whatever this was, whatever I was feeling. Foolishness was what it was, just another "fat-girl crush," as Dana used to call them, desiring the un-attainable instead of dealing with your own reality.

Well, I wasn't fat anymore and I had no need to desire another man. I had a husband who loved me and a God who loved me more. I pushed the weight up another time and then another, shoving it all away. I heard Mark say to do two more at the same weight, so I pressed up again.

"You're a warrior, Mama. You can do it."

He was right. I was a warrior, a warrior for the Lord. There was no way I was going to let the Devil mess with me like this. No way.

"One more. Come on." He was facing me now, leaning forward, staring into my eyes.

I looked away, gathering myself, putting everything I had into the last rep, into the last lift of everything pressing me down. My eyes landed again on that vein pointing the way to the scar. I remembered now what had been there before—a tattoo. For some reason, he'd had it removed. Though the ink was gone, I could make out the word.

Juicy.

The weight clanked down. I grabbed my towel.

He gave me a funny look. "What's wrong? Are you hurt?"

"Not yet and I'm trying to keep it that way." A sigh whistled out of my mouth. I tugged at the bottoms of my outfit, which suddenly seemed too short, too tight. "Mark, I'm going to have to go. This probably wasn't the best idea. Though I'm ashamed to say it, I had some kind of crush on you back in Leverhill and I think it's still having an effect on me. I know you said that the session was a gift, but I'll leave your money at the desk on my way out."

Instead of freaking out like I thought he would or asking me more questions, he flared his nostrils, licked his lips. "You don't owe me anything, okay? I decided five minutes ago that this would be our last session, anyway. Willow asked me not to train you. I fought with her on it, told her that there was only friendship between us, but since you've been here today, I know she's right. This won't work." He paused to look me up and down. "Not that you need me, anyway."

My nails dug into my palms to stop the flutter in my belly. My baby was in there. I was getting too old for this stuff. I stepped back, almost tripping over a weight bench, much the same way that Mark's girlfriend had tried to dive off my front porch. Now I was totally confused. Dana'd had it all wrong. I wasn't a fat girl and Mark wasn't unattainable. His fat-free model girlfriend was worried about…me? How did that happen exactly? Even worse, he agreed that we shouldn't train together, either. He didn't seem surprised by what I'd said at all.

We were walking toward the locker rooms now, alone in the hall. I crossed my arms. "Thanks for understanding. And for the record, I do need you. To train me, I mean. I think that's obvious. It's just that…"

It's not needing you I'm worried about. It's wanting.

As if he'd read my mind, Mark pulled me toward him and kissed me.

The whole thing shocked me, but the kiss turned from sweet to bitter as quickly as it had begun. There was no use discussing it. I had to get away.

I jerked away and ran for the locker room.

"I'm sorry!" Mark called behind me. I didn't turn around. There was nothing else to say, really. Nothing that wouldn't lead to more trouble. I didn't bother to shower and change. I grabbed my bag from the locker I'd left it in and made a run for it, not stopping to leave a check at the desk on the way out. My only concern was to get out of there as quickly as possible.

Ryan was waiting when I got to my car. My heart raced at the sight of him. How had he… GPS, no doubt. The good stuff always cuts both ways. Ryan looked as if he'd been through a war. "Nice outfit, Hot Mama."

I saw my husband, still in his suit, with swollen eyes that only I would notice. He'd sprayed his face with one of Dana's rose hydrosols, no doubt. I couldn't tell by his voice if he was angry or being cute, but from his eyes, I saw that it was neither. He was just sad.

My fingers slid easily into his. Willow pulled past us in the parking lot, slowing down to give me a bold stare. She stopped in front of the gym and Mark came out and approached his girlfriend's car, but at the last minute, he bypassed it and headed for us instead.

Despite my prayers for me to disappear or for Mark to turn away, he just kept coming, heading straight for Ryan.

My husband looked at me with questions in his eyes. I turned away without saying a word, thinking that it was too bad that Willow didn't do muffins. I could use a huge one.

"You kissed him?" Though Ryan had been silent while Mark talked with him, he was screaming like a wildcat now.

I was no better, yelling right back. "*He* kissed me, okay? And I didn't stand there and watch him walk away, either. Oh yeah, we forgot the hotel key, too."

He turned into the church parking lot. "That's not fair."

"Isn't it? Let's just be honest. You've been having something going emotionally with that woman for months. I admit that I've had some kind of Mark fantasy for a while, too—"

"You think? Nice to hear you admit that while you're carrying our son. This is rich, Tracey, really rich. I can't believe you."

At this point, I started doing my Lamaze breathing and not because I was having contractions. It seemed the most sensible course of action. If I kept breathing maybe Ryan would, too. "As I was saying, any feelings or thoughts about Mark were all in response to being rejected and dejected by you. Sierra, on the other hand, had your mind in a twist from the beginning. She probably didn't even know I existed until I pulled up."

Ryan rolled his eyes. "So he came to my house and ate my food. Is that somehow better? He knew about me and kissed you, anyway. You obviously didn't make him think that would be a problem."

This required more than breathing exercises. I grabbed a bottle of water from my bag and gulped some down. "Has it ever occurred to you how it could be possible for a man not to care that I'm married? When is the last time you took me out or we did anything as a family, huh? When? There has to be more to our marriage than making up, Ryan. You say that I don't need you enough. Well, I do need you. Maybe a little too much. Maybe I need to play like Sierra and let you watch *me* walk away."

My husband snatched off his jacket and threw it in my backseat as though he was preparing for a fistfight. "You wouldn't. I know you better than that, Tracey. You wouldn't leave me now, take my children from me. We're in a bad place today, sure, but this is one day. Things have been going well for us."

"No, things have been going well for you. Things for me have just been going. They've had to. Our church, our friends and family, that's been going well for me. You've just been going. Now it's time for me to go, too." I grabbed my bag and started walking, this time to Ryan's car. I had no idea where I was going or what I was even saying, I just knew I had to go.

I could hear Ryan's shoes hitting the pavement as he finally ran behind me. If only it wasn't too late. He stopped running for a second and cupped his mouth with both hands. "What about Lily?" he screamed.

Figures. It wasn't me he was running after, but the babysitter. "I'm sure you'll figure out something," I said, feeling hot and dizzy as I pressed the button to unlock his door. I held on to the handle to pull myself up onto the high seat, but I never made it. Something hot and hard hit my head and everything, Ryan, Mark, the babies, the church…it all faded into blackness.

"Is she going to be okay?"

Ryan's voice broke into my darkness. Light pricked my eyes. My head throbbed. I tried to speak but couldn't quite find the right words. Sleep offered her arms to me and I moved closer into her embrace, not quite ready to deal with whatever had happened.

"Yes, she's stable now," the stranger, who must have been the doctor, said. I couldn't quite make out his face in the dim room.

"And the baby? Is he all right?" Ryan's voice cracked a little, sounding nothing like his CEO tone.

"Everything looks good for now. We'll have to keep an eye on it. Your wife took quite a fall out of that car. She was dehydrated, too. Stressed. I'm going to watch her for another day. She may have to stay off her feet for a few weeks. We'll see how it goes."

"Thank you, Doctor. That won't be a problem at all. I resigned from my company today. I'll be here until you release her."

What? Resigned? Maybe Ryan had fallen out of something, too. A spaceship, perhaps? I tried again to speak, but after only managing to sound like Porky Pig signing off at the end of a cartoon, I gave up and closed my eyes.

Ryan stroked my head, then kissed it. "Lily is with Mom. I'm here for you, babe. And I'm going to be here, as long as it takes. I am so, so sorry about everything. That whole fight was my fault...." He took a seat next to my bed and began to pray.

So did I. Maybe talking was overrated. I'd done a whole lot of talking lately and none of it had gotten me very far. Maybe God needed to do the talking and Ryan and I needed to do the listening. I took Ryan's hand and threaded my fingers through his, just to let him know that I understood.

He understood and so did I. My twenty-four-hour observation turned into a week-long ordeal. Ryan stayed with me every day, bathing me with gentle hands, rubbing my feet with some of the products I'd made before our latest blowout. He came every day without fail, going home only to fill the stack of orders clipped to the front of our refrigerator. He called Adrian and Dana often to ask questions. He even sent samples from each batch to them by FedEx and took digital pictures of all his final results.

Finally, on the next-to-last day of my hospital stay, Ryan realized that the business that he'd thought was child's play (or Mom's play) had serious potential. "We need a name for this thing."

I smiled. "We? So you're into it?"

He shrugged. "I'm into you and I'm out of work, so yeah, I guess I'm into it. Mostly, I don't want to get sued again, so I want to get you some liability insurance."

That got a giggle out of both of us, though I knew Ryan hadn't really meant it as a joke.

He scratched through something on his list. "Wait, what was that you put on the spa day notice? A play on words?"

My back started to hurt. "Mom Thyme?"

Ryan looked pleased. "Yes, that's it. That's it exactly. You've got a great business mind, did I ever tell you that?"

"Nope, but I figured you must have thought so. It's not like you married me for my body or anything."

A pained look came over Ryan's face. "Honey, don't. Okay? I love your body. I love you. I'm sorry that I ever did anything to make you think less of yourself or less of me. I'm a meat-and-potatoes man, you know that. I love every part of you."

The doctor cleared his throat behind us. We broke into a fit of giggles. He shook his head. "Newlyweds. They almost kill themselves fighting and the next thing you know you can't get 'em off each other," he said under his breath before announcing that I'd be going home the next day.

Ryan shook the doctor's hand. I gave him a hug. "Thank you. I feel a lot better. You've been wonderful."

My husband agreed, but he expressed concern about how to take care of me once he got me home. "What can she do? Is she on bed rest?"

The doctor made some marks on my chart. "Let her rest through the weekend and then I'd say that she can do anything she did before, within reason, of course."

It was Ryan's turn to clear his throat. "Anything?"

The doctor sighed. "Yes, Mr. Blackman. Anything."

We never got around to talking to the pastor. Once I'd rested through the weekend, we didn't do much talking at all. The only sounds for a while were clothes hitting the TV, the floor, the walls…and the creaking of Lily's baby swing that she was obviously too big for. Her toes hung almost to the ground and her little baby butt weighed the whole thing down.

I finally had to insist that Ryan not put her back in that thing. It was comical for one and I'd just burst out laughing in the middle of our romance at the sound of her, barely swinging like that. Then there was the fact that it just didn't look comfortable. After a few days of that, we were too tired to care, anyway.

Being the corporate mogul that he was, Ryan couldn't be satisfied with my little garage workshop for our new business. He wrote business plans, made calls and presentations. In the meantime, I did testing on the ladies from the Hallelujah Club and our neighbors. I'd thought that the previous ones had been hits, but the Mango Mama line went off the charts.

It was certainly working well on the home front, though I wasn't sure whether it was the scent or my fall that had knocked some sense into the both of us. Still, wherever I lotioned or sprayed, kisses were sure to linger. When I wobbled around the house now, I saw a new look in his eyes, the same look I saw pass between

Mother Redding and her husband sometimes at church. A look of understanding, a look of love.

Sometimes I still worried that understanding and love wouldn't be enough, that without talking through every detail of our lives, our marriage wouldn't make it. Then one day, Ryan pointed out that exposing every flaw didn't always work. Every couple who'd done a reality show on TV had pretty much gotten a divorce not long after, he said. It was a weak point and a bit out of context, but I had to admit that it was true. Sometimes you just had to eat what was on your plate and trust that it was good for you. Sometimes, like today, seeing my husband's satisfied smile was all that I needed.

"You hungry?" He was resting on one elbow, running his fingers through my hair. I closed my eyes, thinking that it felt as good as anything that had come before. When I'd trudged to the salon every week to keep my hair straightened, Ryan had stroked my hair like the mane on a prize horse. Once I went natural, he'd acted as if he didn't know what to do with it. Evidently curls didn't translate into that kind of touching. Not until now, anyway.

Was I hungry? Yes. Was I hungry for food? I wasn't sure. One thing that losing over a hundred pounds had taught me was that what I often mistook for physical hunger was hunger of my soul. The Mango Mama scent, also in my hair, came to me again. "Do we have some fruit?"

"Peaches," he said in one breath before kissing my ear.

"Peaches," I whispered back, savoring another kiss, given freely, unlike the stingy goodbye pecks I'd often received. "That sounds good."

So bold in some ways and so modest in others, Ryan gathered the sheet around him and headed for the kitchen. I shook my head, watching all that beautiful thread count drag on the floor.

That man had no respect for good linens. None whatsoever. He'd still be doing oil changes with my tea towels if he thought he could get away with it. And yet, watching him go, my heart did cartwheels. This was my gift, my man. He wasn't perfect, but neither was I. We had each other, though, and I was glad.

Doing one last tour of duty in the baby swing, Lily sat staring at me with her wise eyes. She seldom cried and always seemed to be watching. We tried to stay under the covers, but that child knew when something was up. Seeing me undressed seemed normal to her, though. Despite my lifelong weight drama, I'd never been one to hide my body. Lately, though, since reaching my third trimester, I'd started to try, and not just my body, either, but my whole self. My whole heart. Ryan wasn't hearing it. He uncovered me on every occasion. Now, if we could only get to the heart of some of his issues, we'd be getting somewhere. Time, I guess.

Uncomfortable under Lily's gaze, I went to the closet and whisked on a dashiki, my Umfoo-foo clothes as my husband called them. He teased that I'd gone from a buppie to an earth mama while we'd been together, but

I didn't see it that way. I'd never really fit the black urban professional mold. For me, life was a journey with turns to take as they came. For Ryan, it was something to be mastered and controlled, something that could be made constant and consistent with the right tools. Whatever those tools were, I wasn't interested. Chaos wasn't my thing, but micromanaging wasn't, either. There was a time to be bare, before God and before yourself.

I picked up my laptop and shot off an instant message to Dana.

InHisImage: The Hot Mama rocks. This hot mama says she wants to try the candles next. The hair butter is awesome, too. I guess we could just contract some of this stuff from you and sell it here locally. Call me this weekend. We need to talk before Ryan drives me nuts with this stuff.
Tracey

Before clicking send, I deleted the last sentence. It was time for me to lie bare, but my husband still needed to be covered. Even if it hurt me sometimes to do it.

Chapter Seventeen

Chick flicks, soda pop, pepperoni and a bunch of cool church ladies. I was so happy, I could have pinched myself. After weeks of counseling sessions at our house with the couples from the ministry team, it was time for a slumber party. It was all I could manage at this stage of my pregnancy. There'd be pain enough to go around soon enough and not just from labor. A small circle of ladies had shown up: Hyacynth, Brenna, Lynn and, to my surprise, Mother Redding. I decided that we should do some of what my mother-in-law had done—show some of our scars.

The stories came easily, between sips of Diet Coke and munches of salad. When it was finally my turn, I danced around the edge of my problems while pizza crusts formed a heap in the center of our circle. As my pastor had been with my husband, the ladies were patient with me, especially considering that two of them already knew the tale. As we swung our feet around and massaged the person's shoulders nearest to us, I found the courage to tell the latest installment of my own story, complete with my cute workout gear and the kiss that followed. When I finished, I closed my eyes, not sure what to expect.

"Are there any more soy crisps?" Lynn said after what seemed like an eternity of silence.

When we all collapsed in laughter, she looked confused. "What? I'm still hungry. Girl talk always makes me hungry." She patted my knee. "I hate to say I told you so, but I did. Some lessons are learned the hard way. At least now you know."

Hyacynth reached over and gave me a hug, switching places with Brenna, who'd been massaging my neck. "It happens. To be honest, it's as bad with the women in ministry as it is with the men. That's why these types of talks are important. And don't think pastors and their wives are immune, either. With Dre being young and fine, trust that there's always some woman with an eye out for him. On one trip we took, I thought that one of the female ministers was going to lose it when she saw him. I've had my share of inappropriate attention, as well. We have to keep lifting each other up, keeping each other accountable. None of us are as saintly as we think."

"I know that's right," Mother Redding said. "And don't think that the old folks are any different. Sometimes I think they're worse. Have you ever been to a pastor's wife's funeral? Have mercy. It's like a beauty pageant. And don't let a woman know how to cook…."

We all laughed before joining hands in prayer. Hyacynth closed out the prayer sessions, sharing her concern that Mark or Sierra, both Christians, hadn't respected our marriage. It turned out that though I'd never seen him there, Mark attended Promised Land occasionally, too. What a trip.

Mother Redding gave a hearty amen. "Well, with everyone going in different directions in church nowadays, it's a wonder that anybody knows who's married to whom. Most of these children don't even see their parents worship in the pew anymore. I'm all for having ministries, but we have to go back to building the family, as well. Without strong families, the church is weak."

I had to agree. I wondered if for all my concern for the women and Ryan's working with the teens, we hadn't been focusing on the symptoms instead of the problems. What good was a growing church with broken families? It was something to think about.

I clutched a pillow to my belly as 'Cynt started in on my hair (or should I say "her hair"; she'd brought a whole bag of it along). "Speaking of families, all of you were at the Mother's Day brunch, when my—my mom talked about her life with Ryan's father. I've tried to get him to open up about it, but that's his final thing that he won't give on. Can I ask all of you to pray with me each morning at five-thirty, when Ryan's shaving, that he will talk to me about this? I know it's early."

Mother Redding was first to sign on. "Early? Baby, you young people don't know a thing about early... I've seen that man of yours zipping about town and I think it's a good plan. Prayer is the best weapon in any fight."

Fight? Was that what this was? I just wanted my husband to talk to me. Maybe that's what I was missing, the spiritual aspect of everything that was going on in my marriage. As much as God wanted us to reach our promised land, to walk in victory, there was an enemy set against us, keeping us moving laterally in many areas instead of forward.

"I'm going to have to pray hard, girl. That's early," Lynn said. "But I've already seen a lot of changes in my life from the prayers you all have spoken over me. Count me in."

I reached under the pillow to press my stomach, hoping to quiet Christopher's incessant kicks. Though I'd had apple juice instead of Coke, he was having a party in there. Hyacynth was having a party, too, having moved on from sewing two pounds of weave in my hair to applying blue eye shadow to my eyes. (Did they still make such things?) When she finished and ushered me into the bathroom (my purple one, of course), I didn't know what to say.

Lynn, munching soy crisps behind us, found the words I was looking for. "Now that's a fakeover! Trace, is that you under there?"

Nodding, I confirmed my identity, stunned at how different I really looked. Something about the look seemed eerily and painfully familiar. After a few more minutes, I recognized where I'd seen this hair, these eyes before. I looked down at the press-on nails Hyacynth had deftly applied.

Sierra. That's where I'd seen this look before.

Though I said it was because I didn't want to ruin all Hyacynth's hard work, perhaps that wasn't the reason I kept my makeover. Now, sitting in the Cry Room and catching a glimpse of my reflection from this side of the glass, I realized how easy it was to wear this kind of mask all the time, to hide behind fingernails and hair and never face anyone, including myself.

Maybe I just wanted to see if Ryan would react to me differently looking this way. He hadn't said much of anything, except to say that the weave made him itch while we were sleeping.

This morning, while applying my makeup (I had to let that blue eye shadow go, I just could not do it), I'd decided that today would be the last day for this particular beauty treatment. It had been fun. Maybe I'd try it again with a little less hair and minus the press-on nails. One thing marriage was teaching me was that like anything else, change could be good if you let it be.

I couldn't help thinking the same thing about my surroundings every Sunday. Though I was now quite excited about having another baby, the thought of spending a lot more time in the Cry Room didn't exactly thrill me.

For a while at least I'd been back in the service when

Lily first stopped nursing. Now my little angel had moved up to the one-year-old class, where she began screaming like clockwork about ten minutes into the service, usually during someone's prayer. I could fight with her about it, but I was too tired. Maybe after Christopher was born. At least now, I knew the ladies better and we had our moments of fun here and there. The important thing was hearing God's word, not socializing, right?

Right.

Just as I was focusing my eyes on the back of Queen Elizabeth's plume hat, Hyacynth plopped down beside me. I straightened quickly in surprise.

She looked just as shocked. "Girl, my cousin is here from North Carolina and she wasn't feeling well this morning so I volunteered to bring the kids. Little did I know that her son was going to freak out in his class and I'd have to come in here."

That made me laugh. "Leave him, girl. One of us will watch him. Go back out there with your man and minister. We've got this."

Someone grunted in agreement behind me, but 'Cynt didn't move. "Uh-uh, girl. Something tells me I need to see what's going on up in here. God knows what he's doing. I know it needs to be quiet and everything, but this is sort of depressing—"

"Excuse me, but could you please be quiet! We're trying to actually listen to the sermon over here."

'Cynt gave me her no-she-didn't look and I held my breath to keep from cracking up. None of that stuff fazed me anymore. I was long over the whole behind-closed-doors phenomenon that was this place.

We passed the sermon in silence, but 'Cynt kept writing me notes.

I feel like I'm in third grade, she wrote.

My belly moved up and down.

And in prison at the same time, she scribbled again, this time netting a stifled giggle from me.

We were good for the rest of the service. So was Lily, playing quietly with her blocks. Every now and then she paused to wave at Hyacynth, whom she was very fond of. The sermon topic was the spirit of Jezebel and what happens when we focus on power instead of people. It reminded me of the talk my mother-in-law had given on Mother's Day. I made a note in my Bible to give more study to the queens of the Old Testament. I had Esther down pretty well, but didn't everyone?

When the last song ended and the lights came up, Sister Hawkins strode toward us with purpose, ready to give her speech. I tried not to enjoy it when Hyacynth turned to face her with a look of rapt attention.

"First lady? I had no idea you were in here. Why didn't you let us know that you'd be joining us today? We could have—"

"Could have what? Welcomed me? I know that the situation doesn't exactly make room for socializing, but something about this just doesn't work. Are you the one over this ministry?"

Sister Hawkins looked away. "Not officially. No one

has ever actually considered it a ministry. I guess I just took it upon myself."

Any remaining humor left the room. I could see in Sister Hawkins's face that she'd taken a lot more on herself than just this room. We all had.

Hyacynth sensed it, too, and reached out and gave Sister Hawkins a hug. "Maybe it's time for someone else to take this on, sis. Several someones. What do you think?"

Sister Hawkins nodded. "The sermon today really convicted me. I think I found power in here instead of in people and I'm sorry. I could probably use some time back in the service. I could actually sit with my husband now and again, I guess. If he still recognizes me, that is."

As everyone laughed, I stared at myself in the mirror, thinking again of how easy it was to cover over the things that hurt the most.

Hyacynth asked all the women to look for a survey at the front doors the next Sunday to see what changes they'd like to make in the room. Next, she gave me the look that I was starting to learn meant that I'd be a part of this somehow, too.

"I'm not asking for you to do it per se, but do you think that this is something your tiara team could handle? I know they mostly work with you on the Hallelujah Club, but there are other areas where we could use all of you if you're willing."

I agreed to ask the other women, but didn't get too caught up in the possibilities. Sister Hawkins and her tears were more important at the moment. With almost everyone gone from the room now, I walked over and gave her the best hug I could manage with my belly in the way.

She received me with open arms. "I guess I was wrong about you. Your husband, too. Don't let me shy you off listening to what the women have to say, though. Just take what you use and leave the rest."

Sounded like a plan to me.

With our counseling sessions completed, Ryan and I were now on staff at the church full-time. My husband treated the ministry just as he had his own company, rising early and retiring late. In the midst of it all, we'd managed to pool all our quasi business ventures together, with a shared office space on our unused third floor. So far, Internet orders for our products had been high enough for us to order from Dana wholesale and still make a profit.

Though Ryan worked as hard as he had before, the stress had the opposite effect. The more he went out to pray with the sick, check on the teens, meet with the men, the more energized he seemed to feel. I was happy for him, but couldn't really relate. At the end of my pregnancy, I was moving in what seemed to be an opposite direction, winding down. Especially today.

"Guess who showed up at Keepers of the Door this morning?" Ryan said, moving past me to change into a suit for his nursing-home visits. Though he said it was what the older ladies preferred, I knew he got a kick out of dressing up, too.

I had no clue who he was referring to as far as his meeting, though. "I have no clue, honey. Just tell me."

Ryan paused, his eyes on mine. "Your boy, Mark Johnson."

"Are you for real?" This could be awkward.

Hangers scraped in the closet as Ryan selected a suit. "I'm totally for real. And you know who else was there?"

This time I was scared to guess. "Um, Jesus?"

He groaned in the closet. "I'd sure hope so, babe. Yeah, Jesus was definitely there. Marquis, Sierra's husband. I'd never met him, but he obviously knew who I was, he made a beeline straight for me, even before talking to Dre. What do you think that means?"

A sigh of relief escaped my lips. Sometimes Ryan could be so smart but so dense at the same time. What it meant was that Marquis was watching out for his marriage, just like I was looking out for mine. That said, I wasn't in any rush to see Sierra at my next women's event. "He's just letting you know that he knows who you are, honey, just like I did with Sierra. It keeps things simple."

"What's that supposed to mean?" He was dressed now and nursing yet another nick on his chin. Lately, he looked as if he'd been through a meat grinder from the mouth to his neck.

"It means nothing. Now, what's with you and the shaving accidents? Am I going to have to shave you in the morning or what?"

Ryan lay down on top of the comforter, careful not

to disturb Lily, who was sleeping next to me. I'd been too lazy to put her back in the crib after breakfast. "As if you'd even be up early enough to shave me, woman."

Oh, I'm up then, praying for you.

He touched his chin, checking the clock. He had an hour and a half before he was due at the nursing home, but I knew he liked to be early. So when he loosened his freshly knotted tie, I didn't know what to think.

"About the whole shaving thing. I need to talk to you about some things. God keeps bringing it to me when I'm shaving and it's getting worse and worse. I'd better get it over with before I slip and slit my throat or something."

"I think you're being a little dramatic. We prayed for you to be healed, not kill yourself."

His eyes narrowed. "You've been praying for me at that time? I should have known. I thought you were out here talking in your sleep, girl. Wow. When people say that prayer changes things, that is no joke. Anyway, here's the deal…"

An hour and a lot of tears later, my hands traced the tears of my husband's scars, smaller yet just as painful as his mother's. The circles on his back were cigarette burns, but most of the lashes had been words.

"Stupid."

"Ugly."

"No good."

"Lazy."

"Never going to amount to anything."

The words echoed in Ryan's head still, even though

he was old enough, saved enough to know better. It wasn't until he'd heard some of the teenagers speak negatively about themselves that Ryan had realized just how deep his own wounds went. Oh, and the shaving nicks, of course.

I told him about my father, too, what I remembered of him. How I wasn't as strong as Ryan thought I was, how sometimes I was still that little orphan girl in my mind. We didn't analyze each other or offer any solutions. We just listened to each other, held one another. And when the nursing home called to say that they wouldn't be taking visitors that day, well, out came the Mango Mama lotion for a quick massage.

It would have been really romantic if I hadn't fallen asleep in the middle of it. Not to be outdone by my napping, Ryan got an idea for a Guys' Night Out, complete with a basketball tournament and barbecue all in my backyard. By the time I woke, it was on and popping, as the kids like to say.

Literally.

My water broke while Ryan was choosing the menu.

Chapter Eighteen

People tried to tell me that having girls and having boys was different, but I thought they were kidding. I still do. I think it's just having my boy that almost drove me crazy. How in the world could a child take after his daddy's tendency to be early and break my water before the due date and then stay in there reading a book like me? I wasn't sure, but my son managed to do just that.

Ryan tried to put up a good front, but I could tell he was worried. Having Lily had been pretty simple (to watch, anyway), but this was beyond his idea of normal. Contractions came and went throughout the afternoon and night, but nothing strong enough to actually get a baby in my arms. It wasn't until Queen Elizabeth showed up and sat in a rocking chair in the corner, finishing off a blue blanket, that the real pains hit me. Or should I say leveled me. It was like riding in Lynn's Porsche, zero to high speed in seconds.

After a few contractions that made me check my forehead for a line to see if I'd split in two, the doctor on call (Dr. Thomson was on vacation) seemed convinced that I was just getting started. I watched in shock as he and the midwife left the room, saying that they'd be back in a few.

A few what? I wondered. Years? Days? The way my lower body was turning inside out, they'd better be planning to return in a few minutes. (I later learned that they'd been on duty for about forty-eight hours between the two of them, so maybe it was good that they'd wandered off for a few.)

In the end, I think I passed out or something because I didn't remember falling asleep. A nurse had come in and walked out a few minutes before and that was all I could remember. When I opened my eyes this time, I gripped the railing and started to bear down. Queen Elizabeth put down her crocheting, whipped back the sheet (just what you want your mother-in-law to see—not!) and caught Christopher Michael as he made his angry entrance into the world. A fist at each of his temples, he cried as loud as he could before grabbing Ryan's finger.

When the nurses ran in, I collapsed in a fit of hysterical laughter. It was a fitting end to a funny pregnancy. Six months ago, I would have fainted at the thought of Queen Liz even being in a room with me in a bathing suit, let alone helping me give birth.

When all the faces around my bed leaned in, asking

a million questions, I waved them away, pointing my thumb at Ryan. "Ask him. I did the hard part."

Everyone laughed and my son had his first meal as I faded off into sleep. As I did, my hand went instinctively to my throat, to my necklace of apples of honey, right words strung along with pearls.

Lord, thank you for Christopher. Help me to say the right things, do the right things that will help him to become all You want him to be.

Just when I'd gotten the ladies to stop bringing gifts, the men started in. Ryan joked that there probably wasn't another toy truck left in the entire state. Lily eased any worries I had of jealousy when I caught her standing over Christopher's bassinet, smiling as if she'd had him instead of me.

Everyone from Leverhill came, like a caravan of nomads, taking up the entire street. Adrian kept commenting on how good I looked, which made me feel good until I realized what he really meant.

"Seriously, T, you look good. More like yourself. Stay like this."

I stared at my husband. "What's that supposed to mean? I look more like myself? How is that possible?"

Ryan, being a reasonable man with a desire to live a long life, disappeared from the room to find diaper pins for the curtains or some other nonsensical thing.

Just as he left, it hit me. "Adrian, I think you have just given me an insult. Are you trying to say that I look fat again? Wow, I guess you are a regular guy after all."

All of the guys suddenly had something to go and find after that. We all laughed about it for a long time. That night when everyone had left, I got up and looked at my face in the mirror. I smiled when I saw what Adrian had meant. I didn't look fat. I looked happy.

After three weeks in my pajamas, we set off for church for the first time as a family of four. Upon my arrival, my tiara team met me at the door and ushered me into the newly named Ladies' Room. Light ran down the walls in soft columns and couches and recliners replaced the metal chairs. A refrigerator stocked with bottled water, juice and other snacks were on the far wall. There were some seats equipped with headphones for those who wanted to tune out any other distractions, along with areas farther away with a small table and set of chairs. A sink, counter and cabinets rounded out the space and were the last things I saw before tears blurred my vision.

"It's perfect," I said, hugging Brenna, Lynn, Rainy, Pam and Susan, each of them returning my embrace with enthusiasm. "How did you come up with it so quickly?"

Lynn smiled. "It's your kitchen, Tracey. Don't you see? We just put in the things that made us feel comfortable when we're with you."

I swallowed hard so that I could speak again, but the words took a while. "Pardon the hormones," I said, clutching all nine pounds of my little linebacker, who didn't seem to have any problem being squished into the bosoms of strangers. Not that they were strangers really. He'd heard the voices all of his little life.

The room was such a hit that all the grandmas wanted in, too. The ladies treated me like a queen when I arrived for every service, which I found a little unnerving. As the weeks passed and I gained my strength, they got the message that I wasn't looking to be waited on.

Sierra and her husband showed up in early fall, after months of Marquis meeting with the Keepers of the Door. God surprised me by giving me great compassion for the couple, but as Mother Redding had taught me, I kept a close eye on my man, even from my perch in the Ladies' Room.

Christopher was three months old when they arrived and Ryan preached a stirring sermon on emotional healing. I was as surprised as anyone to see my husband step into the pulpit, but when he began to speak I forgot that it was Ryan and received just like everybody else. When he closed the final prayer, though, I knew that something, everything had changed. I bowed my head, hoping that I'd be ready for it.

Pastor Dre's voice boomed through the microphone, cutting my prayer short. "One more thing, can you all pray for my mother, Sister Irene Redding. She was a little under the weather today with a cold and missed her first Sunday service in about twenty-five years. So keep her in your prayers. Mama really wanted to be here for Ryan's sermon this morning. I'd say she missed a treat, amen? We'll get her the tape…."

He said something more, but I was already stuffing my diaper bag and preparing to tell my husband that although I wanted to celebrate his first sermon, I needed to go and check on Mother Redding. Now. I wasn't sure why I felt so urgent, but I didn't stay to chat with the ladies like I usually did. Ryan had a throng of people around him, shaking his hand.

"Baby, I'm going to get you for not telling me about you preaching, but that'll have to keep. You did marvelous and I know you want to go to lunch, but—"

He lifted Christopher from my arms and shook someone's hand and managed to make it look natural. He grabbed the diaper bag before the next couple, Sierra and her husband, stepped up to shake his hand. "Let me know how she's doing," he whispered before turning to them.

Brenna, who already had Lily in her arms, gave me a nod to let me know that she had things in hand there, too. I paused, though, watching Sierra's plastic body move as she shook my husband's hand.

People probably think I'm nuts putting my baby off on Ryan after he just got done preaching. And look at her. Maybe I should stay....

GO. NOW.

And so I went. Though my mind had hesitated for a moment, my feet made up for every second, both on the ground and against the gas pedal. I hated to miss the celebration for Ryan that was sure to follow, but sometimes I just have to move.

When I got there, Queen Elizabeth's car was already

in the driveway. She opened the door and gave us a hug. "I just gave her some tea," she said. "Come on in. Is Christopher with Ryan?"

I nodded as I stepped inside.

"People are already calling me about the sermon. They say it was beautiful. I know it was."

Something hit me hard then. Liz had lived her life to see Ryan in that pulpit, but she'd missed it to be with her friend. That told me two things: my mother-in-law had really changed and Mother Redding had something worse than a cold.

Still, neither of them let on. When I entered Mother Redding's room, she looked as healthy as a horse (What did that mean exactly? Are horses the picture of health?) and as beautiful as ever. Her hair fanned out like a silver sun on her pillowcase.

She wagged a wrinkled finger at me. "Morning, sugar. I knew you'd come. You shouldn't have, but I knew you would. You can't do that, though, baby, worry about old women when your man is giving the Word. It's just a cold, that's all. Nothing so much for you to ride way out here. Anyway, don't do it again. You have to be there. People are watching you. They always watch the first lady. Always."

First lady? I looked behind me. Was she hallucinating? Did she think that I was Hyacynth? "Mother Redding, it's me. Tracey. Ryan's wife? 'Cynt is the first lady, not me."

Thank God for that.

The old woman rolled her eyes. "Do I look senile to you? I know who I'm talking to. I've known since I set eyes on you, same as I knew it about Liz out there. You're a queen, baby. My son, Andre, is a good boy, even a good preacher, but he's no pastor for a church like Promised Land. An evangelist, yes, but not a preacher. You have to love unlovable folk to be a preacher, even when they make you mad and treat you bad. Andre can hardly stand the church people when they're treating him like a king. No, Liz's boy, your man, he's the one. And he had the good sense to pick a hardworking, good, loving woman to marry. Not that I don't love 'Cynt now, 'cause I do."

Swallowing hard, I pulled the covers up around Mother Redding's neck. "Don't you upset yourself now." I felt her head for a fever. She was a little warm, but nothing to warrant this nonsense. I'd have to text 'Cynt on my cell phone when I left so that she could get over here as soon as possible.

Mother Redding swatted my hand away from her blanket before being almost shaken off the bed by a series of coughs. "Umph. Hand me that water. Fooling with you is working me up—"

"Exactly. I came to make you feel better, not worse. Now drink up and rest up. I'm going now."

She sat up in bed, crossing her arms, shiny and brown. She cut one eye at me so hard that I sat down in the seat next to the bed and shut my mouth. Though my home training might have been lacking, one thing I did know was that there's a time to speak and a time to listen. I didn't have the lesson quite down, but I was working on it.

"Thank God. Somebody in this house has the sense to shut up. Now listen here. I couldn't tell you until now because you would have run off from me, but mark my words, sis. Mark them well. My man and I have seen sixty-three years together. Many seasons and trials. Summers, winters, springs and falls. I asked the Lord to let me serve Him all my days with a clear mind and clean hands. He granted me that. One day soon, they will gather Red and I to the Father and my son is going to be on the first train out of here. Watch for it now and remember that your preparation is for your destination. Today's trouble is tomorrow's resource. Pray it through, write it down and when the time comes, tell somebody...."

Her voice trailed off into a snore, with her hand hanging in the air. I pulled the covers back up over her and situated the pillow just right under her head. None of what Mother Redding had said made any sense to me, except that one day she wouldn't be around. I said a quick prayer in hopes that day was far, far off.

My mother-in-law joined me in adjusting the covers. "That's a good woman lying there, you know that?"

I jumped a little. I hadn't heard Queen slip in. "Yes ma'am, I do know it." I tensed as Queen put her arm around me, then relaxed. Though it wasn't the first time, I still wasn't quite used to it.

"You know what else, Tracey?"

"What?"

"You're a good woman, too. I'm glad to call you my daughter-in-law. No, my daughter. You are everything I could have hoped for in a girl. I always wanted someone to stand up to me, to be real with me. I'm sorry that I couldn't see who you were for so long. You have to understand that much of that was because I couldn't see myself."

I did understand. There were so many things to bring people together and just as many things to keep us apart. Though Queen had hurt me often and hurt me deeply, the journey had been worth it. Without realizing it, I'd given her what she'd sought her entire life, the approval of her peers. Having Mother Redding see good in me was as important to Queen as someone seeing something good in her.

That's all she wanted, Tracey. Just some acknowledgment. Someone to point at and lay claim to.

Yes. Wasn't that what everyone needed? Love. Not more programs, not more ministries, just love. I laughed to myself at the simplicity of my thoughts sometimes.

I'd be a wipeout as a pastor's wife. Totally.

Mother Redding never saw another Sunday. Her husband, Reverend "Red," was buried beside her six weeks later. Everyone said he just wilted without her, like a plant plucked from the ground and left without water. It sounded bad, but I smiled when I thought of it.

Having even seen a love like that was a blessing. To live with it all your life? Well, that was just more than I could dream of.

But I did dream of it. Though my marriage hadn't started out on the best of terms, Ryan was a different man without the stress of his business. That last cog in his wheel, the big house he thought I couldn't do without, was let go when I took the time to create a profit-and-loss statement for the next five years. There was no way for us to stay in that house and be free to do what God wanted us to do. What was it really about, anyway?

For me, I'd miss the people most. Evidently, the church felt the same way, because when we sold the house through a blind deal with a Realtor, Promised Land Christian Center turned out to be the buyers. Our home had become a community ministry center, they said, and they didn't want to lose it. If we wanted to live there, they would work that out as long as we were willing to conduct Bible studies during the week and put on regular ministry events.

Though Ryan's faith was strong, that one had driven him to his knees in his best suit. "So God was just waiting on me to let go all along?"

"Yes," I'd whispered, kissing his clenched fists.

With the house off his back, Ryan truly got free. I knew it the first time I saw him look into the mirror and laugh out loud, telling himself how great the day was going to be.

Things between us were different, too. It was like

meeting Ryan for the first time all over again. Only this time, I didn't have stars in my eyes or thoughts of a Cinderella ending. This time, I knew that marriage meant starting a business with someone, making a commitment to stay around even when things weren't so great, to invest time and energy when I didn't feel like it, to work at our relationship each and every day. And even then, to realize that it would never be perfect.

And it wasn't perfect.

But it sure was good.

That's what I was thinking while nursing Christopher in the Ladies' Room while Ryan preached on "Getting Out of God's Way." He'd had plenty of material for that one. At an odd interval, the piano started to play and I heard my name on the speaker just as Christopher threw up in my hair.

One of the ushers ran into the room and waved me toward the door. "Sister Tracey! They need you in the sanctuary."

Grabbing a paper towel on my way out, I went out into the church, still with the burp cloth over my shoulder. Brenna snatched it off me as I passed by. Ryan was on the stage looking as confused as I and maybe even a little upset. Now that he'd gotten a taste of preaching, he liked to take it through to the end. He shrugged his shoulders to let me know he'd had no part in this.

Pastor Dre took the mic. "Forgive me for embarrassing these folks, church. They have no idea what I'm about to say. Some of you do, though. I can tell by the looks on your faces. Hyacynth and I have enjoyed very much being your pastors here at Promised Land. We've learned so much, in fact, that we've decided to step down…."

Ryan took a sharp breath. "What?"

Bo, the minister of music, looked shocked. "Is he kidding?"

Alarm started about four rows back and moved back into sheer panic.

Dre hushed the crowd. "Oh, hush now. It ain't all that and you know it." Everyone laughed. "We've been praying about who would replace us and these two folks up here keep coming to mind. We're not pressuring them for an answer and we're not pressuring you to accept them. What we want is for you to pray for them and for 'Cynt and I, as well."

I reached around Christopher and pinched my wrist. No change. I was still awake, though right now a nap sounded really good.

"Uh-huh. We'll do that, Pastor, but where you goin'?" someone called out from the back.

Pastor Dre laughed. "See now, I can't slip a thing past you all. My wife and I have been asked to go and start a church plant in Las Vegas of all places. So whenever you hear coins jingling, pray for us. I think we've got the bling part down at least, wouldn't you say?"

More laughter. At least that's what I thought I heard. The sounds of the room blurred as I searched the crowd for the one face. There she was, Queen Liz. Though everyone else was laughing and talking among themselves, my mother-in-law was sitting forward on the second pew, hands raised, lips moving.

I watched her mouth and read the words.

God did it, Richard. Do you see them up there? God did it. In spite of you. In spite of me....

My pastor (he was still my pastor as far as I was concerned) passed Ryan the microphone again. "Well, Brother Ryan, what do you think? I can understand if you need more time. Look at your mama down there praising God. Ladies, do you know that's a proud mother? You remember that when your boy asks what he should be when he grows up. There's still honor in being a man of God, amen?"

Amen. I just wasn't sure if I was the right woman.

I stepped off the stage, shoving my paper towel into the pocket of my suit jacket. I climbed down the stairs slowly at first, then faster. (Boy, that pulpit is up high!) By the time I reached Queen's row, the people were already standing to let her out. Or to let me in.

I squeezed through them, almost falling into Queen's waiting arms. Behind me, I heard Ryan's voice, breaking to hold back his own emotions. "Well, I guess it will be all right with my wife and my mother," he said slowly.

The crowd broke out in relieved laughter.

"I don't want to give a quick answer because right now I'm enjoying teaching the youth so much. I don't want them to think that I'm abandoning them—"

"We love you, too, Pastor Ryan!" called a bunch of high-school boys lined against the back wall. "Do your thing. We've got this."

Ryan's lip started to tremble. "Well, I guess that about does it then." He stopped talking for a minute, then started again, waving his mother and I back onto the stage. We arrived just as he began to speak. "Church, if you all will have me, my family and I would be honored to serve you."

Before anyone could respond, my husband pulled me away from his mother and kissed me the way I wished he had at our wedding. He kissed me good and lifted my hand up in the air before taking the microphone again. "One thing, though, this lady here is mine. Y'all be nice to her."

Pastor Dre started the clapping. I don't know when it ended. All I remember is looking to the back of the sanctuary and seeing the glimmer of light coming out of the top of the Ladies' Room. The long pane of glass across the front of it looked different from up here, too. It looked radiant.

I didn't know what God was doing, but I'd learned God used even hard things to reflect Christ's image in my life. Everyone waited quietly as I gave my nod of approval. Tears blurred my vision as I realized that somewhere between the first and last song, I'd gone from a former fat girl to a first lady.

Liz blew me a kiss and took her seat. Finally, it was my turn to be Queen.

* * * * *

Dear Reader,

Thank you so much for joining me on the final leg of my journey with the Sassy Sistahood. It's been a blast. This story, Tracey's story, is very close to my heart and I look forward to hearing what you think about it. Please send me an e-mail at MarilynnGriffith@gmail.com and let me know how you enjoyed Tracey and Ryan's not-quite fairy tale of living happily even after. Thank you for your continued support of my books and my family. We appreciate it.

Blessings,

Marilynn

DISCUSSION QUESTIONS

1. Tracey feels like an outsider in her church at the beginning of the book. How do things change when she starts spending time with the women in the Cry Room? How do you think Tracey handles having to sit there?

2. Ryan has his problems, but he really wants to be a good husband. What were some good things he did to let Tracey know how he felt about her? Would those things have worked for you? What are some nonverbal ways that you communicate your feelings to your loved ones?

3. When Tracey moved away from her friends in the Sassy Sistahood, she probably never thought she'd be that close with anyone again. What do you think of her new group of friends? Who is your favorite?

4. Tracey's secret bathroom is her safe place to be queen once a week, even if the scale gives her bad news. Where is the safe place in your life you go to be alone with God? If you don't have a place like this, describe what it might be like.

5. Queen Elizabeth starts off as a very aggressive, manipulative character, but showing her own scars seems to change her. Contrast the effect of Mother Redding's influence on Tracey with the effect of her mother-in-law's influence. What did you think about the relationship between Hyacynth and Mother Redding?

6. Though Tracey fantasizes about being a queen, God grants her request in a very unexpected way. Has something like this ever happened to you? If a friend gave you a tiara for your birthday, would you wear it proudly or stash it away?

7. What did you think of the Hallelujah Club? Would an e-mail list like this appeal to you? Would you have been willing to be a Promise Princess and send a scripture to the list? Or would you have been a lurker who never posts anything?

8. Lynn is coming back to church after a long absence and she often sees things differently from the other women. Though it's uncomfortable for Tracey when she asks certain questions, Lynn's honesty also helps Tracey to see herself more honestly. Do you have a friend like Lynn who tells it like it is? Does that work for you or does it get on your nerves sometimes?

9. Sierra caused a lot of problems in Tracey's marriage with her reckless flirting. How would you have responded to Sierra if you were Tracey? Are you a flirt? If so, have people misunderstood you before because of it? Has it caused trouble in your relationships?

10. Ryan works very hard to be able to provide for Tracey all the things he thinks that she needs. In the end, though, he learns that God is his provider and that only when he lets go of what he thinks he needs most can God help him. Have you experienced a situation like this before? How has it affected your life?

Back to Russia with Love

SUSAN MAY WARREN

Newly married Josey Anderson will be the perfect
wife. She just has to find the perfect cape-style house
while learning how to bake and sew. That shouldn't
be too difficult, right? However, when her husband,
Chase, lands a new job in Moscow, Josey's dreams
disintegrate. After all, she's been there, done that as
a missionary, and moving back to a city without year-
round hot water—or decent maternity clothes—leaves
much to be desired. But what's the perfect wife to do?

Chill Out, Josey!

Available wherever books are sold!

www.SteepleHill.com

SH585

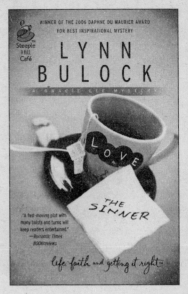